SHOW ME
BETRAYAL

SHOW ME MYSTERIES – BOOK ONE

ELLEN E. WITHERS

Scrivenings
PRESS
Quench your thirst for story.
www.ScriveningsPress.com

Published by Scrivenings Press LLC
15 Lucky Lane
Morrilton, Arkansas 72110
https://ScriveningsPress.com

Printed in the United States of America

Paperback ISBN 978-1-64917-291-4

eBook ISBN 978-1-64917-292-1

Editors: Elena Hill and Susan Page Davis

Cover by Linda Fulkerson www.bookmarketinggraphics.com

For my family and a Heavenly trifecta of fantastic women: My mother, Ruth Gorrell Erdel, who nurtured my love for reading; My Aunt Juanita Ulrich Erdel, who became my mother figure when mine passed too soon; and Louise Pruitt Withers, my former mother-in-law, turned "mother-in-love," who seemed to adore every word I wrote.

Chapter One

Liesl
November 1

Liesl raced across the porch steps of the grand Victorian dwelling, through the house, and up the stairs.

What happened? Aunt Suzanne was fine, but now she might not make it?

At the doorway of her great-aunt's bedroom, she gathered courage around her like a cloak and stepped into the room.

"Hello there."

Aunt Suzanne's frail body was small and pale against the cream-colored sheets. Her gray hair hung loose around her narrow, oval face. If she'd heard Liesl, she gave no sign.

Liesl felt gut-punched by her aunt's drastic decline.

Crossing the polished hardwood floor, she dropped her purse on a nearby chair—no need for medical training. One glance hinted at Aunt Suzanne's dire condition. She should be in a hospital bed, not her own bed. Aunt Suzanne's cheek felt afire against her kiss. With a soft caress, Liesl smoothed her mussed hair. Still no movement. She hadn't considered the possibility of life without her aunt in her twenty-seven years. She dropped onto the chair next to the bed and silently prayed for a miracle.

God, this wonderful woman means everything to me. Must you take her so soon?

"Hello, Liesl."

She jumped at the unexpected greeting.

Patricia Sizemore, Aunt Suzanne's friend, rose from a chaise longue in the far corner of the bedroom and moved toward Liesl. She offered no handshake or hug. Her usual rigid personality had not softened, even under these circumstances.

"Mrs. Sizemore." Liesl ran her fingers through her hair. She must look hideous to the prim and proper woman before her. "Thank you for being here."

Mrs. Sizemore tried to straighten her navy pantsuit, but the wrinkles remained, likely the result of a long vigil at Aunt Suzanne's bedside. It was the first time Liesl had seen her look less than perfect. This morning, dark circles framed her cool, blue eyes hooded by puffy lids. Her mouth, sans lipstick, twisted from a grimace into a slight smile.

"We weren't expecting you so quickly," Mrs. Sizemore said.

Liesl shrugged. "After Doreen's call last night, I threw clothes in a bag and drove all night. How is she?"

The two turned toward Aunt Suzanne.

"No better." Mrs. Sizemore spoke in a low voice. "Before she left, Doreen called Dr. Johnson again. He'll be here any moment."

"This was so sudden."

"Yes, she was fine at the Butterfly House board meeting three days ago."

"I appreciate you and Doreen taking care of her." Liesl

turned and noticed her bloodshot eyes. "Would you like to go home and rest?"

Mrs. Sizemore shook her head. "No, dear. You might need help."

"Thank you." Liesl returned to the chair beside the bed.

When Mrs. Sizemore left the room a few minutes later, Aunt Suzanne's eyes fluttered open.

"Liesl … sweet Liesl," she whispered.

Liesl blinked back tears, leaned down, and repeated her kiss. "You got sick, so I thought I'd come for a visit."

Aunt Suzanne's lips forced a smile, and her liver-spotted hand burrowed out from under the covers. Liesl held it against her cheek and felt the warmth of her aunt's gnarled fingers. These fingers had bandaged her skinned knees and squeezed her hand in reassurance when she'd lacked faith.

"Don't worry. I'm here to take care of you." Liesl gave her hand a little squeeze with the hope her aunt would have the strength to fight her illness. *Stay with me. Have courage.*

"So good to see you," Aunt Suzanne said. Her voice seemed raspy. "Love you to the moon and back."

"Love you to the stars, Aunt Suzanne."

They smiled at the affectionate phrases they'd always exchanged.

After a moment, the old woman's smile faded. "You must find my book."

"You mean *my* book?" Liesl had published several romance novels. "You want one of my books?"

Aunt Suzanne's brow furrowed, and she shook her head.

What book was she talking about?

Her lips moved, and Liesl leaned closer.

"Must … stop the killer," Aunt Suzanne said.

"Did you say killer?" Liesl squeaked her response with astonishment.

"Yes ... who killed Winnie ... all there ... in my book."

Aunt Suzanne couldn't be talking about Liesl's books. Hers were romances, not murder mysteries. "Where is this book?"

After a moment, Aunt Suzanne blinked her watery green eyes. "Don't trust anyone who was there."

"Where?"

Was she hallucinating? With all the medicine on the table beside her aunt, had something caused her to be confused?

After a deep breath, Aunt Suzanne continued. "Everyone there was ... is dangerous."

Liesl squeezed her hand again. "Don't worry. Everything will be firre."

Her aunt mumbled incomprehensibly and closed her eyes. Her breathing grew steady and slow in sleep.

* * *

At the large picture window in the entryway, Liesl paused and inhaled. The faint smell of old wood permeated the room. How she loved this house and the woman who owned it. Aunt Suzanne was so ill. She'd always assumed the iron-spirited woman would outlive her. The tears she resisted earlier spilled.

Footsteps on the front porch caught her attention. She hurried to open the door before the bell could disturb Aunt Suzanne's sleep.

Dr. Johnson, a tall man wrapped in a heavy wool coat and leather gloves, smiled his welcome. He stepped forward and encircled Liesl in a bear hug. "I figured you'd be here when I finished my hospital rounds."

She stepped back and brushed the tears from her cheeks. "Thank you for coming. I know you don't do house calls."

"Nonsense. For your aunt, I'll do anything. You know she was my first patient."

She took his coat and gloves. "Really?"

"I knew her as a boy. She volunteered at a Boys and Girls Club. Encouraged me to 'do big things.' When I returned here to practice medicine in 1998, I figured the citizens wouldn't accept a doctor from the wrong side of town." Liesl followed Dr. Johnson upstairs as he continued. "But on the first day of my practice, Suzanne marched in and welcomed me. Her attitude helped attract other patients."

"She's done so much good." Liesl bit her lower lip. "What's wrong with her?"

"Likely some type of flu. Doreen called, stating her symptoms were nausea, diarrhea, and general weakness, but no fever. She's had all the recommended vaccines, but they don't protect against all strains. Let's go check and see if I need to admit her to the hospital."

"She looks terrible."

"I'll be that judge." He turned and crossed the hallway.

"I'll be right back. Just want to grab my suitcase."

Outside, the air was crisp. A soaring pine filled the early November air with its wintry tang. Liesl's boots crunched through the light frost in the shaded areas of grass.

The garage was once a carriage house. In the 1920s or 1930s, the owners redesigned it to suit automobiles. The wooden double doors weighed a ton. Aunt Suzanne's handling them nearly every day offered proof of her strength, even at age seventy-nine.

Her aunt's white Cadillac hugged the right wall and left plenty of room for Liesl's Jeep to park in its former place. After unloading her suitcase and laptop, she turned toward the house and paused, taking in its grandeur. This two-story architectural treasure was a hundred and thirty years old, yet it stood majestically in well-kept condition. She loved the colorful gingerbread at the eaves, the wrap-around porch spanning half the house, and the turret that rose from the northeast corner.

Liesl was lucky to have grown up here in Mexico, Missouri, in this house that influenced her writing. Her first published manuscript, a historical romance set in the Victorian era, featured a similar house. Aunt Suzanne had replaced the slate roof and added two bathrooms and modern conveniences to the kitchen. Little else had changed since her aunt's grandfather built it.

A faint siren blared in the distance. Liesl glanced up to Aunt Suzanne's second-story window. Mrs. Sizemore rapped on the glass, beckoning her to return. The siren roared as flashing lights filled Liesl's peripheral vision.

Heart pounding, she scrambled up the porch steps. Dr. Johnson must have sent for an ambulance.

No. I can't lose her.

Chapter Two

Liesl
November 7

Mr. Van de Berg's paralegal led Liesl down a narrow hallway, then turned into the spacious office that smelled of leather and men's cologne. Bookcases filled with legal reference books lined two walls from floor to ceiling. A massive mahogany desk served as the room's centerpiece. Two chairs faced the desk, and the paralegal seated her at the one not stacked with files.

Liesl nervously fingered the stitched seams and brass studs on the chair's arms. Fifteen minutes later, Mr. Van de Berg burst into the room.

"Thank you for coming," he said. "Someone should horsewhip me for my delay." His neatly groomed white hair showed his advanced age. He was short and wide and wore a double-breasted blue suit that lent him a dignified air.

Liesl stood, towering six inches over him as he clasped her hand in his enormous paw. "Not a problem, Mr. Van de Berg."

"A client cornered me at Diner 54. It was hard getting away. I'm inclined to send him a bill." He gestured for her to sit.

He snaked past the stacks of files teetering on the floor near his desk and claimed his chair. "It was not appropriate to tell you at the funeral, but I have to say, you've grown into an admirable woman. Suzanne's pride in you was not misplaced."

His compliment caused her cheeks to flush. "Thank you."

"Now, we have business to do." He frowned. "I'm so sorry we've lost her. She was one of my dearest friends."

"Did she seem ill the last time you saw her?"

"No. She was her usual chipper self." He grabbed a thin file that sat to his right and pulled out a legal-sized document. "We had lunch together before the Butterfly House board meeting last Monday. She looked great."

He fished reading glasses out of his jacket pocket and placed them on his nose. He silently studied the page in his hand and then looked up. "Your aunt made several bequests."

"I'm not surprised. Did she donate the house to her brother, Myron, or one of her favorite charities?"

"No. Myron and his family have established themselves in California. They don't want that house. She's left it to someone who loves it." He peered over the top of the glasses. "You. She also left quite a bit of money for charities."

Liesl hesitated, contemplating what little money she'd tucked into a savings account. "If there isn't enough money in her estate to clear her bequests and pay her funeral expenses, I have some put away."

"What?" His face bloomed as red as a tomato in Aunt Suzanne's summer garden. "You mean your aunt never enlightened you with the details of her financial situation?"

Liesl shrugged. "She never talked money."

"Your aunt should have gone over her finances with you a long time ago." He glared at her as if this was her fault. "Some things should be family matters, not left for her attorney to explain, even if Suzanne knew me since I wore diapers."

He took off his glasses, pulled out a hankie, and rubbed them clean. After an inspection, he replaced them on his nose. "I repeatedly told her to educate you about her affairs. Obviously, she ignored me."

"Please don't be angry."

He mumbled a bit about Suzanne's "charm," lightening Liesl's heavy heart.

"Other than some sizeable bequests, your aunt left her estate to you. Any idea how much that might be?"

"Not a clue."

"Liesl, in addition to her house and her car, after her donations, you will inherit approximately thirty million dollars."

Liesl blinked. Was he kidding? She studied him to see if this was a joke, but his face bore no sign of humor.

Her mind raced to make sense of this news. "Did she win the lottery and not tell me?"

"Oh, that's a good one." His lips trembled. Then he threw his head back and laughed. "Win the lottery? Can you imagine her buying a ticket from Mrs. Kavetti at the liquor store?"

They shared a chuckle until Liesl asked, "Where did all the money come from?"

"Originally? Your aunt's father. He was quite a fine accountant and learned to invest money."

She nodded. "I knew he made a lot of money, but I thought Uncle Myron had some type of business failure after their father died."

"That, my dear, is exactly what Ms. Suzanne wanted the

9

town to believe. When her brother Myron needed money for his business, she bought out his half of their parents' house. Then, she did nothing to stop the gossip that the money was gone. She probably even encouraged it. No, no. A brokerage firm in St. Louis has handled her investments for decades. The local townspeople know nothing about it."

"But Uncle Max must have known." Surely Aunt Suzanne wouldn't have kept something that huge from her husband.

"He did, but it all belonged to her, not him. Not that he cared about money. He was more interested in talking about golf."

"Why would both of them have kept it a secret?"

"Perhaps this will help you understand." He pulled a lumpy, legal-sized envelope from the file and handed it to her.

Tears burned her eyes as she read her name, written in Aunt Suzanne's exacting penmanship. They'd been so close. Why hadn't she told her about the money? Was it a matter of trust?

"Mind if I read this now?"

"Be my guest."

She hesitated before opening the envelope and shook it upside down. Three keys fell onto her lap. They were long, thin brass keys with tags attached.

Liesl flipped through the manila file folders inside and found copies of some of Aunt Suzanne's trusts and her will. There was a smaller envelope, still sealed, addressed to her. She ran her thumb under the sealed edge and removed its contents. The date was three years past.

My dearest Liesl,

I've not been able to tell you about the money. It is both a blessing and a burden. You will understand when it belongs to you.

There's fun in the control of a secret stash of money. Sometimes Santa Claus wears high heels. Whenever there's a need for money to improve someone's life, I step in and anonymously make the change. An example of the fun of giving involves Dr. Johnson. I noticed his intelligence when he was just a boy. Both of his parents worked two jobs just to raise him, leaving no question that scholarships had to fund his higher education. I secretly created a scholarship fund that only one smart young man applied for and received. It awarded tuition, books, and a small living expense for his college career, as well as his medical school. I've enjoyed that gift the most because I've reaped the benefits as his patient. He's the best physician this town's ever had, and I'm proud to have had a hand in it.

It's your decision whether people know about the money. Secrecy has allowed me to escape pressure from those who crave money. You may decide otherwise. Do what's right for you.

My dearest Max never cared a whit about my money. He simply loved me for me. I wish the same for you one day. Too bad things didn't work out between you and Kurt. He really loved you.

Of course, she'd mention Kurt, but a woman can't forgive certain things. His betrayal, for one, could not be forgotten.

Every day, I thank the Lord and your parents for giving you to me. I love you to the moon and back.

11

Aunt Suzanne

When she finished, Mr. Van de Berg nodded at the keys. "Those are safe deposit box keys, all for Mexico Bank." He pushed up his glasses. "We'll have to open them together. Part of the estate, you see. I'll file her will in probate court now, and in a week or two, we'll meet again and go through her investments."

"Won't people discover her sizeable estate when you file?"

"No. Long ago, we designed her estate so the financial information is in trust. No financial details will go in the public records. No one will know unless you tell them."

"I'm at a loss about my apartment in Houston. I have two months remaining on my lease and a part-time job there."

"You have options." He waved his arms in the air like a magician. "You don't need a part-time job with this inheritance. You've written some books, but you don't have to continue unless you choose."

Could she possibly stop writing? Writing was like breathing.

"Liesl, you're a very wealthy woman. Don't do anything hasty until you've digested this news. Take some time to decide how you will live your life."

She reached for her purse and stood. "Mr. Van de Berg, Aunt Suzanne didn't want people to know about the money. I'll respect her wishes in that regard. I just don't understand why she didn't tell me."

He rose and moved toward her. "When you've figured her out, let me in on the secret. I knew her more than sixty years, as her friend and as her attorney, yet she remained an enigma. Only your Uncle Max seemed to understand her."

He glanced down at the carpet. "I'll miss her, Liesl. She was … a delight. I'll miss her for the rest of my days."

Her eyes burned. "Don't you find it odd that she was perfectly well on Monday, then ..." she stammered, unable to say the words.

"I do, Liesl. That I do."

She gave him a quick hug and longed to use her money to bring Aunt Suzanne back.

* * *

Afternoon sunlight filtered through the picture window and shone on lacquered wood floors. Brass chandeliers hung from the high ceilings. Glass transoms topped the openings to the various downstairs rooms. Carved wooden rosettes dotted the upper doorway trim. Wainscoting on the walls gave the entry warmth, even though it was a large space.

Aunt Suzanne's—no, Liesl's house.

It would take some getting used to before she could consider this beautiful house her own. There was a small fireplace in the corner, where photographs of Uncle Max, Aunt Suzanne, and Liesl dotted the mantel. On the right, a hallway led to the formal dining room, butler's pantry, and kitchen. To the right of the hallway entrance was a massive, hand-carved mahogany staircase. To her left, a hallway of pocket doors led to several rooms. The first space was the music room. It opened into the library, used as a study or den, and finally, the screened sun porch.

She shrugged free of her wrap and hung it on the antique oak and brass coat rack behind the door, next to Aunt Suzanne's coat. Without hesitation, she pulled the camel hair material to her face and inhaled. The reward was the faint scent of Aunt Suzanne's perfume. Fighting back tears, she fingered its soft texture. This needed to go to charity. Aunt

Suzanne would kill her if she didn't donate all her clothes to worthy causes.

But she wasn't capable of removing her aunt's things from the house today. One day soon, but not yet.

Chapter Three

Liesl

The following morning, Liesl stood shivering on the front porch, balancing a dented foil pie pan stacked with brownies.

"Do you know what your aunt did at the book club fundraiser a few weeks ago?"

"Actually, you told me about it." She resisted looking at Mrs. Detmeier's eyes. They looked cartoonish, magnified by her coke-bottle-bottom lenses.

"Well, we all sat around the table, when she ..."

Liesl mentally rolled her eyes. Although Mrs. Detmeier's story was worthy of a chuckle at the visitation, it was less amusing the second go-round after the funeral. Faced with a third rendition, Liesl fought the urge to scream.

Poor Mrs. Detmeier. Her cheese was slipping off her cracker, and she was blissfully unaware of its imminent departure.

At least Aunt Suzanne had been fully alert until the end. Or had she? Her strange ramblings that last day were so out of character. Did her sickness cause Aunt Suzanne to get confused? Talking about a killer and a *book*. Had her long search for Winnie Whitcomb's killer spun out of control at the end?

A red Chevrolet Suburban turned the corner and stopped in front of the house. Liesl's heart skipped, and she couldn't help smiling. A petite, brown-skinned woman jumped down from the car. She was saved.

Nicole shouted a greeting to the departing Mrs. Detmeier, then threw her arms around Liesl, taking care to avoid the perilous tower of brownies.

After their hug, they watched with morbid fascination as Mrs. Detmeier made her way to the Buick parked mostly in Aunt Suzanne's front yard. With a growl from the engine, Mrs. Detmeier threw the sedan into reverse, crushing a hedge and nearly sideswiping a hefty maple tree before she found the brick-lined street.

"That blue-haired land torpedo barely missed your Suburban, Nic." Liesl's breath showed in the frigid air.

"I'm going to call her son when I get home and insist he take away her keys. She's a lethal weapon behind the wheel."

Liesl smiled. "You always know when I need you."

"I *am* amazing like that."

Liesl chuckled. "You have great instincts."

"It was Lee. He asked me how you were doing. I figured I'd better see with my own eyes. How'd your meeting with Mr. Van de Berg go?"

"It was sad, but there was one good thing. I'm to inherit this house."

Nicole squealed with joy. "Oh, praise the Lord. Does that mean you're moving back home?"

"I'm leaning toward that, but I don't want to rush my decision. I've really enjoyed living in Houston."

"I know you have, but I've missed you. My husband, daughter, and I have a good life together. But I'd like my friend nearby."

"Come in. Let's have coffee and brownies for lunch."

Nicole gave Liesl a wry smile. "Don't you have any healthier leftovers? Perhaps the angel food cake Mrs. Williams made from scratch, swimming in her homemade strawberry preserves?"

"We also have the option of carrot cake with cream cheese icing, broken into large chunks over ice cream."

"Vegetables. Now you're talking."

Liesl stowed the stack of brownies on the counter, already overflowing with homemade baked goods. They chatted while she brewed a fresh pot of coffee.

"Can you believe Aunt Suzanne ground her own coffee beans?"

"Sure." Nicole removed her knit cap and fluffed her wavy brown hair. "She had good taste. Enjoying excellent coffee is as important as the new furniture she donated to the hospital waiting room. She was a connoisseur of life's finer things."

"For others. She hardly spent a dime on herself."

"You're right." Nicole walked over and touched Liesl's arm. "Are you doing okay? Really?"

Liesl gave Nicole a bowl of ice cream and cake. "I'm trying to get my mind around this. It was so sudden. She was fine when she came to Houston over Labor Day. We talked on the phone every couple of days. She never mentioned feeling bad."

"Not a groan or an arthritic gripe?"

"Nothing. It shocked me when Doreen called to say she was so sick."

"You sound as if you blame yourself because she came

17

down with a nasty virus. The flu is a serious threat to the elderly, as well as the rest of us."

"Of course." The chair squealed its resistance as Liesl pulled it out from the kitchen table. "I can't help but believe I should have done more."

They ate in companionable silence. Then Liesl asked, "When did you last see Aunt Suzanne?"

Nicole twirled her spoon in the ice cream. "Sunday. When she was leaving early service at her church. We were heading for our church. She was in the parking lot. I waved at her, and she waved back."

"How'd she look?"

"She looked great. She wore that purple suit you bought her. At that distance, I couldn't see more than her suit and her smile."

Liesl grinned, remembering the bullying necessary for Aunt Suzanne to accept that suit as a birthday present. "It makes me happy she wore it near the end. That suit was my last gift to her."

"I'm sure she loved it." Nicole sipped her coffee. "This bowl of dessert is decadent, but an excellent change from my usual lunch."

"Everything tastes better with ice cream." Liesl launched a large spoonful to her lips.

Nicole sighed. "Be grateful you were raised by some of the nicest, godliest people I've ever met."

Tears filled Liesl's eyes. "You always say the right things. Aunt Suzanne loved to tell me how shocked she was when she found out she and Uncle Max were my guardians. My father talked to Max when I was born, and he'd agreed to it, never giving a thought to letting her know. She always claimed I was the best surprise in her life."

Nicole nodded. "She told me. It's a great story. Just think, if you'd gone to one of your father's brothers or sisters, you'd have been one of many in a big family. Being raised by Mr. and Mrs. Schrader as their only chick gave you their complete attention. You've turned out great under their inexperienced tutelage."

Liesl nodded. "God has a plan. We might not understand it in the beginning."

"Exactly. Anytime you want to visit their graves or do something that hurts your heart, call me. We'll do it together."

"Thank you. You know I'll call." After a pause, Liesl added, "I thanked Aunt Suzanne repeatedly for the wonderful life she gave me. She worried that since her own mother was difficult to love, she wouldn't be a good mother, but she was wonderful."

Nicole wiped a tear. "I'm glad you did that."

"There's something I want to discuss. Just you and me."

"Talk. I don't have anything until"—she glanced at the clock—"one thirty today."

"Okay. When I arrived last week, Aunt Suzanne was rather delirious. She said something about a killer and finding a book." Liesl turned to Nicole. "I couldn't tell if she was hallucinating or lucid. It's haunted me ever since."

"I never experienced her being confused about anything." Nicole stopped eating, and her brow furrowed. "She was always talking about her friend's murder. What was her name?"

"Winifred Whitcomb. Aunt Suzanne called her Winnie. She was killed when Aunt Suzanne was in high school."

"Maybe someone has written a book about it. Or she wanted you to consider writing a book about it."

"I write romance, not nonfiction." Liesl swirled her spoon in her bowl. "But that's not the point. She specifically said,

'You need to find my book,' which means she'd either bought a book about the murder or had written one herself."

Nicole pulled out her cell phone.

"What are you doing?"

"Searching for any books about Winnie." After a moment, she shook her head and stowed her phone. "Nothing. I suggest you look around for a book your aunt was writing. You haven't lived here for several years. You've written books. Maybe she wanted to do the same."

Liesl pondered Nicole's suggestion. Aunt Suzanne could have hired a ghostwriter or a historical researcher, or both. Her financial records would show payments or charges for that. The Historical Society might have information about the murder. They'd know if Suzanne had been there to look at their documents. Then a third option came to her. "Remember those appointment diaries Aunt Suzanne always kept?"

"Sure."

"She called them journals, or just books. Maybe she'd found some new information about that murder and wrote about it there."

"That's plausible," Nicole said. "She always had one in the butler's pantry, by the phone, back when she had a house phone. Once she got rid of her landline, I don't remember seeing those books around anywhere."

"She brought one to Houston with her over Labor Day. Wonder where those are? Especially her current one."

"Keep your eye out for them when you sort through everything. They'd be fascinating to read."

"I'm not ready to go through her stuff yet."

Nicole looked around the kitchen. "I figured she'd leave this wonderful old thing. It's your home, and I'd love to have you back in town, but don't rush your decision. This has been a great shock. You're gonna need time."

"I need to take my mind off my grief." Liesl's voice shook. "Otherwise, I'll dig myself into a deep depression."

Nicole reached over and patted her arm. "I won't let that happen."

"Thanks, my friend." Liesl rose. "More coffee?"

"Since you're up, I'd love a refill." While Liesl topped off her coffee, Nicole said, "My grandmother mentioned that murder occasionally. Winnie's murder. Apparently, it terrified everyone. They thought some lunatic was in town intending to bludgeon all the young girls. Grammy said she wasn't allowed to walk anywhere alone until she was an adult. It took years before the town returned to normal."

"They never caught Winnie's killer."

When Liesl returned to the table, Nicole eyed her for a moment. "Would you consider writing a book?"

"Possibly. The murder's interesting and might lead to a good story."

"It has potential." Nicole whittled another bite from her mound of ice cream.

Liesl considered the idea. "I wish I knew more about it. Aunt Suzanne didn't talk much about it because it upset her. Did they ever determine any serious suspects?"

"Grammy believed it was a railroad hobo. The train station was relatively close to the house where she was killed. Grammy said riffraff would wander through her neighborhood begging food."

"Isn't that a little random? A hobo hops off a train, beats a young girl to death, and then jumps on the next train out of town. And how did your Grammy know so much about town? I thought she was raised on a farm."

"Gramps was the farm boy. Grammy was a townie until she married him." Nicole changed the subject. "Your Uncle Myron gave a beautiful testimonial at the funeral."

"Didn't he? I'm sorry he had to fly back to California so soon. He promised next time he'd stay longer."

"I figured many people would attend your aunt's funeral. I had no idea the entire town would try to squeeze into the church service."

"Not the entire town." As soon as the snide comment burst from her mouth, Liesl added, "Sorry. I shouldn't have said that."

Nicole frowned. "No, you're right. I expected Kurt to be there. He should have been there."

All of Liesl's anger, pain, and humiliation at his slight against her aunt's memory rose to the surface. She forced her lips shut but saw her emotions duplicated in Nicole's eyes. When Liesl suffered, Nicole suffered.

The old-fashioned doorbell sounded before Liesl could change the subject again.

"I'll get it," Nicole offered and scurried away.

Liesl recognized the voice in the entryway. She stiffened and wished she could vanish as completely as Amelia Earhart.

Chapter Four

Suzanne Thatcher
Thursday, March 10, 1961

The distinctive tones of the ancient front doorbell echoed up the stairs. Suzanne prayed it was one of her friends to rescue her from studying for a test in Algebra II, even if for a short time.

Moments later, Winnie Whitcomb sighed and fell backward on her bed. "Only a week until my party. Can you believe it?"

Suzanne grinned from her desk chair. "Of course I can. You've given me a daily countdown for a month."

Winnie remained outspread on the bed, her long black hair fanned around her head. "Suz-zanne. It's going to be the most exciting party we've ever experienced in this town. Comparable to no other."

"Thank goodness you dropped the idea for a costume party. The guys kept complaining about that."

"All that matters is that Edgar is there."

"There'd better be more than one guy or it'll be a bust."

Winnie gathered the edges of her brown sweater and buttoned it as she spoke to the ceiling. "This house is always so cold."

"It's heated through a boiler. In the basement. You should be used to it. You almost live here."

"Hence the sweater, my friend." When she finished with the buttons, her arms fell back on the bed. "Did the boys honestly complain to you?"

"You know I always tell the truth. At least we don't have to figure out a stupid costume now that we're wearing our new dresses."

"With your imagination, I can't fathom why you weren't bewitched by the costume idea."

"I told you. The guys kept harping about it. We might like the idea of Cinderella's ball and a handsome prince, but they'd show up looking like the cast of *Rawhide*. No point in wearing a ball gown with the guys in string ties and cowboy hats."

Winnie sat up and launched a pillow at Suzanne.

Suzanne caught the pillow and giggled.

Winnie swung her feet to the floor and sat up. "Let me see your dress again. It's just divine."

Suzanne gestured at the Algebra II textbook lying on the desk. "We have a test tomorrow. Have you even looked at the chapter?"

"The things on my mind matter more than math. Why are you even in my class, anyway? You're almost two years younger."

"I'm only a year and four months younger. They placed us in that class based upon Iowa Basic test scores, not age." Suzanne winked at her. "The real question is, why you're in that class?"

"Ouch!"

"The truth hurts."

The second ring of the doorbell, followed by approaching footsteps, alerted them to another visitor. Doreen, clad in winter gear, crossed the threshold of Suzanne's room. She grinned and then dove onto the bed beside Winnie, her brown curls bouncing.

"Doreen, take off your coat," Suzanne said. "It's not that cold."

"I can't stay. I escaped mother because I told her I had to go to the library for my English paper."

Suzanne frowned. "You lied to your mother?"

"No. I *am* going to the library. I just didn't tell her I was stopping here first."

"Stay for a second," Winnie said. "Suzanne's going to show us her dress for my party."

"I only have a second, but I'd love to see it."

Winnie gave Doreen a slight push. "Off we go."

They trooped to the other side of the second floor. Mother and Father's bedroom was usually off-limits, but Suzanne felt she could justify the trespass. With Mother putting her new dress in their wardrobe, she should expect it to be visited occasionally.

"I forgot how big this bedroom is," Winnie said.

Suzanne smiled. "My grandmother designed it. She insisted on room for the bed, that enormous wardrobe, and a reading area."

Doreen ran her hand across the chaise longue. "The house and furnishings are divine. So unusual."

"Unique, that's true," Suzanne said. "I believe Grandmother wanted to hide from her servants. In those days, household staff did all the work. In the hall between this bedroom and the bathroom, we even have a dumbwaiter to the butler's pantry and a laundry chute that runs to the basement.

The help still climbed the stairs to serve tea and gather linens, but they didn't have to lug everything up and down."

"How fun to have been rich and lived during that time," Winnie said.

"But if you were poor, you'd be someone's servant," Doreen said. "That would have been awful."

Winnie and Suzanne exchanged a glance. Doreen wasn't blessed with the family wealth they experienced. Her parents had recently divorced, and money was tight.

Winnie pointed to the wardrobe. "Come on, Suzanne. Dig out that dress."

"I used to hide inside this wardrobe when I was little."

Winnie made a face. "I'd have hidden in there, too, if your mother had been my mother."

Doreen turned on her. "That was ugly."

Winnie raised an eyebrow. "It's true, and you know it."

Suzanne spread the doors, and the skirt of her new dress leaped to freedom. The girls sighed in admiration when she removed the gown from the wardrobe.

The emerald green, A-line dress made of lace and tulle had a scoop neck and three-quarter sleeves. At the narrow waist was a wide band, and the skirt held enough tulle to choke an elephant.

"Oh, Suzanne. It's the prettiest dress I've ever seen," Doreen said.

"When you see mine, you'll say it's the second prettiest," Winnie interjected. "It's a beautiful pink with a white lace collar and cuffs. This dress, however, is heavenly and comes in at a close number two."

Suzanne felt a pang of guilt about owning it. Such a dress deserved a better model. "Too bad my face isn't anywhere near as pretty as this dress. Mother had to order this from Famous-Barr in St. Louis because I can't carry off a lesser dress."

"That's not true," Winnie said. "You have a pleasant face."

Doreen nodded. "I'd give anything to look as intelligent as you do."

Suzanne held up her hand. "Stop. Both of you. We all know my features don't quite fit my face. I'm not begging for misplaced compliments. I'm just telling you why my mother bought me such a magnificent dress."

Doreen touched the tulle. "It's a beautiful color. It'll bring out the reddish highlights in your hair."

"That's it!" Winnie gasped. "I knew this dress reminded me of something. I couldn't put my finger on it. Scarlett's curtain dress in *Gone with the Wind*."

Suzanne chuckled. "Only because it's green. It's not velvet."

Mrs. Thatcher's voice rose from the first floor. "Are you girls in my room?"

Doreen's eyebrows shot to her hairline. In a whisper, she asked, "How does she know?"

Suzanne smirked. "It's nothing magical. There's a squeaky board up here. You can hear it in the kitchen." She shoved the dress back into the wardrobe and stepped to the doorway. "We're leaving, Mother. Just admiring my new dress."

"Gotta go!" Doreen ran out of the room and down the stairs before anyone could say goodbye. The sound of the front door closing verified her departure.

"Your mother petrifies poor Doreen. I don't understand why."

"She may petrify all of us at some point, but her mother, my grandmother, was way worse."

"I don't remember your Nana being scary."

"That's because she wasn't. Nana was my father's mother. Grandmummy, mother's mother from England, was terrifying. She died before you and I started hanging out together. My mother seems warm and cozy compared to her."

Winnie shuddered. "If that's true, she must have been awful. Why don't I remember her from church?"

"She went to a different one, closer to what she was used to in England."

Confusion sparkled in Winnie's eyes. Her family would never divide ranks and attend different churches.

Winnie shrugged. "I'd better go too. Need to avoid those 'evil eyes' your mother gives when I've stayed too long." She started down the staircase, then whispered back to Suzanne. "And that voice. Her 'controlled anger' sends shivers up my spine." Raising her voice to normal level, she called out, "Talk to you tomorrow."

Chapter Five

Liesl
November 8

Liesl shivered involuntarily. How could a voice produce such reactions? Would she melt into a puddle when face-to-face with him?

Get a grip, girl. She searched the kitchen for something to busy her hands. After collecting dirty dishes from the table, she sped to the sink. Soapy dishwater would hide her shakiness.

Nicole's voice echoed down the hall as she chatted with the visitor. When she crossed the kitchen threshold, she said, "Liesl? Kurt's here to see you."

With deliberate slowness, Liesl glanced in his direction and nodded. Was her face a pale shade of green? Her ice cream lunch wasn't sitting well. She stared at him and didn't invite him to sit down.

Other than slight crow's feet near his eyes, he looked the same—tall and muscle-bound like a linebacker. His presence filled the space between them. His tweed sport coat fit snugly, wide at the shoulders and nipped at the waist. The dark sapphire shirt he wore caused his multi-hued eyes to shine blue.

He transferred his weight from one foot to the other as if waiting for someone to break the silence. Finally, he cleared his throat.

"I ... I came here as soon as they told me about your aunt. I'm so sorry I missed her funeral. I was at a convention in Colorado."

"I see." Liesl's voice sounded steadier than she felt. Thank the Lord. "Must have been a long convention."

He frowned at her comment. "My cousin Ronny lives near Colorado Springs. You remember him, don't you?"

She nodded, recalling a rail-thin fellow with blond hair.

"He's been after me for years to go elk hunting. With the convention there, I could do both. I was told about Miss Suzanne this morning." He paused. "Today's my first day back at work."

Liesl sighed. "Sorry to be snippy. I didn't know."

He took a step, then hesitated. "What a loss for you and for our town."

"Thank you." In the past, all her problems disappeared when he wrapped her in a hug. Today she remained tethered to the floor, problems tethered with her.

An awkward silence stretched. Liesl returned to scrubbing dishes while Kurt ran his fingers through his brown hair. His gesture revealed a pistol in a shoulder holster. Since when did he carry a handgun?

"I was told she became ill and never recovered. Do they know what it was?"

"So far, they're calling it the flu. Dr. Johnson promised he'd review her records and all the tests from the hospital. He didn't expect her to deteriorate so quickly. He wants answers as much as I do."

"If anything suspicious comes out of it, please call me. I want to help."

Why would she call him?

Nicole jumped in, directing a question at Kurt. "How do you like being part of the detective squad now?"

Kurt turned to Nicole. "It's both a challenging experience and the most exciting thing I've ever done. A gigantic leap in my career."

Nicole told Liesl, "They promoted Kurt to detective last month." Then she said to Kurt, "I'm sure you'll do a great job."

They continued to chat while Liesl studied him. She'd hoped the years would have allowed her to get over her feelings for him, but the rollercoaster sensation in her stomach showed otherwise. Why couldn't she leave her affection for him in the past? Especially after his betrayal.

"Liesl?"

Nicole's expression told her she'd missed something. "Sorry."

"Kurt asked if you were going to move back to Mexico."

She looked from Nicole to Kurt, then back, and shrugged. "I haven't decided anything."

Nicole turned to Kurt. "Like I was saying, Mrs. Schrader left her this house. As a real estate agent, I cautioned Liesl against making a quick decision after such an enormous loss."

They faced Liesl again, and she continued attacking the dishes. "It's going to be a hard decision. I love my apartment in Houston, and I have great neighbors. Thankfully, with several months remaining on my lease, I have time to decide."

"This house is amazing, but it'll cost a fortune on upkeep alone," Kurt said.

Although with the size of her inheritance, the point was moot. Liesl nodded as if considering the operating costs.

"Whether you stay or go, install an alarm system," Kurt said. "Crimes against property have become a problem."

"Do you know a local company?"

He held up two fingers. "Either will do you right."

"Our star quarterback, Donnie Davis, owns Mexico Security Service," Nicole said. "He'll take good care of you."

Kurt's face clouded.

Liesl secretly enjoyed Kurt's discomfort. "Thanks. I'll give Donnie a call."

Chapter Six

Liesl

That night, Liesl boxed her pillows like a prizefighter, haunted by her immature behavior in front of Kurt. Her crushed pride had tortured her for nearly seven years. When could she let it go? No matter what she said or did, nothing would change the history between them.

His betrayal was complete, but wasn't it time to move forward?

She flung off the bedcovers and groped for her robe. Her brain would not allow sleep, so she headed to the couch in the second-story living area. The pull of silvery moonlight lured her to the large second-floor window at the front of the house. She made a nest on the padded window seat and wrapped herself in a plaid fleece laprobe. A whiff of Aunt Suzanne's perfume remained on the blanket, making her simultaneously happy and sad.

Faint, rhythmic pings from the basement boiler belched heat. Steam hissed through the pipes. The musical sounds blended into a jazzy combo when joined by the occasional creaks of the house. This familiar symphony was like her second heartbeat, and she relaxed. This house was almost a living entity to her.

As a child, she'd imagined a giant worked in the basement, blowing heat through the pipes to keep them warm. After tiptoeing down the narrow stairway to capture a glimpse of him at work, her courage had vanished when confronted with the massive metal door dividing the playroom from his boiler room lair, which sent her Strawberry Shortcake sneakers flying upstairs.

As teenagers, her friends would arrive for a sleepover with high expectations. They'd drag sleeping bags and pillows to the playroom side of the basement, blare rock music, and eat popcorn until some unearthly clank frightened them back above ground.

She and Kurt had shared many chuckles generated by the boiler. At the end of countless dates, entwined in a romantic clutch or a kiss, they'd crumble in hoots of laughter as the rattle of the steam in the pipes sounded more like passing gas.

She was now the new owner of the metal beast. Uncertain of its care and feeding, she'd also need to get it examined for safety—another item on her ever-expanding list of "Things That Must Be Done Now That Aunt Suzanne Is Gone." A sad list.

The double window showed the absence of traffic on the boulevard, which signaled the lateness of the hour. Circles formed by the streetlights resembled spotlights on a stage, as if they waited for someone to step into the glow and sing. Frozen dew shone silver in the moonlight, and the wheat-colored grass of winter spiked in all directions. Clumps of snow winked beneath trees and bushes.

Movement across the street caught her eye.

Was it a branch dancing in the wind? Someone else sleepless tonight? She stared at oversized bushes beneath the neighbor's picture window. That house was vacant. The Murrys had packed up their empty nest and retired in South Carolina.

Again, there was movement. Someone was out there. Before she could react, a dark figure threw a large object through the window, and the splintered shards fell, sparkling in the moonlight. Two black-clad figures pushed glass debris from the lower ledge and pulled themselves into the home. Tiny lights blinked in the room, then went out.

She bolted from the window seat, skidded across the polished wooden floor in her effort to get her phone from the bedroom. With it in hand, she tapped out 9-1-1.

"Nine-one-one. Please state your emergency," a woman's voice said.

"The house across from 1105 South Jefferson Street is being robbed. I saw them break in."

"How many people did you see?"

"Two, but there could be more." Liesl walked back to the window. The neighbor's house remained dark. "Two at the front of the house. There could be more in back."

"Did you see any weapons?"

"Too dark to tell."

"I'll dispatch the police. Please stay on the line."

The dispatcher called for response and relayed Liesl's address.

Liesl tried to correct her, "No, across from 1105 South Jefferson. The Murrys' house," but the dispatcher was still talking to the responding officer.

When the dispatcher returned, Liesl explained the location issue and held while the address was corrected.

"Are you calling from the Schrader residence?" asked the dispatcher.

"Yes, ma'am, my aunt is ... er, was Suzanne Schrader."

"I'm sorry for your loss."

Small-town condolences. It warmed her heart. Even the emergency dispatcher knew her aunt. "Thank you."

"Can you still see the intruders?"

"I've been watching the house. The ones who broke in haven't come out, at least not out where I can see."

"Please describe the suspects."

"Two figures, could be men or women, wearing black. Hoodie sweatshirts or jackets, black pants or jeans, dark sneakers or boots."

"Did you see the suspects' vehicle?"

"They came on foot from behind the house. They shattered the big window, and it caught my attention."

The wail of a siren cut through their conversation. Dogs howled. "I hear 'em coming."

"Please stay on the line," the dispatcher said. "I'd like you to confirm they're heading to the right place."

"No problem." Flashing blue lights signaled the imminent arrival of the squad car. A white sedan with bar lights flashing across its roof skidded from the boulevard onto South Jefferson Street. When it screeched to a stop in the middle of the street, there was a scream of rubber on pavement. "They're here."

The car doors burst open, and two uniformed officers exited. They approached the dark house quickly, with caution.

"They are heading to the right house."

"Thanks for your help," the dispatcher said. "Disconnecting now."

Within seconds, two more cars appeared. One of the first responders climbed through the broken window while one remained outside. The two fresh additions ran around toward the back of the house.

Liesl let out a breath she didn't realize she'd been holding.

A fourth car squealed to a stop, this one dark with blue and red lights flashing in its grille. A non-uniformed driver exited the car. He approached the officer stationed in front, and they conversed. Then both heads turned to stare at her.

The one dressed in civilian clothes walked toward her house. She recognized that loping walk. Kurt. Why was he coming here?

* * *

Liesl careened down the flight of stairs in her slippers, hesitating only to grab her coat beside the door. When she stepped onto the porch, the burst of frigid air made her shiver. She pulled on her gloves and rushed down the steps to meet him.

Kurt's long strides made crunching sounds as he drew near. "Are you all right?"

She nodded.

"Did they try to break into your house?"

"I don't think so. They were in the bushes at the Murry place. When they broke the window, I called 911."

"When your address came across the scanner, I nearly jumped out of my skin. I got here as fast as I could. How many are there?"

"Two, I think." Liesl hugged herself to keep warm.

"Did you see a car?"

"Nope."

He reached out and gripped her arm. "I told you to get an alarm system."

She jerked his arm away and hissed, "Yes. This afternoon. I

can't move mountains, Kurt. As soon as you left, I called for an appointment. It's tomorrow."

He frowned. "Sorry. I'm just concerned about your safety." He glanced over at the other house. "I've got to get back."

"Go. I'm certainly not trying to keep you here." Liesl rubbed her runny nose on her sleeve.

He scowled. "You need to come to the station and file an eyewitness report."

"Tonight?"

"No, morning will be soon enough."

"Fine. Uncle Max always said no good deed goes unpunished. He was right."

She spun and marched across the frozen grass. Her anger evaporated when a large black-and-tan object lying on the porch brought her to a halt.

She fell to her knees. The moonlight provided enough illumination for her to see that it was Aunt Suzanne's camel-hair coat, burned black in spots. She moved to gather it into her arms, but stopped when she realized it might still be hot.

Kurt's voice boomed beside her. "What is that?"

His flashlight winked into action and confirmed her fears.

"Aunt Suzanne's coat."

"Did you do this?"

She spun toward him and asked through gritted teeth, "Why would I set my dead aunt's coat on fire?"

He ignored her venom and squatted beside her. Holding his palms above the coat for a moment, he pronounced it cool. With the handle of his flashlight, he pushed the material forward and studied the boards of the porch where it had been lying.

"It wasn't burned here." He touched the area the coat had covered. "No heat damage like blistered paint. Someone burned this elsewhere and brought it here." He bent down and sniffed. "Smells like lighter fluid." He turned to her. "When did you last see this?"

Liesl rocked back on her heels. "It was hanging by the door inside. Today I ran some errands after you and Nicole left. I didn't notice if it was still there when I left or returned."

"You're sure you locked up?"

"Of course. I'm obsessive about it."

"Notice anything disturbed?"

"Nothing."

Kurt's radio squawked. He stood and tugged it from the clip.

She wiped her nose again and studied him as he conversed with his people.

He returned the radio to his belt and jerked his head at the other house. "They've captured two men, and I've got to go down to the station with them. Let me walk through your house first and make sure everything is secure. You'd better come down there with me tonight. This has to be reported. It's both arson and vandalism, if not outright theft. I don't like this one bit. Fire is usually a sign of anger and aggression."

She considered that and looked down at her robe. "I need to change."

"Hold on a second. Let me look for tracks." He circled the house while she stood on the porch and shivered.

On his return, he asked, "Was this out here when you rushed out?"

"I don't know, I was looking at you. I could have missed it."

"Right. It's doubtful I'd have missed seeing someone sling this onto the porch while we talked."

"Why would anyone steal, burn, then bring back my aunt's coat?"

His hazel eyes didn't provide any answers.

Liesl shivered, this time from fear rather than the cold.

* * *

Kurt made a quick check of the house before giving Liesl the okay to change clothes. When she'd dressed, she found him pacing downstairs.

"I checked your downstairs doors and windows, and they're all secure."

"Thank you."

"Does anyone else have a key to the house?"

"Several of Aunt Suzanne's friends would probably have one."

"You need to look into that or consider changing the locks."

"Will do."

"Can you go grab a paper bag? I'd like to use it to transport the coat."

On the porch, they carefully transferred it to the bag without touching it.

"I'll take you to the station."

"How will I get home?"

"I'll bring you back." They walked to his car, and he opened the passenger door for her. "I need to talk to the other officers for just a minute."

She slid into the car as he strode toward the house suffering the break-in.

His car was a welcome oasis of warmth on such a cold, strange night. The heater stirred the scent of aftershave. She glanced at all the radio and police gear, resisting the urge to touch.

Movement in the back seat made her scream and catapulted her out the passenger door. She huffed white clouds of panic into the frosty air, peering with caution through the open door into the back seat. A boy's head popped into view, and she breathed a sigh of relief. She returned to the front seat to take her first look at Kurt's son.

The boy's wheat-colored hair framed a face similar to Kurt's, but the softness in his chin and lips must have come from his mother's gene pool. He was wrapped in a blanket, wearing Dallas Cowboys pajamas.

"Hello, there. I'm Liesl."

"Sorry I scared you. I'm Ross. Where's my dad?"

"He'll be back soon. He's helping with the arrest of some burglars."

"Were they breaking into your house?"

"See that house?" She pointed to the scene of the crime. "That's the one broken into." Tapping the passenger window beside her, she added, "That one's mine. I saw them break in and called the police."

After wiping sleep from his eyes, he looked around.

"Do you always ride along with your dad when he's called out?"

"He won't let me stay home alone, even though I'm six years old."

"I have to agree with him, although you're awfully grown up."

Her stomach, already in knots because of the evening's events, ached. For six years, she'd avoided confronting the physical proof of Kurt's betrayal of their relationship. Why did she have to face him tonight?

Ross scooted to the middle of the back seat and then climbed to the front, dragging his blanket with him. He settled behind the wheel and looked at her. "How did you see the bad guys? Were you outside?"

"No, I was in that big window on the second floor."

"Your house looks spooky."

She couldn't argue with him about that. From his

perspective, a big Victorian house might be scary. "There aren't any ghosts. Although, when I was little, I believed there was a giant in the basement."

"Really?" He grinned, exposing a hole where a tooth used to be. "Could I see it one day?"

"Ah ... sure. I'll take you on a tour anytime, but the giant was only in my imagination."

"I wanna go into that round area up at the top."

"That's a turret. When I was a child, my aunt let me play there. I pretended to be a princess in a tower, kidnapped by an evil queen. Kind of like Rapunzel, except no golden hair."

"I have golden hair."

"Yes, you do. You must have inherited it from your mother."

Ross frowned. "I don't have a mother."

The look on his small face made her regret her words.

He turned and stared out the driver's window.

"I'm sorry. It's tough growing up without a mother. I was two years old when both of my parents passed away. My great aunt and uncle raised me in *that* house."

He looked at me. "Really?"

She nodded. "Truth."

"Daddy and I do just fine by ourselves."

"I'm sure you do. Can your daddy cook?"

"He makes great pancakes and hamburgers. I make the macaroni and cheese."

The driver's door opened, and Kurt said, "Hey buddy, move it to the back seat."

Ross dove over the seat, dragging the blanket in his wake. "Did you get the bad guys?"

"Yep," Kurt said, settling into the car. "Now buckle up." He turned to her. "You too."

She did as Kurt requested but refrained from looking at

him. If he saw her face, he'd see how tough it was for her to meet his son.

"Did you all get acquainted?"

Ross piped up. "Her name's Lisa, and she didn't have a mother or a dad when she was a little girl."

Kurt chuckled. "It's Liesl. Miss Liesl to you. And she's an old friend of mine."

"Did she see you play football?"

"She did. All of my games."

All but one. Because of that one night, there was a little boy named Ross in the back seat.

Chapter Seven

Suzanne
March 12, 1961

S uzanne rarely begged, but she needed her mother's car for hauling supplies and decorations to Winnie's house. Winnie expected party attendees to decorate. After several minutes of bickering and eliciting Suzanne's promise to return the car before noon, her mother handed over the keys. With a false tone of humility, Suzanne thanked her and silently prayed for her own car one day, even if it was a jalopy like her brother's car. Anything to keep from having to plead a vehicle from her mother.

At Winnie's house, cars and trucks of various ages and colors dotted the long driveway. At a glance, she associated owner names to most of the conveyances outside the home, including bicycles, similar to the way she knew who was home by the shoes at the back door. That was small-town life. If you spotted an unknown vehicle, it must belong to someone new to town or a stranger passing through.

She was leaning deep into the trunk of the car, wrestling with an uncooperative, oversized box, when someone shouted.

"Suzanne, stop. You're making me laugh. I'll get it for you."

The offer from her soon-to-be savior made her smile. "Edgar!" She abandoned the struggle. "You're a lifesaver."

He grinned as he approached. A ball cap covered his hair, but he wore no coat or jacket to protect him from the cold.

"You're gonna freeze. I know you gave your letter jacket to Winnie, but don't you own other coats?"

He chuckled. "Sure, but I only ran outside to throw something in my truck, not stay in this arctic wonderland." He reached into the trunk and lifted the awkward box with ease. "Now, if you would, I'll take this straight up to the third floor." He peered at her over the box. "Assuming that's where it goes."

"Yes. Thank you. I'll just grab these two smaller boxes, and that does it."

"Is Myron coming to help?"

She shrugged. "He left the house before I pried mother's car keys out of her hands. As the annoying little sister, the less I know, the happier he is."

"He's constantly saying you don't rat him out. He appreciates your silence."

"Must be why he keeps me in the dark. The less I know, the less I'm tempted to tell."

"Maybe."

When they crossed the snowy yard to the front sidewalk, she spotted someone she didn't recognize standing near the street corner. It was a man. Older. Wearing a brown hat. Dressed in a well-used overcoat and pants. A laborer?

Before she could ask Edgar if he knew him, he asked her a question.

"He's coming to the party, isn't he?"

"Who? That man?"

"What man?"

She gestured with her head toward the general direction of the man near the street.

Edgar glanced at him and chuckled. "No. I was talking about your brother. Is he coming tonight?"

"I guess so. Mother wants him to, and she's usually the deciding vote." After a pause, she asked, "Who's that man?"

Edgar eyed him. "I don't think I've seen him before." Then he climbed the porch stairs.

She followed him and opened the front door of the three-story Craftsman-style house. It was a charming place, perfect for the party. The dancing would occur in the third-floor attic space.

Winnie's mother waved at her from her seat at the dining room table. Spread out in front of her were varying shades of pink, red, and green tissue paper. By the look of things, she was constructing paper flowers.

Winnie's family was going to decorate the downstairs for the time of eating cake and giving presents. Teenagers would decorate the attic they'd claim for the rest of the evening.

* * *

Elvis Presley was crooning, "It's Now or Never," when Suzanne and Edgar reached the summit of the stairs. The number of people scurrying around doing chores amazed her.

Winnie had already organized groups. She had a future in management or event planning. She possessed the ability to make young men fall at her feet to do her bidding, and gals appreciated her suggestions of improvement. A collection of the more athletic guys was shifting boxes and old furniture into the corners of the room while Winnie supervised. She waved at Suzanne and returned to bossing around the fellas. Once the primary space was cleared, decorating could begin.

A year's dust had accumulated in the attic since last year's shindig. Several groups, mostly girls, currently attacked this issue. Doreen seemed in charge of one group.

The four corners of the attic had roof rafters that slanted from ceiling to floor. They were hazards for head hitting. The center of the floor, however, was amazing because of the vaulted ceiling. Each side of the attic had two windows, filling the space with light until sundown. At night, some people used the dark corners for requisite smooching and handholding. So far, no one had ever invited Suzanne into a corner.

Standing near one corner, not even pretending to work, was her pal Patricia. She wore a round, pale green skirt, crisp white blouse, and a wool sweater draped across her shoulders. The rest of them wore jeans and sweatshirts, clothes suitable for labor. Patricia stood alone, peering at the workers as if they were a science experiment she monitored.

Patricia's lack of exertion needed to be rectified, so Suzanne moved toward her, planning what actions to take. Edgar's voice interrupted her thoughts.

"Where do you want this, Suzanne?" He stood in the middle of the chaos, balancing the box.

She pointed at a table near Patricia. "Why don't we put Patricia to work?"

He winked at her and moved to the table.

Patricia stared at the box as if it were something to fear. When Edgar placed it on the table, she stepped to the side, as if to leave.

Edgar grinned at Patricia, which caused her to hesitate then flash her brightest smile.

"No flirting," Suzanne said. "You don't get to make eyes at

Edgar, my dear. You and I are in charge of the contents of that box." She turned to Edgar. "Thanks for your help."

"Anytime."

They watched him go, then Suzanne turned to Patricia. "So, even though it was you who broke up with him, you still like him?"

"No, I just can't resist smiling at a handsome man, even if he isn't the man for me."

"How long have you been doing nothing, watching everyone else work?"

Patricia glanced at her wristwatch then crossed her arms, readying for a fight. "You just got here yourself. It's not like you've been slaving away for hours."

"It took hours to convince Mother to loan me her car. That's different from being here and pretending work is beneath you."

Patricia frowned. "It's not that work is beneath me, it's that I'm not willing to get dirty."

"Nor are you dressed for it. For heaven's sake, don't you own a pair of jeans?"

Patricia stared at Suzanne as if she'd asked her to go fishing. "You should have called me. I would have picked you up, and whatever things you needed to bring."

"I didn't think about it. I forget you have your own car. Lucky girl. I'll have to make a habit of asking you for a ride."

Patricia smiled and relaxed her arms. "And what a car it is too. I love it. Call me anytime. I mean it."

"Who wouldn't want to ride in a 1961 white Ford Thunderbird convertible with red leather seats? How silly of me."

"That's right, and don't you forget it." Patricia's fingers danced through her perfect hair, then she gestured toward the table. "So, what are we doing with this box?"

"Winnie asked me to bring the decorations from my birthday party. This attic is gigantic. She thought we could use my stuff on and around the punch and cookie table." Suzanne waved her arms. "It was serendipitous to find you standing so close to what will be the punch and cookie table."

She opened the box, and they worked to decorate the area until a loud noise startled them. They both whirled to see what happened.

Angry voices came from the far side of the room. Ray Thompson, one of the senior classmen, reach down and picked up a wooden ladder off the floor. The guy next to him appeared to shove someone in front of him. She couldn't see who was pushed because a crowd had gathered.

Suzanne took a step to go over, but Patricia grabbed her arm.

"You have no business getting involved in some guy fight."

"How do you know it's a guy fight?"

"There are only guys over there. You could get hurt."

Suzanne shook off Patricia's grip but stayed in place. Patricia had a point. A guy fight could erupt into swinging fists and rolling around the floor.

Winnie's mother came bounding up the stairs. "What in the world happened? Is someone hurt?"

Ray turned to Mrs. Whitcomb. "No ma'am. Billy, there, banged into Tom, and it knocked this ladder out of his hands."

Billy was Edgar's eight-year-old brother. The older boys picked on him, which made the ladder's "fall" suspicious. Tom or Ray probably tore it out of Billy's hands and threw it on the floor.

Mrs. Whitcomb approached the red-faced Billy. "Is that right?"

Billy pushed up his glasses and then looked from Tom to Ray. He nodded at Mrs. Whitcomb.

She patted Billy's shoulder. "No harm done, right?" She waved at the crowd standing around. "Show's over. Get back to work. Anybody know where I can find Winnie?"

Suzanne turned to Patricia. "Have you seen her? She was here when I arrived."

"She was flitting around organizing everyone. I don't think I've seen her since you arrived."

"I saw her managing a group of the guys moving furniture when I came up. But I don't see her now."

Doreen approached Mrs. Whitcomb. "I know where Winnie is. Do you want me to go get her?"

Mrs. Whitcomb smiled and nodded. "That would be lovely, dear."

A smug look crossed Doreen's face.

"Look, Patricia." Suzanne nodded toward Doreen. "What's she up to?"

"My guess is, she knows where Winnie has disappeared to with the handsome Edgar. She probably wants to break up their fun and rat them out to Mrs. Whitcomb."

Suzanne speared Patricia with a look. "That's not very nice."

"Not nice, but true. Admit it. Everyone loves Edgar. He's as handsome as Elvis. Doreen has a crush on him, like every other girl in this town. It'll make her happy to break up whatever private moment they're having."

"Not *every* girl has a crush on him," Suzanne said. "I don't. He's a nice guy, but he's like another brother to me."

"You may be the only girl able to resist his charms. I suspect Doreen has it bad for him. She's a little strange that way."

Suzanne threw up her arms. "You call her strange, yet you came here under the guise of helping with the party, when all you're doing is checking out the guys."

Patricia raised an eyebrow. "You think there's something wrong with that?"

Suzanne laughed. "Come on. We need to finish hanging these decorations. I've got to take Mother's car back before noon."

"When you need to go, I can follow you and bring you back here."

"Great idea."

Suzanne noticed Billy trying to stay away from the older guys. "Just a second. I'm going to get Billy to help us. He'll be safe over here until Edgar reappears."

"Must you?"

Suzanne grinned. "Yes, I must. Now be nice to him. He's only a little boy."

"And therein lies the problem."

"Not everything in the world revolves around handsome guys."

Patricia fluffed her hair. "Not in *your* world, perhaps."

Chapter Eight

Liesl
November 9

The aroma of freshly brewed coffee teased Liesl's nostrils as soon as they pushed through the door of the public safety department. A hail of greetings erupted, all of them directed at Ross.

The desk sergeant waved at Ross and pointed to a bowl near her. "There's a candy bar in there with your name on it," she said with a wink.

Ross skipped to her desk, grabbed the candy, and stuffed it into his mouth with glee.

"Roxy, I'm coming to you when his teeth rot," Kurt said, with a look of disgust.

She laughed and waved away his comment. "There's milk in chocolate. It's good for you." She turned. "Right, Liesl?"

Liesl smiled. "Good to see you again." Roxy had been friends with Aunt Suzanne and attended her funeral.

Kurt groaned. "The two of you are ganging up against me."

He jerked his head toward the back of the building. "Let's go to my office. Ross, you can watch television in the breakroom."

Liesl followed him as he snaked his way past empty desks and stopped in front of a glass door that read: Detectives.

Kurt paused at the door. "I'm very proud to be part of the detective squad. It's exciting to be doing this now."

"Good for you."

He flashed her a grin as he opened the door. "Thanks."

The room had a faint odor of musty papers. One wall held windows hidden by drooping vinyl blinds. Grey metal, three-drawer file cabinets fronted the other three walls. File boxes, stacked three high, towered on the vinyl floor. The center of the room held four metal desks, pushed into pairs facing each other.

He crossed to one of the battered desks, pushed files and papers aside, and indicated for her to sit in his chair. Then he plucked a piece of paper from a stack on his desk. "This is an incident report form. Complete it with as much detail as possible."

"Paper? There's no electronic form?"

"Not exactly. You'll fill out the paper form, and I'll scan it into the system."

Liesl shuffled around the desk and plopped into the squeaky wooden chair. "What do I say? That I witnessed two black-clad, unidentified individuals break into the neighbor's house and then found my aunt's burned coat on my porch? That's going to be great."

Kurt frowned. "No, Miss Sarcastic. You're going to say you witnessed the vandalism and attempted robbery of the neighbor's house. While providing details about said break-in to a detective, you found a vandalized coat belonging to your deceased aunt on your front porch. The item suffered fire and heat damage. You note it's likely someone removed or stole it from your house at an earlier time. It appeared the coat was burned at an unknown location, as no fire or heat damage occurred to your porch. This made you conclude it is likely that a person or persons unknown deposited it on your porch. Because of these unfortunate events, you request your home be added as a special interest drive-by on the normal patrol route."

She glanced away from his piercing gaze, glowing with restrained fury. "Okay. Your version is better. I'll do my best to write it that way."

He nodded. "I've got to check on the booking of our vandals. Be back in a minute. Want coffee?"

"No, thanks. I'd like to sleep sometime tonight."

At the close of the door, she grumbled about his bossy and brash demeanor. When they'd dated, the only conflicts they'd experienced, until his betrayal, related to his bossiness. Obviously, this hadn't changed.

With a sigh, she found a pen and started on the report, using Kurt's version of events. Once finished, she perused the file cabinets and boxes filling the room. Were these active investigations? Maybe old murder files were stored here. Should she search for the original investigator's report on Winifred Whitcomb's death?

Kurt stuck his head in the door. "Finished?"

"Yes."

He crossed the room and started reading her report. After a moment, he said, "Pretty good. I'll get this scanned."

"Considering your words are on that paper, it should be good. Is that all we need to do?"

"That's all for now."

She stood and moved over to the file cabinets. "You have a lot of stuff."

"We're bursting at the seams. Our recent cases are

digitized. The plan is to digitize our old records, except for physical evidence, as soon as we have enough money." He waved his hand at the file boxes stacked on the floor. "We've moved the closed cases and our older, unsolved ones into the basement. We're overflowing."

Winifred's murder would definitely be an older, unsolved case. Could she get her hands on that report? She resented asking Kurt for any kind of favor, but she'd set aside her pride if he'd consider it. Would a Freedom of Information Act request get her hands on it? She'd look into that. In the meantime, she wanted to go home.

"Have we lost Ross?"

"I'm sure he's with Roxy, stuffing candy in his face." Kurt motioned her toward the door. "I'm sending the coat to the State Crime Lab for testing. That takes some time. I'll try to pull some strings to find out quickly what accelerant was used to burn it. My best guess is lighter fluid." He turned to her. "Once you've had some sleep, the plan is for us to have a discussion about why someone would burn your aunt's coat."

Chapter Nine

Liesl

The ancient revolving doors of the downtown Mexico Bank branch whistled when Liesl pushed into the building later that morning. Mr. Barnaby sat at his desk behind a glass wall. He waved and snaked his way toward her through the lobby.

Tall and olive-skinned, he'd been a fixture at the bank as long as she could remember. Kind brown eyes searched her face, and his neatly clipped mustache drew attention to his sincere smile. His only flaw was a toupee that resembled doll hair more than human hair. It didn't match the brown and gray fringe at the sides of his head.

Liesl smiled and let her negative thoughts dissipate. As a child, he'd given her a sucker on every bank visit. Other than his unfortunate choice of toupee, she held him in the highest esteem. At Aunt Suzanne's funeral, his eyes had filled with tears expressing his condolences.

"Good morning, Liesl. Good to see you. Van de Berg hasn't

arrived yet, but that's no surprise. Cup of coffee while we wait?"

"I'd love one."

"And a sucker?"

She chuckled. After greeting one of her friends and a cousin, both working as tellers, she followed him to the lobby coffee bar.

The corporate world had embraced the casual look, but not Mr. Barnaby. His silk tie and dark suit seemed fancy, even for a small-town bank president. He poured coffee and handed it over.

She inhaled the aroma while he prepared a cup for himself.

"You remembered the keys to the lock boxes?"

She patted my purse. "Got 'em right here."

"You're already a signatory for all of your aunt's accounts here. Would you like new checks in your name?"

"Yes, I'll need those."

"You prefer to keep the mailing address for all the accounts the same?"

"The house is fine. I've inherited it, but I haven't decided if I'm moving back permanently. Nicole says I don't need to make a hasty decision."

He nodded. "I agree. It's a big decision. It's been your home since you were a toddler."

"It means so much to me. Could I stand to sell it?"

"That's a question only you can answer. Keep in mind this checking account automatically pulls from her savings if you write a check beyond the balance, eliminating overdraft charges."

"Assuming there's enough in the savings account?"

He averted his eyes. "I'm sure the amount is sufficient for your needs."

He knew Aunt Suzanne's net worth. Best to confirm that with Mr. Van de Berg.

In his office, he typed the order for the new checks while they exchanged small talk.

Mr. Barnaby monitored the lobby, excusing himself when he spotted Mr. Van de Berg.

Liesl used his absence to perform a fishing expedition in her purse, snagging the lockbox keys. She lined the three of them along the edge of the desk. They looked innocuous but would unlock the past today.

Van de Berg bustled into the office and shook her hand.

"Good morning, my dear. I hope Barnaby hasn't talked your ear off while I extracted myself from a harangue by one of my clients."

Barnaby frowned at Van de Berg's comment. Likely, he'd have lobbed a brusque reply if they'd been alone.

The lawyer set his briefcase on his lap and popped the clasps.

"Please use my desk," Mr. Barnaby suggested, clearing away a small stack of paper.

Van de Berg placed the case in the area offered and then extracted three sets of papers.

"These are your copies." He dealt a set to each of them.

Mr. Barnaby produced reading glasses from his jacket pocket and studied his packet. Liesl flipped through the pages, then turned back to the front for deeper scrutiny.

"The probate court has agreed to my motion," Mr. Van de Berg said. "This allows Liesl immediate access to the bank storage boxes in her aunt's name. You and I, George, must produce an inventory of the contents for the court."

Barnaby nodded. "Of course."

Van de Berg faced Liesl. "Did you bring your keys?"

She waved her hand at them, lined up like a squad of soldiers.

Barnaby examined each key, then pulled signature cards from a manila file near his elbow. After matching a card with each key, he tapped a card in his hand. "There's one more box. Do you have another?" He looked at her expectantly.

Liesl shrugged. "I don't have any others." She turned to Mr. Van de Berg. "Do you have another key somewhere?"

He looked surprised. "No, I sure don't." He pulled his cell phone from his pocket. "I'll call the office and ask them to look for any other keys. I don't remember any."

"It's probably somewhere in the house, Liesl," Mr. Barnaby suggested as he pointed to the card. "Suzanne shows recent use of this one. About a week before she passed."

After a brief conversation with his office manager, Mr. Van de Berg pocketed his phone. "My staff isn't aware of another key. Let's open the ones we have." He turned to Liesl. "You'll need to locate the key for the last box."

* * *

While Liesl was driving to meet Nicole for lunch, Mr. Van de Berg called her.

"I didn't say anything in front of Barnaby, but all your aunt's investment information is with the accountants and investment firm she used in St. Louis. That's why so few financial documents were in the bank boxes."

"That makes sense."

"You should meet with them as soon as possible. They'll explain what they're doing, and you can decide if you want them to continue."

She sighed. What did she know about investments? This

was something else she needed to learn. "Could you give me their contact information?"

She pulled over while Mr. Van de Berg searched for the information. She scrambled to find a pen and paper in her purse. After noting their number and web address, she asked him about Mr. Barnaby.

"How much does Mr. Barnaby know about Aunt Suzanne's money?"

Mr. Van de Berg sighed, "More than I'd like. Your aunt insisted her investment firm use his bank as much as possible. He has knowledge of some certificates of deposit, the money she regularly transferred in from St. Louis, plus her substantial savings and checking accounts at his bank. I doubt if he knows anything about her investment accounts, such as her stocks and bonds."

"He must have kept his mouth shut all these years. The townspeople don't know my aunt had a lot of money. If they did, they'd have talked about it."

Mr. Van de Berg harrumphed. "Regardless, you need to talk to the people in St. Louis about spreading around your assets. There are more banks in this town. It makes much more sense to have several smaller accounts than a few large ones."

Mr. Van de Berg sat on the board of another bank in town. Did he have an ownership interest in it? Perhaps he was jealous that Aunt Suzanne kept her banking business elsewhere. She used his legal services, but maybe he was envious that Mr. Barnaby handled all her banking interests. Maybe that explained the tension between them.

Before she started driving again, she called the accounting firm in St. Louis and made an appointment for Monday.

Chapter Ten

Suzanne
March 18, 1961

The sound of running feet pulled Suzanne out of sleep. She registered that the day had dawned, but it was still early. Footstep grew louder as they approached her bedroom. She sat upright, expecting her mother to enter.

It surprised her when Winnie threw open the door. She was still wearing her coat and gloves, and tears streamed down her face.

"What's wrong?"

She fell onto her bed with a sob. "My life is ruined."

"Ruined? Oh, no. Your mom figured out you flunked the algebra test?"

Winnie raised her head and wiped her nose with a gloved hand. "No! I don't care about the stupid algebra test. It's Edgar."

"Is he okay?"

"He's fine, but I'm not."

Suzanne reached for tissues and tossed the box in Winnie's direction. "Here. Get ahold of yourself. Tell me what's going on."

During a combination of coat removal, sniveling, and blowing her nose, Winnie explained. "Edgar has to bring Billy to my party tonight, or he can't come."

"What?"

"Isn't it awful? All of his focus will be on stupid Billy. Like I'm not even there."

Suzanne stared at her, stunned. "You mean you're this upset simply because Edgar is going to be a responsible brother?"

She nodded and dabbed at her eyes with a tissue. "Isn't it awful?"

"I hardly think so. At least their mother is allowing them to come. She could have made them stay home."

Apparently, this was the wrong thing to say. Winnie fell back on the mattress with another wail.

"For Pete's sake, Winnie. It'll be fine. Billy tries to fade into the background whenever Edgar takes him places. He's fully aware his presence is unwanted. Poor kid."

Winnie leaped onto her knees and reached for Suzanne's hands. "Only the dearest friend in the entire world would volunteer to stay home and babysit Billy. Just the most wonderful—"

"Stop!" Suzanne pushed away Winnie's hands. "If you think there are any words you could use to make me stay home and not wear my Scarlett O'Hara dress, you're sadly mistaken. I'm going to that party, and I'm going to celebrate your birthday with all of your other friends."

Winnie pouted.

Suzanne watched her for a moment. "What I *will* do is

watch Billy for Edgar when he wants to dance, assuming I won't already be dancing. You can call that my other birthday present for you today. I already wrapped the first gift. Happy birthday, by the way."

Winnie grinned and grabbed Suzanne in a bear hug. "You really are the best friend a girl could ever have."

"You doubted that? Last year, I probably danced two times all night long. You and Edgar can get some punch and keep your eyes on Billy for the few times I might have an invitation to dance."

Winnie blew her nose. "I'll bet your dress increases your odds of dancing. It'll be the second-best dress at the party."

"You forget about Patricia. That girl is going to walk in with something stunning. I guarantee it."

"I hadn't thought about that." Winnie frowned. "And poor Doreen. She'll be lucky to have a tolerable dress."

"If she wasn't so proud, we could give her some of our dresses to remake. I tried it once, but it offended her."

Winnie shrugged. "At least you tried. She reacted the same to me last week. After we showed her your dress, I felt for her, so I called to invite her over the next time she was going to visit her father."

"Her father?"

"She walks past my house to visit her father. He moved into that big house on the next block. The one converted into apartments."

"I didn't know. Doreen doesn't talk about him."

"Understandable, considering … She visits him on either Saturday or Sunday. I told her she could pick something from my closet to wear to the party. She turned me down."

"She didn't mention any of this to me. So, her dad's living in an apartment?"

"Rumors say he lives with a girlfriend who's half his age."

"Oh, no. I'm sure her heart is broken. Think she'd talk to any of us about it?"

"I doubt it. She's private."

"Poor thing. She must feel pulled between her parents."

"She hasn't been happy for a while, and she wasn't happy when I offered her a dress."

"You did the right thing. Sorry it offended her."

Since Winnie seemed distracted, Suzanne asked her something else. "Where did you and Edgar go on Saturday morning?"

Winnie shot her a sly grin but refused to answer.

"I became suspicious when Doreen volunteered to hunt you down."

Winnie sighed. "We went to 'our' place. We call it the SS, the secret shed. We've met there several times."

"Where? What do you do there?"

"I have a mother, Suzanne. I don't need you to volunteer for the job."

"I'm serious. You could ruin your reputation."

"It's not *that* bad. We meet in the gardener's shed on the Willinghams' property." She stuck out the little finger on her right hand. "But you've got to swear never to tell anyone about it."

"I swear." They performed a pinky swear against Suzanne's better judgment. "Do you really need to trespass on the Willingham property? Can't you just play 'back seat bingo'?"

"He doesn't own a car. When he's at my house, Mother watches us like a hawk. If we are ever at his house, Billy's there and tells their mother everything. We have no privacy."

"I know nothing about dating, but it seems you could find a better place. I mean, think about it. A shed?"

"Doreen almost caught us there on Saturday. We were

walking back when she found us. I think she wanted to discover us. Wanted to get me in big trouble."

Suzanne reached over and patted Winnie's hand. "It worked out, and I'm glad."

"So am I. Mother would have blown a gasket."

"You're lucky to have a mother who's like June Cleaver. She's affectionate. I didn't even know there were mothers like her until we became friends."

Winnie glanced at Suzanne with sadness in her eyes. "I wish you had a mother like mine too. Your mother is ... well ... rather stiff."

Suzanne threw back her head and laughed. "You're the queen of understatement. Now, we'd better get ready for school." Suzanne shrugged on her robe, slid into slippers, and walked Winnie downstairs.

Father called out from the dining room. "Suzanne, you and Winnie, come here for a moment."

Winnie shot Suzanne an embarrassed glance as they entered the room.

"Mr. Thatcher, I'm sorry for disturbing you so early this morning."

Suzanne's father sat at the far end of the long table, his empty plate pushed to the side. He wore a suit and tie, ready to head to his accounting office. The top of his head, covered with gray hair, was visible over the top of his newspaper. He lowered the paper to peer at them over his reading glasses, eyes twinkling with mischief. "What a delight to see you're feeling better now, Winnie."

Winnie turned to Suzanne. "Your father had the unfortunate experience of letting me in with all my misery."

"You're fine," he assured her.

"Dad, did you wish Winnie a happy birthday? Today's the day."

He smiled. "Well, happy birthday, my dear. I'm sure your party will be a great success. Olivia and I will see you there." He winked at Suzanne. "I'll make sure all the mothers stay downstairs tonight."

"That would be a miracle."

"I was young once." With a chuckle, he disappeared behind the newspaper.

"See you later, Mr. Thatcher."

"Before you go," he lowered the paper again and pointed to an article. "Did your mother or father see the fire at the Willingham place last night? It's being called an arson fire. We haven't had one in two years, and that one was a prank gone awry. Some kids fired up the homecoming bonfire the night before the actual bonfire."

"The Willingham's house?" Winnie seemed perplexed.

"No, sorry, not their house. It was just one of their outbuildings near the highway. I thought you or your parents might know something about it, since you live so close."

"Now that you mention it, we heard sirens. But neither of them said anything to me about a fire."

"No matter," Mr. Thatcher said.

Mrs. Thatcher called from the kitchen. "Suzanne?"

"Yes, mother."

"Well, you're up early today."

Winnie turned and hissed, "I need to go."

"Go," Mr. Thatcher said. "I'll ask your parents tonight at the party."

"I'm sure it was another prank, Dad," Suzanne said.

They scurried out of the room and into the butler's pantry. From there, Winnie shot her a look of fear. Suzanne held up a finger to her lips to silence Winnie. They held their tongues through the main living room until they got to the front door, to keep Mrs. Thatcher from overhearing.

"Oh, Suzanne! I hope that fire didn't burn our Secret Shed. We couldn't have had anything to do with a fire."

"Didn't Dad say it started last night? You were there on Saturday."

"We were there yesterday after school too. Just for a few minutes."

"Were you smoking? A cigarette could smolder for hours."

"No, silly, the only fire was between us. We were necking."

"Then it must have been stupid boys playing with matches or smoking."

Winnie grabbed Suzanne's arm. "Please don't tell anyone we were there. We'd get in a lot of trouble."

"I won't tell another soul. Pinky swear." They performed the ritual again.

"Thanks for monitoring Billy."

"Yeah, yeah. Get home and start working on de-puffing that beautiful face of yours. And happy birthday. I'm glad you feel better. See you in algebra class."

Winnie pulled on her gloves. "Mom's going to kill me when she finds out about that test. But it will be after the party."

Chapter Eleven

Liesl
November 10

Liesl rushed through the doors of the local barbeque restaurant.

Where was Nicole sitting? They were supposed to meet fifteen minutes ago, but Nicole would forgive Liesl's tardiness once she showed her the lockbox loot.

There. The enormous shopping bag thumped against Liesl's leg as she hustled over to the table for two in the center of the room. As a realtor, Nicole always wanted to be front and center—she called it "being seen."

Good. Nicole had already ordered. Salad bowls sat in the middle of the table. Liesl was starving but too excited not to show off what she'd brought before eating.

"Have a good shopping trip?" Nicole stood and hugged her, the entire time eying her bags.

"I had to bring in these treasures. Look what we uncovered at the bank this morning." Liesl pulled out a small notebook from the shopping bag and handed it to Nicole. "You can see this is the earliest version I've found so far."

The book was small, made of stiff brown leather and had the word "ledger" stamped in gold lettering on the front. Inside, instead of a long column of numbers, there was cursive writing. The interior front cover read, "1962 to 1963, Property of Suzanne Renee Thatcher." Each page bore the date scrawled across the top. Some had additional notes, like "rainy and cold" or "three inches of snow." Many notations involved what appeared to be stock prices.

Nicole peered at Liesl. "This is amazing. Too bad it's after the date we're interested in. When you're through with it, put it on display in a shadow box."

Liesl smiled. "What a great idea." She pulled up a picture on her phone and handed it to Nicole.

"Are those coins?" Nicole asked.

"Some silver, some gold. Mr. Van de Berg thought they might be worth some money. I left them with Mr. Barnaby. He's taking them for an appraisal. All I know is that they're old and pretty. Aunt Suzanne never mentioned coins to me."

"You think she could have forgotten them?"

"Maybe. There was some silver and gold jewelry too. A few cameos and clip-on earring sets that looked ancient. I wonder if they're historical items. None looked familiar."

Nicole shrugged. "Cameos are coming back in style. Are you able to keep them, or do you have to get those appraised too?"

"They have to be appraised to be added to her estate. We also found a gold watch and a handkerchief, both bearing the initials TMT. Thomas Myron Thatcher, Aunt Suzanne's father. The pocket watch also had a fob. I wonder why Aunt Suzanne had it instead of her brother?"

"Luckily, Myron is still alive. Ask him."

"I will. The best finds were old pictures, the original plans for the house, and many more journals. Myron may want some of that too."

"You have the house plans?"

Liesl nodded.

"May I?"

Liesl searched through her bag until she came up with a large roll of dark-colored papers, then handed them to Nicole.

Nicole pressed them flat on the table while Liesl stood and peered over her shoulder. "Here's the first floor." Nicole released the edges, and it curled away to reveal the second-floor layout. "Then, here's the attic, and finally, the basement." Then she pulled up the first-floor plan again.

Liesl studied the page. "It's not quite the same. The bathroom by the kitchen isn't here."

Nicole pointed to the bottom right corner. "It's dated 1893. This is the original plan. Since then, they've upgraded, adding electricity and plumbing."

"These are fascinating."

"You might frame these. They'd be terrific wall art, and intriguing for guests."

Liesl dug in her bag for more treasure. "Take a look at this. It's the abstract."

Nicole's eyes shone with glee. "Did you know some of these old abstracts trace back to land grants from former presidents, both pre- and post-Civil War? They make fascinating reading." She looked at Liesl. "Can I take this with me? I promise to give it back."

Liesl chuckled. "That's why I brought it. I knew you'd love it." She picked up her fork and pulled the salad closer. "We could make some copies and frame them as well."

Between bites of salad, Liesl said, "Do you know that Aunt Suzanne had a tiny pair of my sneakers in a lockbox?"

Nicole beamed. "You must have worn them when you first arrived. They were probably the only 'baby' shoes she had for you. Toddler shoes."

Liesl blinked away the moisture in her eyes. "I'm sure you're right."

"Anything else in that bag I need to know about?"

"It's stuffed with journals of various sizes and colors. But you need to hear what happened last night."

Nicole leaned forward. "What? What happened?"

Liesl explained about spotting the burglars.

"That's horrible. They could easily have robbed your house."

"I agree. Donnie's coming today to figure out what kind of alarm system I need."

"Good. I don't like you in that big house alone. Especially with thieves just across the street. It sends shivers up my spine."

"That's not all. Someone stole Aunt Suzanne's coat from the house, burned it, and threw it onto the front porch. Kurt had me file a report about it."

Nicole sputtered. "They what? What was Kurt doing there?"

"He heard the call about the break-in across the street and came to help. He was there when I discovered the coat."

"Why would someone burn that?"

"No clue. I lock the house whenever I leave, so either I didn't hear an intruder or they have a key. Kurt was sure they burned it elsewhere and returned it."

Nicole put down her fork. "How creepy. That's sickening."

"It scared me. Kurt said it was a sign of anger."

"Anger at you or Aunt Suzanne?"

"I honestly don't know."

"Your exploits from last night terrify me. First burglars, then the whole 'burning coat' thing. Aren't you freaked out?"

"I appreciate your concern, but I'm fine. The biggest threat I'll have this afternoon is a close encounter with Donnie Davis. In fact," she glanced at her phone, "I really need to go."

Chapter Twelve

Liesl

Donnie Davis had drastically changed over the years. His captain-of-the-football-team days were over. Unfortunately, some things don't improve with age, and Donnie was one of them. Liesl had to credit herself with some sense in high school. She had never been interested in going out with him, unlike many other girls. His bad-boy reputation was off-putting then and probably hadn't changed much since.

She tried not to stare as his belly jiggled above his cinched belt. Jowls hung from his puffy face and matched the flesh hanging beneath his chin. It seemed he was living a hard life. Too many beers? He sported a baseball cap with his alarm company logo. She speculated whether it covered an absence of hair.

His eyes evaluated her, lingering on her curves.

"You sure are looking good, Liesl."

She frowned. It was going to be a long afternoon. Kurt's

face when she'd opted to use Donnie's alarm company suggested the rivalry between the two former teammates still existed. However, now that she'd seen Donnie again, the temptation of making Kurt jealous wasn't worth the trouble. Also, why make Kurt jealous if her feelings were gone?

"Getting an alarm is a great idea, Liesl."

She held up a hand. "Whoa. You don't need to sell me on an alarm. I'm sure you're aware the house across the street was burglarized last night. Just explain what choices I have, and I'm buying one."

"Nothing like crime to protect my security business. Too bad the police aren't doing a good job keeping the riffraff under control."

She bit back a sarcastic reply. No way would she defend Kurt. "Let's get started."

They went from room to room, discussing her options. He was quick to mention his newly divorced status from his second wife. Liesl had known the first Mrs. Davis, a nice girl who'd been in a class two years behind her, but she hadn't met the second wife.

It became clear Donnie was deliberately violating her personal space, casually bumping into her or patting her on the back or shoulder. After the third "accidental encounter," she exploded. "If you want my business, you'd better keep your hands to yourself."

"Ooh, the quiet ones can be feisty, can't they?"

"You're here to install an alarm system. I never dreamed I'd need an alarm to deal with you."

He took a long look at her and changed his demeanor. "Sorry, Liesl. I'm not trying to offend you. I've always found it hard to resist a good-looking woman."

"Is that why you have two ex-wives?"

He shot her a frosty look and then turned to examine the kitchen windows.

While he evaluated her needs, she threw a stale bag of chips into the garbage and thought about adding Donnie.

An hour later, he'd written an estimate and arranged for a crew to start installation the following week. They'd agreed on a high-grade system, which included alarms to sound if an emergency exit in the basement was used, plus heat sensors near the boiler and the large appliances.

She refused to damage the beautiful wooden front door, with its antique doorbell, so no doorbell camera. Donnie suggested he wire a camera above the door that worked on a motion sensor. She agreed to that and had him add two heat sensors to the ceiling of the front porch. After finding the burned coat there, the potential return of the arsonist was a paramount concern. She wanted no fire damage to this beautiful home. After writing a large check, she escorted him to the door.

* * *

Liesl spotted Doreen Martin, one of Aunt Suzanne's best friends, limping along beside her overweight beagle mix, Barney. The dog looked like a watermelon walking on four Vienna sausages. Doreen wore a heavy coat with a colorful scarf wrapped around her curly, gray-streaked hair.

Liesl grabbed a jacket and headed out the door to talk to her. She'd helped take care of Aunt Suzanne and coordinate the church ladies with food after the funeral. Liesl needed to thank her again for all she'd done, and Doreen's perpetual smile was a bit of sunshine—just what she could use on a cold, gray day.

After a few minutes of chitchat, Liesl broached the suddenness of Aunt Suzanne's illness.

"Well, sweetie, I know you're upset. As you should be, mind you. I didn't hesitate a second to call you when I realized she was getting worse. That was Wednesday, wasn't it?"

"You called me Thursday night."

Barney tugged on the leash toward a bush, so Doreen hobbled a couple of steps to accommodate him.

Liesl followed her. "I arrived Friday morning."

"Oh, that's right. I'd left several hours before you arrived. Patricia and I were taking shifts."

"I can't thank you enough for that."

"Oh pshaw, child." She waved her gloved hand in the frigid air. "What're friends for?"

"Did Aunt Suzanne speculate on why she became ill?"

"Not really. I figured they wore her out after the Butterfly House board meeting on Monday and our ladies' church circle meeting at Pauline Roberts's house on Tuesday night." The dog, tired of wetting the bush, tugged again at his leash. This time, Doreen held firm.

"Did you attend the Butterfly House meeting?" Liesl asked. "Mr. Van de Berg saw her there and said she looked fine."

Her face darkened. "No. When my term on that board was over two years ago, I resigned. I've had enough fights with Patricia to last a lifetime. I left it to her to run, and your aunt to control her spending. I washed my hands of it, I tell you."

"But you and Patricia are friends, aren't you?"

"We've tolerated each other, mostly for Suzanne's sake, but never been close. Even when we were young. When she spent so much money refurbishing Butterfly House, I was ... offended. That's the best word I can use."

Liesl blinked in surprise.

"Patricia's always been wealthy. Only the best was good enough for her." The dog continued to fidget, but Doreen continued. "I felt the board had a duty to economize. It's a nonprofit, you see. She spent hundreds of dollars on things I didn't believe were necessary. Nothing to preserve the structure. She wanted brighter curtains, new carpet and such."

Liesl hadn't realized the personality differences between the ladies. Everything Doreen said was a legitimate gripe, and Mrs. Sizemore had never been a favorite of Liesl. To move on, she turned the questions back to Aunt Suzanne. "When did you find out Aunt Suzanne was sick?"

"She seemed pale after ladies' circle. That was Tuesday night. I'd warned her not to eat certain things. When I called her Wednesday afternoon, she sounded awful, even though she made light of it. I went to check on her the next morning and stayed when I realized she was so nauseous."

With a whimper, Barney finally settled into a sitting position as Doreen rubbed her chin. "Patricia stopped by, so I ran to the pharmacy. Picked up some over-the-counter stomach medication. After that, I went home, and Patricia stayed. I came back after supper and tried to send Patricia home, but she wouldn't go. Because Suzanne seemed worse, we both stayed the night. Suzanne couldn't keep anything down the entire night."

"So it was the flu?"

"Either that or food poisoning."

"Did she blame food for making her sick?"

"I commented about her looking a little 'green around the gills.' She questioned Dee Wainwright's ham salad. Dee is notorious for bringing leftovers to the circle. Smart women steer a wide berth around her contribution."

There was a quiver in Doreen's voice. Her eyes misted, so Liesl rushed to change the subject. "Are you getting along okay?"

Doreen's voice grew firm as she relayed her latest complaints and laughed about getting old. "You know you're old when you take a lot of medications." She tugged on the leash. "Well, better run."

"Just one other thing." Liesl bent over and petted Barney, who was now standing near her feet.

"Sure." Doreen pulled her coat collar up around her neck against the wind.

"If I move back, do you know of anyone who could help me with this house? Someone to clean and cook? I'm not a very dedicated housekeeper. An expert should handle that big place."

Doreen chuckled. "Your mind has always been elsewhere. Even as a child, you'd be in your own make-believe world. You stayed busy for hours, not a bit of trouble."

Liesl smiled. "That ability has allowed me, as an adult, to sit at a computer playing make-believe with my characters."

"And you've been successful at that. Perhaps made some money?"

Would her newfound inheritance negatively affect her writing? Liesl pushed those thoughts away. "Can you recommend anyone?"

"Oh, I got side-tracked. I might know one or two. How about I have them contact you if they're interested?"

"Sounds good. I'm going to St. Louis on Monday, so have them call rather than stop by."

"Need me to pop by and pick up your mail? I assume you'll stay the night?"

"No, thanks. Just a day trip. But I am having an alarm system installed."

Doreen frowned. "You want me to return my key?"

Liesl had forgotten Doreen had a key to the house. Patricia Sizemore and other friends probably did too. "No, no. When the system is in, I'll walk you through it."

"Fascinating." Doreen smiled. "I don't know anything about alarm systems."

"Doesn't the Butterfly House have one?"

"Yes, but I don't believe anyone on the board's ever touched it. At least they didn't when I served."

Liesl watched Doreen and the dog waddle down the street. That dog would benefit from fewer calories and more exercise. With Doreen's gout causing her such problems, maybe she should offer to take Barney on some longer walks.

As she retreated back inside, her phone rang. Dr. Johnson.

"Liesl?"

"Yes."

"I've been looking over your aunt's medical records and ... well, I'd like to talk to you. In person, if possible."

A niggling concern coursed through her. "Of course. I can meet with you. When?"

"I've finished with today's patients and can wait to do my hospital rounds. Can you come by the office right now?"

"I'll see you in five minutes." Her hands shook as she reached for her purse.

Chapter Thirteen

Suzanne
March 18, 1961

Suzanne was going to be late to the party.

Even though they were in the kitchen, she overheard Myron and Mother fighting. Her brother didn't want to drive her because she was an embarrassment. He was picking up friends on the way and didn't want his little sister there. Myron had a point. She embarrassed him the same way Edgar was embarrassed about having to drag Billy along. No wonder Myron and Edgar were good friends.

Myron lost. He would drive her to Winnie's house first, then would pick up his friends. After a few minutes of silence in the car, he tried to make amends.

"You look fabulous in that dress."

She glared at him, full of fury. No compliment could erase the wounds her ego suffered while he battled their mother. Being a younger sister was humbling. Being the reason for a fight between a rebellious brother and an overbearing, controlling mother was miserable.

"Hey, Suz. You know I didn't mean none of that. Back there with Mother."

Silence.

"You must be boiling if improper grammar doesn't force you to correct me." He sighed. "Look. I'm sorry. You know your mother tries to control everything. I have to fight her, even when it's a losing battle."

"She's your mother too. And you're not winning any points for forgiveness by saying that driving me is punishment for a lost battle."

"You're not a punishment. Taking a stand against her is the losing battle. I will not surrender, not like Dad."

She sighed. He was right. Their father did whatever their mother said. Both yearned for him to stand up for himself. For years, they'd prayed and hoped he would put his foot down. At least occasionally.

When her feelings weren't hurt, she was sympathetic to Myron. Their parents saw him as the responsible firstborn, preparing to step into the career path they envisioned for him. Myron was under a lot of pressure to conform to their wishes; a proper education, a specified career path, an acceptable marriage, and a brood of children.

She could relate to his rebellion, his refusal to put himself into that yoke. She understood his fear of the straitjacket life path they planned. Their expectations for her were different. Mother believed Suzanne was too clever and not pretty enough to attract the right man. Her parental "path" was to marry and have babies.

Mother demanded a rich spouse, while Father wanted her mate to be intelligent enough to carry on a conversation during a holiday or be a sports fan to watch games with him. It might be a blessing to have so little with which to conform. With Suzanne's "unique" looks, men would never fall at her feet. If they didn't mind her looks, then her witty repartee scared them away.

Who needed men? In these new times, women didn't have to hang on to a man to have success.

Myron tried again. "You're gonna knock 'em dead at the party."

In better circumstances, she would have told him their mother was responsible for her fantastic dress. Yet, there was no need to rub salt in his wounds. Their mother's motive for buying such an extravagant dress was to compensate for Suzanne's plain features. It was an odd gesture of love. Now people would look at the dress, not the face above it.

When they reached Winnie's house, she didn't thank him or say goodbye. Why should she? He'd lost a battle to drive her, and she wanted him to feel guilty about her humiliation.

* * *

On the porch, Suzanne shook off her hurt feelings. This was a night for celebration, dedicated to fun, dancing, and laughter. The daily tussle between Myron and their mother shouldn't take that away from her.

Inside, she became the door greeter and take-your-coat girl, running outerwear and purses to the guest room. Standing around exchanging chitchat in sizeable crowds was not her forte. She much preferred a duty to perform. This chore functioned in her favor, as every new arrival, including most of the teenage guys, complimented her dress. She enjoyed this bit of fluff to her ego after suffering such a deflation inflicted by Myron.

Her parents were the last to arrive, but that was their mother's intention. It was also why she hadn't wanted Suzanne to ride with them. Her mother was purposely late to everything to make a statement. If Suzanne rode with them, they'd have been forced to arrive earlier.

When her mother handed over her coat, she nodded her approval. "You look lovely, darling, but a bit more lipstick would add that extra glow." Her last word was a breathy whisper, for dramatic effect, as she moved into the living room.

"I'll take care of it."

Her dad hesitated in the hall with her. "Pay no attention to her. You're stunning."

After she gave him a quick kiss on the cheek, Suzanne took their items to the bedroom. The smile her mother wiped off her face returned, brought back to life by her wonderful father.

The party downstairs lasted about an hour—long enough for cake and ice cream to disappear and presents to be unwrapped. Eventually, Mrs. Whitcomb let the teenagers, plus one eight-year-old, start the party in the attic. The adults divided into cleanup crew, television basketball watchers, and those who gathered around the dining room table to talk.

In the attic, the senior boys ignored all the junior girls, including Suzanne and Doreen. They flirted with Patricia and Winnie, who looked much older than high school seniors in their fancy party dresses.

Doreen huffed and stalked away.

"Wait, Doreen." Suzanne rushed to catch her. "You need to look at this guy thing logically. We're younger, and therefore less desirable, than Patricia and Winnie. Try not to let your feelings get hurt. After all, guys are pigs."

Doreen turned to her with surprise. "Did you just say 'guys are pigs'?"

She laughed. "Absolutely. I have a brother. I know." She put an arm around Doreen's shoulder. "Come on. Let's go get some punch while it's just us. Pretty soon I'll have to entertain Billy."

Within a few minutes, Doreen and Patricia fell into a disagreement. Suzanne felt caught in the middle, which was a terrible place to be, but could understand why it happened. Doreen, feelings hurt from lack of male attention, took her frustration out on Patricia, who was drowning in fawning fellows.

"Why in the world do you want to go to a college in a town that none of us can spell?" Doreen demanded.

Patricia froze her with a glance. "Poughkeepsie is not that hard to spell."

"Says the girl who thinks glockenspiel is easy to spell." Doreen ignored Patricia's icy glare. The only sign of Doreen's nervousness was her right index finger twirling one of her curls.

Patricia, three inches taller than Doreen, looked down her nose and wisely kept her mouth shut.

Winnie and Suzanne shared a glance of panic.

Suzanne turned to Doreen. "Have you tried those crackers with Meng cheese? I'm crazy about them. That cheese is the best thing sold at Moore's grocery." She looped her arm around Doreen's and shuffled her a foot closer to the food table.

Winnie waved over Edgar and Myron.

"Myron, take Patricia for a dance. Maybe you can impress her with your footwork."

"You can always hope," Edgar teased.

Winnie took Edgar's hand. "Hey buddy, how about showing this girl your own dance moves?"

Edgar called out. "Suzanne? Will you watch Billy while we dance?"

She nodded. "Sure."

Billy joined Doreen and Suzanne, making his way through the nearby snacks while Doreen cooled off. She eventually talked about her father's new place and his new girlfriend. Suzanne was as sympathetic as possible.

* * *

An hour passed while Suzanne enjoyed Billy and watched everyone dance. He was a joy to entertain with word games because he was a smart eight-year-old. He liked the challenge and found additional happiness in the nearby food.

With Edgar's approval, Suzanne and Billy took Winnie's Jack Russell terrier, Zest, for a short walk around the block. Zest needed some relief from her party-time quarantine in Winnie's room. Billy needed to burn off some energy. It was a frosty night with slick spots on the sidewalk, but Billy helped Suzanne navigate in her party shoes.

During dancing breaks, Edgar came over to check on Billy. From the looks Suzanne received from Winnie, she was grateful for her help. Her friends were having a great time.

Suzanne was giggling with Billy over a wild guess he'd made for a definition in a word game they'd been playing when she spotted someone familiar walking up the stairs. Initially, she couldn't place him. Was he someone's relative? There was some curl in his light brown hair. He had an athletic build and sun-darkened skin. Who would have a suntan in the middle of March?

It surprised her when the new arrival topped the stairs, saw her, and strode over.

As he approached, recognition pulsed through her like an electrical surge. She spotted a sparkle in those green eyes when they registered her recognition. It was pure magic. Unexpected joy filled her heart, and a smile reached her lips. No wonder she didn't recognize him. They'd both matured since their last encounter several years past.

His answering smile reflected a promise of fun. For the first time in her life, Suzanne dared to dream there might be a date in her future.

"Nice to see you, Suzanne. You look fabulous."

Billy pushed his way between them. "Hey, who are you?"

Max's smile never dimmed as he acknowledged Billy. "Are you this beautiful young lady's chaperone tonight?"

Billy turned to her. "I don't know what that means."

She smiled at Billy, then turned to Max. "Why, this is no mere chaperone, sire. May I present Sir William Van de Berg of The Netherlands."

Max ran with the humor and bowed to Billy. "Pleasure to meet you, Sir William."

She put her arm around Billy. "Although Sir William is small of stature, you can see he is brave and true. Sir William, I'd like to introduce you to Sir Maximillian Schrader, from our neighboring community of Rush Hill."

To Billy, Max said, "You may call me, Max, Sir William." In a theatrical whisper, he added, "Although it is not wise to correct a woman, the fair maiden Suzanne is uninformed of my new land. I am now Sir Maximillian Schrader of the east of Mexico."

"A new home?" she asked in surprise.

"More like a bunkhouse of brothers. The family bought a cattle farm, and four of us boys are living there now."

"Without killing each other?"

He grinned. "We have our moments, but so far, so good."

"A new farm is exciting."

"That's nothing compared to seeing you tonight." He offered a hand. "Care to dance?"

She turned to Billy. "Will you be okay if I step away to dance?"

Doreen approached and shooed them away. "Go ahead, Suzanne. I'll keep my eye on him."

"Thanks, Doreen."

Max took her hand, and they walked to the center of the room, where the group was dancing the stroll. The configuration placed girls in one line and guys in another, with space for dancing between the lines. Some eyebrows rose when Suzanne joined the girls, but Winnie seemed thrilled. Even Patricia shot her a smile.

Suzanne caught Edgar's attention and mouthed "Doreen." He nodded, understanding that Doreen was watching Billy.

When it was their turn to dance down the aisle as a couple, Max spun her around while they made their way, camel walking. He was a superb dancer and swept her away in the moment.

Dancing was such fun. She had a handsome partner, and they didn't do crazy, gyrating moves. Perhaps practice could make her comfortable with the twist. The only experience she'd had was in front of a mirror, where she thought her moves looked ridiculous.

In a lull between songs, Myron approached them.

"Good to see you, Max. It's been too long."

She gave Myron an icy look. If he dared embarrass her in front of Max, she wouldn't hesitate to tell embarrassing secrets about him.

Myron acknowledged her unspoken threat and kept the conversation mundane. He didn't comment on Max hanging out with her, either. He spent his time discussing Max's new cattle operation.

"How many acres does it have?"

"Right at two hundred, with a couple of streams running

through. We're going to run a cow-calf operation with an eye to expansion."

"All five of you boys are working it?"

"Four. Buddy is working the Rush Hill farm with Dad."

"Even with four," Myron said, "I can't fathom how you get along well enough to live and have a business together. Good for you."

When "Put Your Head on my Shoulder" played, Suzanne breathed a sigh of relief. They returned to dancing, a slow dance this time.

Being close to Max in the slow dance was exciting and nerve-wracking all at once. Was he having fun? She pulled back to glance at him, but a movement near the floor to her right caught her attention.

Zest, Winnie's dog, was dragging her leash, racing around the dance area. Suzanne stopped moving. "Oh no, Zest must have broken away from someone."

"Want me to catch him?"

"If you can."

She bent down and made a kissing noise. "Zesty, come here, girl." The normally hyperactive dog seemed twice as nervous. "Come here, Zest." Suzanne clapped her hands, and that caught her attention.

Zest raced toward her. Suzanne grabbed her leash and plucked her from the floor. When she patted her back, the dog felt wet. Had it started to snow outside? Suzanne pulled her hand away and saw blood. "Oh, no. She's hurt."

Max took Zest and examined her. "I don't see an injury."

A scream of agony rose above the music, primal and gut-wrenching.

Where was the scream coming from?

Downstairs. Must be downstairs.

Suzanne and Max exchanged a glance and moved swiftly toward the stairs, Zest still in Max's arms.

Chapter Fourteen

Liesl
November 10

D r. Johnson's office was in a medical park on the northeast side of town. The screech of Liesl's tires heralded her Jeep's stop in the parking lot. His waiting area was deserted, and so was the reception area. She knocked on the sliding glass between the waiting room and reception.

"That you, Liesl?"

"Yes, Dr. Johnson."

"I'm in my office. Come on back."

The door from reception to the examination rooms opened to a narrow hallway. She barreled toward Dr. Johnson's office, sidestepping a large scale, and nearly tripped.

He stood when she entered and shook her hand over his paper-strewn desk. "I hope you don't mind the short notice, but I wanted to talk to you in person."

"No problem," she assured him.

"I'm reviewing all of Mrs. Schrader's medical records. I always try to double-check what I've done, especially if my treatment failed." His eyes reflected a deep sadness.

Liesl gave him a sympathetic smile.

"Her illness started with the same symptoms as a gastric virus. After they admitted her to the hospital, we treated her for nausea and dehydration. We weren't able to stop the progression before damage to her organs was so significant, it shut them down. She suffered a full multi-system organ failure."

"Was it painful for her? It was hard to tell in the hospital." Liesl's fingernails dug into her palms, awaiting his answer.

"No, she was slipping in and out of a light coma. Not unusual with this type of organ failure. I've reviewed everything I can find, trying to understand what happened."

"What caused her to be so sick?"

Taking a yellow paper from the top of the file in front of him, Dr. Johnson passed it to her. The date, time, patient name, and number filled the upper left corner; the rest of the report reflected abbreviations and other numbers.

"Her blood levels were within normal range, except in two areas. You can see her white blood cell count and liver enzymes were much higher than expected. Blood and protein found in her urine indicated kidney involvement."

"What's that mean?"

"It's possible she ingested something that caused her sickness, rather than a virus or disease."

Her mouth went dry. Remembering her earlier conversation with Doreen, she asked, "Like bad ham?"

He shifted in his chair. "That would be food poisoning. This is more consistent with a substance that shouldn't have been ingested. Something that acted as a toxin."

"A toxin. You mean a poison?" She sputtered. "You believe she mistakenly ate something poisonous?"

He nodded, frowning. "Either something toxic or poisonous. I noticed no signs that she suffered from dementia, but sometimes the elderly ingest something they shouldn't."

"So you're saying she might have poisoned herself? With a chemical or toxic substance?"

"It's possible."

"But her vision was excellent, and she never showed signs of confusion."

His brow furrowed. "Did she, or her friends, ever complain about her struggling to take care of herself? Or having difficulty driving?"

"Never. One of Aunt Suzanne's friends would have called if that was an issue."

Dr. Johnson folded his hands on the desk and sighed. "I'm struggling with this."

Liesl sat in stunned silence, her mind running through the likelihood of Aunt Suzanne getting confused and hurting herself.

"I've gone over her prescribed medications, and nothing she was taking should have caused a negative reaction."

"What was she taking?"

"Blood pressure medication and an anti-inflammatory to ease her arthritis. Nothing unusual for her age."

"When I arrived, she said something strange. Could she have been hallucinating, or was it an example of dementia?"

"She responded appropriately to me when I examined her. Did she do something like that at the hospital?"

"No. What little she said at the hospital made perfect sense until she passed away." Liesl brushed away a tear that slid down her cheek.

Dr. Johnson stood up. "I suggest you search her kitchen for

something unusual. I wouldn't want you to ingest whatever might have caused her sickness. It's a theory, but for your own safety, I knew you'd want to know. If you don't find anything, contact me. I can dig a little deeper into other possibilities."

Liesl nodded and rose, fighting the temptation to burst into sobs. He walked her to the parking lot, looking as sad as she felt.

"I'm sorry, Liesl. I wish I could have saved her. She was a special lady."

Chapter Fifteen

Liesl

Liesl drove home in a brain fog.

Once inside the garage, she turned off the car and sat wrapped in the darkness. She struggled to understand what Dr. Johnson suggested.

Could Aunt Suzanne have poisoned herself? If so, how? She was too sharp for an accidental poisoning. So that left the possibility that someone killed her. Both options were horrifying and preposterous to consider. Yet, consider them she must.

Aunt Suzanne had been an extraordinarily bright woman. Yet, mistakes happen. Did she get confused and swallow the wrong thing? On the sinister side, did she figure out who killed Winnie and confront them? Suzanne had long considered the possibility that Winnie's killer was someone she knew.

Liesl's stomach churned. A friend? Who, among Aunt Suzanne's friends, could have hidden the traits of a reprehensible killer? Aunt Suzanne spent years looking into her friend's faces and wondering if this one, or that one, was responsible for a brutal murder.

Her journal. Could that be the book she'd mentioned?

Aunt Suzanne kept a yearly journal for nearly sixty years. Where were her most recent journals? Was 'the book' in a special hiding place? Somewhere easy to get to, yet hidden from the rest of the world? Or locked away at the bank?

To eliminate the possibility of an accidental poisoning, everything in the kitchen needed examination. After the funeral, guests had eaten food brought in for that purpose, not what was already in the refrigerator or cabinets, except coffee. She and Nicole shared carrot cake and ice cream, to no ill effect. Whatever it might have been could still be there. But if she was purposefully poisoned ...

Liesl vowed to take no chances.

* * *

Determined to search the house, Liesl opened the car door and snagged her purse from the passenger seat. She screamed when a figure emerged from the darkness of the garage.

The dark silhouette jumped back. "Sorry. I wanted to make sure you were okay."

Kurt.

Anger replaced her fear. "Why are you sneaking around here?"

"I saw you pull in a few minutes ago, but you never came out. I figured something might be wrong."

"Are you spying on me?" Her voice rose an octave.

"Of course not. Since the burglary in this neighborhood and your oddball vandalism, I added this area to my personal watch list."

"And you do that by hiding in my garage?" She stomped past him, went outside, and turned to shut the door.

He followed, then beat her to the door. He closed it and secured the latch. "I didn't sneak up on you. I waited for you. When you didn't come out, I thought something bad happened."

She turned and stalked away. The night was crisp. An arctic breeze whipped her coat around her legs as she maneuvered past his car in the driveway.

A small, blond head bobbed above the dash on the passenger's side. Ross waved at her. She slowed her steps and waved back. For him, she changed her scowl to a smile.

"What's wrong, Liesl?" Kurt's steps crunched in the gravel behind her. "You're upset, and not just at me."

She spun around. "You really want to know?"

He nodded, his creased brow reflecting his concern.

She hadn't trusted Kurt for years, but that was a matter of the heart. If someone poisoned Aunt Suzanne, she'd have to report it to law enforcement. What harm would come from asking for his help?

He was a cop, trained to investigate. If Aunt Suzanne's death was related to Winnie Whitcomb's death, he might have access to the old murder investigation. With a sigh, she pushed away old resentments. "Are you busy tonight?"

"No. We were heading home for dinner."

"Does Ross like pizza?"

"Sure."

"Then come in. We'll order pizza, and I'll tell you my troubles."

He nodded and went to get Ross.

When they were all inside, Kurt gestured to his service belt. "I need to put my gun away. I lock it in a gun cabinet at home. Got anything similar?"

She led him to the library, her favorite first-floor room. Aunt Suzanne had called it a den or a study. With the fireplace and floor-to-ceiling bookshelves on three walls, it felt like a library to Liesl. A wall of windows was opposite the fireplace. Once she was old enough to have lots of homework, Aunt Suzanne redesigned the room for her.

Aunt Suzanne had removed the television her father used and recovered his well-worn armchairs. She'd moved her father's old desk closer to the windows. Two armchairs sat close to the fireplace. Liesl had claimed this room as her own library, and Aunt Suzanne and Uncle Max had tolerated her teenaged need for privacy.

Liesl walked over to a small, built-in cabinet on one shelf. "See the lock?"

Kurt peered to inspect it. "This is great."

A brass key, tucked behind an early edition of *Sense and Sensibility*, opened it.

"I'm surprised this house doesn't have secret passages or hidden rooms."

"There are a few surprises. Sadly, I've never discovered a secret passage or a secret room."

A half hour later, Liesl completed a tour of the house with Ross, except for the basement. He declared it was too spooky for nighttime exploration. His favorite room was her old playroom in the turret. The room, encircled on three sides by large windows, was spacious. Every window had a built-in bench, equipped with a hinged top that lifted to reveal a compartment for storage. She used to fit inside these storage areas when she was his age and thought he'd like them.

She was wrong.

"I'm afraid of small spaces," he explained.

"I love them. When I was young and had done something naughty, I'd hide in there." She grinned at the return of this memory. "Aunt Suzanne would be so mad when she discovered me, I'd get double punishment."

Ross laughed.

After the tour, they ate several slices of pepperoni pizza, then settled Ross down to watch one of his favorite television shows in the upstairs living area.

Kurt glanced at her from his end of the couch and raised his eyebrows.

She nodded toward the window seat across the room. They rose from the couch. Ross stretched out on the sofa, keeping his focus on the television screen.

When they'd settled on the window seat, Kurt looked at her. "I didn't want to say anything in front of Ross, but he's claustrophobic."

"You mean when he didn't like my old hiding place?"

"Yes. I try not to have him dwell on it. The doctors say he'll likely outgrow it."

"Gotcha. I eventually outgrew a sleeping problem I'd had as a child. They related it to losing my parents."

He nodded. "I remember you telling me that. So what's upset you now?"

"Dr. Johnson called. He said Aunt Suzanne's cause of death might be because she ate something poisonous or caustic by mistake. She appeared, at first, to suffer from some type of gastric virus. But he reviewed her test results, and he felt I should know there were other possibilities."

"Like being poisoned?"

"That's a tough one, isn't it?" Her eyes filled with tears. "I can't believe she could have done something like that by mistake. There's no sign anything was wrong with her mind."

He spoke, but she cut him off. "Let me tell you the entire story, so you understand all my concerns."

"Okay ... I'm listening."

"Back in the 1960s, someone murdered a girl during her birthday party. They killed her outside her home."

Kurt shifted on the seat. "I remember hearing about that. That women's shelter is a memorial to her. The Butterfly House, right? They never figured out who killed her. Blamed it on a vagrant passing through town."

"That girl, Winifred Whitcomb, was my aunt's best friend. Aunt Suzanne was at the party and believed the murderer was too. Since that time, she's been trying to figure out who killed Winnie. Last week, she said something about a book, as if it related to Winnie's murder. Now Aunt Suzanne is gone, and today I find out her death is suspicious. I've got to figure out if she hurt herself, or if she finally figured out who killed Winnie."

Kurt's eyes narrowed. "You believe your aunt's death could be related to the death of this other girl from so long ago?"

He must think she'd lost her mind. Had she? "What if she discovered who the killer was and confronted them? Or she got close to the truth, and the killer stopped her."

Kurt stood and paced the floor. "If someone poisoned her, and I'm not saying they did, but it had to be someone she trusted. Someone who could offer food or drink without her questioning the offer."

"I agree."

"From the little I've been trained about poisons, most go undetected because they're easy to disguise. Then, finding a poison forensically is like looking for a needle in a haystack. You need to narrow down the possible poisons. Also, for a killer, poisoning is interactive. They often watch their victim suffer and delight in the power of making them experience that discomfort."

He spun toward her with a look of surprise. "The burned

coat on your porch. It takes on a whole new meaning if your aunt was deliberately poisoned."

"Why?"

"Fire expresses anger, 'burning' resentment, so to speak. I'm glad it went to the state crime lab. Maybe they'll find trace evidence, like hair or fibers. I only asked them to test for accelerants. I'll call tomorrow and request tests for everything they can find."

"That's great. Thanks."

He paced for a moment. "Have you eliminated the obvious? Looked to see if she accidentally ingested something harmful?"

"No. I just found out. I was sitting in the garage, trying to make sense of it—as if that's even possible." She ran her fingers through her hair. "Nothing makes sense, not after this news."

He stopped pacing and approached her. "Let's go through everything in the kitchen. Rat poison might be on a shelf with the cereal, for all we know."

"Right. I'm surprised you're taking this seriously."

"Why not? If Dr. Johnson says it's possible, then we should believe it." Kurt turned toward the couch. "Ross. We're going downstairs for a minute, okay?"

"Okay," replied the sleepy boy from the couch.

She stood and Kurt spun around, his face inches from hers. They stared at one another, and she prayed he was unaware of her racing heart. Could he see the attraction she felt?

Lord, please help me let this man go.

Kurt was the first to speak. "I'm glad you asked me to help. Thanks for trusting me. Again. I promise never to lose your trust again."

She bit back a sarcastic comment. Would he break her heart again? Not if she didn't offer it to him. This was about Aunt Suzanne, not them. "I appreciate your willingness to help. You've got to promise to keep this between us and Nicole. I'm going to talk to her about it tomorrow. No one else can know. Anyone could be a suspect."

He nodded. "I promise."

* * *

The entire first-floor entryway was aglow with light from the old brass chandelier. Passersby, who could see the golden hue, could never imagine the search they were about to undertake.

In the kitchen, they started with the cabinet beneath the sink.

"Didn't she keep drain cleaner around?" Kurt asked as he peered behind the pipes and the garbage disposal.

"Hmm." Liesl leaned back on her heels. "She keeps stuff ... or rather, kept stuff like that in the garage, on some tall shelves out there."

"We'll take an inventory tomorrow. It's Saturday, and I'm off for once."

"I've forgotten what day it is. With everything that's happened lately, it's a wonder I haven't lost my mind."

Kurt unfolded himself from the lower cabinets. "Nothing sinister there." After checking a few other bottom cabinets, he asked, "Are you going to stay here? Move here?"

"I don't believe I could ever sell this house. It's my home. I have two more months on my lease in Houston, so I'll need to decide by then."

"I hope you'll consider moving back. I've missed you."

She looked away. Did he mean it as friends? She'd missed him, too, but she'd rather cut out her tongue than admit it. She propelled herself to her feet and opened a drawer of utensils.

Without comment, Kurt opened a cabinet next to her. Spice

bottles of various shapes and sizes lined the shelves. "Something could be in any of these."

"Is there a lab to test this stuff?"

"A private lab?"

"Yes, private."

"It would cost a fortune. Option two is to send it to the state crime lab, but results would take months."

"Well, I have a fortune," she responded without thinking. "Ah—what I mean is, I can use what I've inherited from Aunt Suzanne to figure out whether she was poisoned."

He closed the cabinet and turned. "It would speed up the process. We have cases of empty specimen containers at work. I'll bring some tomorrow. We can ask a private lab to test all the spices, flour, sugar, and condiments to make sure they're what they're supposed to be—and nothing more."

"Great."

Kurt opened the refrigerator door. "There's a ton of food in here."

"Brought in for the funeral. It's the way people express sympathy."

"What about the milk, pickle jars, and stuff?"

"I bought the milk yesterday, and some people brought food after the funeral The rest was here since I got here."

"Have you had any?"

"Other than carrot cake and some ice cream, no. I've mostly eaten out since I came."

"Good thing." He shut the door. "We'll check all that, too, then toss it all. I don't want you eating anything that was already in this house when you came."

"I've had some of her coffee. She always grinds her own beans."

"No ill effects?"

"None."

"Then don't eat or drink anything else, whether it was already here or brought for the funeral. Agreed?"

"Yes, not worth the risk."

In other cabinets, nothing looked out of place. When they finished, Kurt pulled out his phone and tapped on the screen. "I'm making a list of things we'll do tomorrow." He took a seat at the kitchen table.

While he made his list, she decided the kitchen search should include looking for the missing lock box key. The hook by the back door held nothing but the extra set of keys to Aunt Suzanne's car and a spare house key. She returned to the kitchen and started going through the drawers.

Kurt called from the table, "Did you check her medicines?"

Liesl stopped shifting through her large serving spoons. "No. I haven't stepped into her bedroom since we took her to the hospital."

Kurt stood up. "Let's go look."

She hesitated. "I'm not sure I can do that without losing it."

"You're going to have to do it eventually. Better with me than alone."

Reluctantly, she agreed. She didn't want to make a fool of herself in front of him. Again. She'd done that when he'd confessed the events that lead to Ross's conception. They'd rarely spoken since.

Chapter Sixteen

Suzanne
March 18, 1961

S uzanne and Max stumbled as they scrambled down two flights of endless stairs, racing toward the screams. Her heart pounded twice as fast as their feet struck the steps. People ran in front and behind them, all moving toward the horrible sounds.

At the first-floor landing, the front door was open. Guests streamed out into the night, and they followed. Max grabbed her hand and helped her descend the porch steps.

Zest started wriggling in his grasp. "It's okay," he murmured to the dog. They rounded the east corner of the house and stopped.

In that moment, that one moment, their world changed.

In the sideyard, Mr. Whitcomb struggled to hold Mrs. Whitcomb upright as she continued to scream. Beside them was a mound—a wad of clothing surrounded by pink snow.

An adult man pushed through the crowd to Mrs.

Whitcomb. He threw his arm around her and gently steered both her and Mr. Whitcomb toward the house.

When Suzanne took a longer look at the bundle of clothes, she spotted long, dark hair splayed in all directions. It was a person. Her knees gave out when she recognized the beautiful pink dress. Winnie. She moved to run toward the gruesome scene, but Max stopped her.

"No, Suzanne. Something terrible has happened here."

She turned to him and wailed through tears. "It's Winnie. Something terrible ... to Winnie?"

He nodded. Then he shifted Zest in his arms and managed to pull a handkerchief from his pocket and wipe her face. "I'm so sorry. So very sorry." He put an arm around her shoulder. "Hear that?"

The sound was of sirens approaching. She nodded.

"The police. We need to go back inside." He tried to pull her toward the house. "Let them do their job." There was a tremor in his voice.

Through her foggy brain, she couldn't process what had happened. She studied him, trying to focus. His face was pale and scrunched with concern. Beads of sweat dotted his forehead. He released her shoulder and gently tugged her hand.

She stared at their entwined hands. Suddenly, the cold temperatures hit her. She was shaking from fear and from exposure to the night chill.

She glanced up at him again. "Why? How did this happen?"

"Someone hurt Winnie. Probably beaten. There's a woodpile right by her ... where she was ..."

"Okay." She choked out the words. "I can't ... Take me away from this nightmare."

They turned and shuffled toward the house. Several police cars arrived. One uniformed officer ran to the house while another veered toward them. He dodged around them and ran past.

At the porch, her father was waiting. He pulled her into his arms and held her tighter than he'd ever held her before.

Her mother hovered beside him, concern painting her face. She patted her arm. "Oh, my poor Suzanne. I'm so sorry."

Had she lost Max? "Max?"

"Right behind you."

"You still have Zest?"

"Yes. I'm not letting her go. Let's get in the house."

Chaos reigned inside. Law enforcement officers kept arriving, herding the grieving into various rooms inside the house. They were trying to interview everyone who attended the party. No one could leave until they'd given a statement to an officer.

The police pointed her family and Max into the master bedroom downstairs. They told them to wait until they came to get them to give statements. Her father passed Suzanne his handkerchief while her mother found tissues. Together, they dabbed at their eyes and remained silent.

At some point, Myron joined them. She didn't know how long they waited until they called Max for questioning. He handed Zest to her, and she hung on to the dog like a lifeline.

After a few moments, a different officer came into the room. "I need the dog."

"No, don't take her." Suzanne shifted Zest behind her. "Don't hurt her. I won't let her get hurt."

"Suzanne, dear, they'll bring her back," her father said in a gentle tone. He looked at the officer. "They'll bring her right back when they've finished, yes?"

"Of course, sir. We noticed spots of blood on the young

man's attire, and he explained it was blood transferred from the dog."

She handed Zest to him with reluctance. "There's blood on her leash too. Please bring her back when you're finished."

About fifteen minutes later, the officer returned Zest without her collar and leash, but the dog seemed fine. They must have wiped her down because all traces of blood on her fur were gone. That made Suzanne feel better somehow.

Max returned, wearing a different dress coat. "I'm supposed to leave now. You going to be okay, Suzanne?"

Tears filled her eyes. "I don't know."

"I'd like to see you tomorrow."

"Sure."

He reached out and gave her hand a squeeze. "I'll call you in the morning." With a last pat to Zest's head, he left.

At some later time, they called her into the dining room. Since she was a minor, her parents sat in on her questioning, and her father held Zest. The officer cautioned her parents not to say anything that might influence her testimony.

"Suzanne, as you know, I'm Officer Ziegler."

She recognized him as Myron's friend's dad.

He stared for a second at the bloodstains on her dress, transferred from Zest. "I understand you handled the dog a few minutes before the body was discovered."

She nodded. "Yes, sir. Twice, actually. When she first came to the attic, and a few minutes ago when you called in Max."

"Did you notice the blood?"

"Yes. In the attic. I picked her up. I thought she'd run away from Winnie. Then I saw blood on my hands and thought she was hurt. Max held her, and we checked her for injuries. We didn't find anything. Then the screaming started."

He turned to her parents. "We need her dress for evidence.

Mrs. Thatcher, could you find something for Suzanne to change into?"

Instead of a lecture about his inappropriate request and the cost of the dress, her mother nodded and left the room to do his bidding.

Ziegler documented Suzanne's movements in specific detail. When her mother returned with a sweater dress that belonged to Winnie, Ziegler handed her a paper bag. He paused his questions while Suzanne and her mother went to a bathroom to change.

In the tiny powder room, her mother pulled the dress over her head and placed it in the bag. "Suzanne, darling. This is terrible. I'm so sorry. For you to lose Winnie under these circumstances."

Suzanne stood as her mother helped her into Winnie's dress while tears poured down her cheeks. Her beautiful friend would never wear this dress again.

Her mother treated her as if she were a child again. She helped her blow her nose, dried her tears, and held her arm as they walked back to the police.

When Mother handed the sack with her dress to Ziegler, he returned to his questions. Where was she when this occurred? Who was with her? Had she heard anything before the screaming started?

As she explained the events to him, she realized Zest was the key to everything. With Zest found dragging her leash, wet and bloody, it meant she had been outside with someone, likely Winnie, right before or as the attack occurred. If she wasn't with Winnie, she could have broken away from whoever had been walking her. Maybe she'd spotted someone hurting Winnie. For Zest to come back inside, someone must have opened the front door and allowed her to run or sneak in. She came to the third floor because of all the noise up there, even though she'd been barred from the attic all night.

If Winnie took Zest for a walk, Edgar would have been there too. Where was Edgar? Suzanne hadn't seen him since the entire group was dancing.

The officer broke into her thoughts.

"Miss Thatcher. You need to focus on my questions."

"I'm sorry, sir."

Her father interrupted. "I think Suzanne needs to go home. This has been a terrible shock for her. For all of us. Can you finish? Or ask her questions tomorrow?"

Ziegler eyed her for a moment and stood up. "Mr. Thatcher, if I could ask you and Mrs. Thatcher a few questions, I'll let you all go home."

In a sad version of musical chairs, Suzanne moved to the end of the table and took Zest from her father while her parents moved near Ziegler. While they reported their activities, Suzanne wished Zest could tell them what she'd witnessed.

When Ziegler dismissed them, she looked for Mrs. Whitcomb. She found her at the small table in the kitchen, surrounded by several women.

As soon as she entered the room, Mrs. Whitcomb burst into tears.

She looked down at her dress, Winnie's dress. "I'm so sorry, Mrs. Whitcomb. I didn't think." She turned to leave.

"It's not you, Suzanne. It's that dog. That dog caused Winnie to be outside tonight." One of her friends moved close and put an arm around Mrs. Whitcomb's shoulders. "I don't ever want to see that dog again. Ever. Can you take her away?"

Before she could respond, her mother's hand was at her waist. "Of course. Suzanne will take her. She'll have a suitable home with us."

Suzanne stared at her mother as they left the room. No animal had ever been allowed inside the house in her entire life. Zest was a housedog, yet her mother agreed to take her with no hesitation.

While they put on their coats, Suzanne turned to her mother. "Are you kidding? About the dog?"

"No. It's something we can do for Evelyn. We'll discuss it later."

When they descended the steps of the front porch, the sound of baying bloodhounds chilled her far beyond the cold temperatures. She hugged Zest. She prayed God would help the dogs find the person responsible for this nightmare. There must be justice for Winnie.

Chapter Seventeen

Cain's descendant

Winnie thought no one knew about her and Edgar's secret place.

I knew.

It was easy to follow them there after school. Then she left the rest of us to decorate for the party while they ran off necking. Infuriating.

I put a stop to that. Burnt their little hiding place to the ground. Their secret kissing place was gone.

I watched as the flames danced around the old shed. Licking the dried-out wood. Popping and creaking. Fire is powerful. And in my control.

Winnie couldn't leave it alone. I didn't intend to have a fight with her. I certainly didn't intend to kill her. But the more she talked, the more enraged I became.

She had to brag about Edgar. Her secret romance. Their secret plans. Blah, blah, blah. She wouldn't shut up. Then she told me they were getting engaged. Engaged? My fury rose. All

I wanted was to push her down and ruin that beautiful dress. Anything to make her stop.

I spotted the stacked firewood nearby. I knew I could use it to make her stop. I had to make her *stop* talking.

She just fell down in a bloody heap, right at my feet. Winnie was a red and pink lump in the formerly pristine winter wonderland.

I ran. They'd lock me in prison for the rest of my life. I couldn't be caught.

God help me! What have I done?

Chapter Eighteen

Liesl
November 10

Kurt leaned over and stroked Ross's blond hair as he slept, then he covered his son with a lap blanket and turned off the television.

Seeing the tender interaction made Liesl realize some of the resentment she'd harbored over the years had faded. Perhaps she'd matured. Kurt made the best life from a difficult situation, and his reward was the unbridled adoration of a darling son.

For someone who'd accepted the responsibility of being a single father since he was nineteen, he was doing an excellent job raising the boy. All she could show for that same time span was seven years of bitterness. Time for her to move on.

Kurt strode over. "You ready?"

"Yes, but we have three things to search for. One is the possible poison, two is a missing bank lockbox key, and three is a journal Aunt Suzanne kept."

"You mean a diary?"

"I believe that is the book she was talking about the night I arrived. Aunt Suzanne was not functioning well. She mentioned 'her book,' and I thought she was referring to one of my books. This 'book' could be one of her journals. Information from her search for Winnie's killer might be in it."

"Did she always keep a journal?"

"For decades. They were like a daily diary of weather and events. There were a lot of them in the lockboxes at the bank. The most recent one there was 2019. I suspect all but the one she was currently using are in the one lock box we didn't have a key for."

"Where's the key?"

She shrugged. "No clue. That's why it's on our search list. Mr. Van de Berg had the keys to the rest of the bank boxes, along with a letter she'd written a few years ago. Records show she used the newest box about a week before she died."

"If those journals give details of her day, the most recent one could help us figure out if someone tried to hurt her, or show some of her contacts for the last week or two."

"It also might show if she was in her right mind."

"You're right." He pulled himself to his full height. "Ready to go in there now?"

Liesl bit her lip and walked toward the hallway. The wooden floorboards creaked as they approached Aunt Suzanne's bedroom. Kurt opened the wide door and turned on the overhead light. She hesitated at the threshold. Without a word, he put an arm around her shoulder and they walked into the room.

The bed remained unmade, sheets crumpled from the EMTs' efforts to move Aunt Suzanne onto their gurney. Liesl's tears flowed from the memory of her lying there, a diminished version of her former self.

Kurt squeezed her shoulder. They walked closer to the bed, and she resisted the urge to throw herself on it. Her fingers ached to caress the cool linen of Aunt Suzanne's pillow.

The bedside table held a collection of over-the-counter and prescription medicine bottles, along with a tissue box and an empty glass.

Kurt gestured toward the tabletop. "We'll send these in to the lab."

"Yes."

She opened the drawer of the table and shuffled through the items. There were pens, a pair of reading glasses, and articles torn from the local paper—probably for her. Aunt Suzanne always mailed items about people and events she thought Liesl would enjoy. There was a book, Susan Page Davis's latest True Blue mystery, but no journal. A last glance around the bedroom revealed nothing else to consider for testing.

They shifted to do a bathroom search. Kurt got on his knees and began rummaging through the cabinets.

Liesl fingered the toiletry items near the sink. Aunt Suzanne's perfume, makeup case, and toothbrush were lined up as she'd always had them. How could she throw away these personal items? She shook her head. She would have the new housekeeper remove these things once they'd taken samples. Except the make-up case. The contents could go, but she'd keep the case. Aunt Suzanne had used it for years, and it was something to cherish.

Then a sinister thought arose. "Kurt? Should we test her makeup, toothpaste, and things of that nature? Can cosmetics be poisoned?"

He looked at her in surprise. "The toothpaste, for sure. I don't know if you can poison someone through the skin, but I'll check on that."

Other than shower gel and shampoo, nothing else in the bathroom caught their attention. Kurt added these to his list, and they returned to the bedroom.

Liesl tackled the dresser drawers while Kurt entered Aunt Suzanne's walk-in closet.

From the closet, in a tone dripping with sarcasm, Kurt asked, "Did she have enough shoes?"

"A woman can never have too many shoes."

"What size do you wear? I see some sexy-looking brown librarian-type lace-ups with a sensible heel in here."

She chuckled. "Why don't you try them on? A picture of those posted on social media could make you famous."

"Sure. Just the publicity every detective needs."

"A single guy in women's shoes packing a badge and gun. It would keep the women away."

"I don't need anything else to keep women away. One little boy takes care of that."

She frowned. "I'm sorry. Don't they see what a good father you are and consider it one of your better points?"

"They see it as a liability. I don't bring home much money, even with my promotion to detective. My attention is always on Ross. Most women want a man's undivided attention and a good provider. I miss the target on both counts."

"Your comment about women looking for a good provider is a sexist remark."

"Sorry. Is it sexist if a man admits he's looking for a woman who's a good breadwinner?"

"I'll ponder that and let you know." Odd that someone like Kurt wasn't considered a great catch. The downside of dating as a single parent never crossed her mind.

"As much as I hate to admit it, all the locals know the circumstances about Ross. They know I wronged you."

She tried not to preen in satisfaction. With nothing coming

to mind but "karma" or "you deserve it," she held her tongue and changed the subject. "Do you ever consider going to law school anymore?"

Before being saddled with the responsibilities of fatherhood, he'd planned to be an attorney. His father had been a laborer at one of the town's brick refractories and encouraged him to use his brain, rather than his back.

"I'm getting an online degree in criminal justice right now," Kurt said. "I'll finish in another semester. Maybe one day, when Ross is older, I could go to law school. Probably when Ross is in college himself."

The search of dressers came up empty, so she turned to the massive Victorian-style wardrobe. It was her favorite piece of furniture in the house. When the house was built, Aunt Suzanne's grandmother specifically designed the wardrobe for her use. Its ornate carvings were appropriate to the era, and those, combined with a shiny dark lacquer finish, made the piece a showstopper.

The brass hinges of the wardrobe were large and burnished. Part of Liesl's punishment, in the rare instances she was naughty as a child, was to be conscripted into child labor to polish them. Based on the shine of these hinges, either Aunt Suzanne had taken up the work after her departure, or some unlucky child from the neighborhood had recently worked off their crime.

She opened the door, and the aromatic dark wood provided memories of trying to make the wardrobe work magic like the one in the C. S. Lewis books. Aunt Suzanne must have regretted reading them to her because Liesl was constantly in the wardrobe, searching for passage to Narnia.

The bottom third of the wardrobe had cubbyholes for shoes. A rod near the top spanned the width and held hanging clothes. Across the top was a deep shelf filled with old hat boxes. Aunt Suzanne had a family collection of hats and their stiletto-like hatpins. Aunt Suzanne told her women used the hatpins as weapons, if needed, back in the old days.

She inspected every square inch of the wardrobe. No key and no journal. Besides hats, clothes, and shoes, there were many handkerchiefs with the initials of Aunt Suzanne's mother and a few small ones with embroidered ducks and rabbits—obviously Aunt Suzanne's when she was a child. Liesl fingered them and decided these would make a lovely wall hanging. They were too sweet to leave hidden away.

Kurt emerged from the closet with mussed hair and a look of disgust. "I've never seen so many clothes and shoes in my life."

She smiled. "There's a cedar-lined closet in the attic that's bigger than this bedroom."

His eyebrows rose. "You're lying."

"Nope." She grinned. "You never had a reason to go up there when we were dating. But it's true. All the old winter clothes, sweaters, and holiday decorations are there." She stepped back from the open wardrobe and waved her arms. "More clothes in here."

"You could fill a department store with all this."

"I'll go through it and donate the majority. Some stuff in this wardrobe belonged to Aunt Suzanne's mother and grandmother. I'll bet the historical society would like the older outfits."

"Any luck with a key or journal?"

"Not a bit."

He rubbed his chin and glanced around the room. "Did you check on top of the wardrobe?"

"No. I'd need a ladder, and Aunt Suzanne was a foot shorter than me. I can't imagine it could be a hiding place. For the journal, she would have needed to reach it every day."

"Tomorrow I'll bring a stepladder and check the top of every piece of furniture in the house."

"Thanks, Kurt. That'd be nice."

He stood back and marveled at the wardrobe. "It's massive, isn't it?"

"Interested in the story behind it?"

"Sure."

"This was made to order in England from sketches drawn by Aunt Suzanne's grandmother, the original Mrs. Thatcher. Some wardrobes are called 'knock downs' because they could be taken apart and reassembled, making them easier to move."

Kurt appeared to be listening avidly, so she went on.

"Sadly, the original Mrs. Thatcher didn't want it to 'knock down.' They packed this into an enormous crate and transported it to America by ship, and then to Missouri by train. When they tried to move it in, the bedroom door was too narrow. They enlarged the doorway, and someone handcrafted a custom door. No one notices the additional width of the bedroom door, but once pointed out, it's obvious."

"I never noticed it." He glanced around the room. "Is that everything?"

She gestured to the small bookshelf wedged between the closet door and a lounge chair. "This is our last hope of finding the journal in this room." She moved the chair cushions but found nothing beneath but a few crumbs. The floor under the chair was clear.

She sat cross-legged on the rug in front of the bookcase and pulled out half the contents of the bottom shelf. Books of all sizes were stored there. She inspected each one to make sure she didn't miss a journal.

There were books from her childhood, some from Aunt Suzanne's childhood, and a few golf manuals and war novels

119

that had belonged to Uncle Max. In this collection of family's favorites, it was no surprise to find her novels, all in a row.

She thumbed through her first published work, printed in paperback, titled *Lord Henry's Betrayal*. The dedication read, "To Uncle Max and Aunt Suzanne."

"Your aunt was very proud of that," Kurt said.

"Yes, she told me." She looked up at him. "She talked to you about it?"

"She talked to everyone about it. She was a modest person, but she couldn't resist bragging about you."

"I'm glad she was proud."

"I liked the book, but it was obvious you'd modeled Lord Henry after me, and he was an awful character."

"You've read this?"

"I've read everything you've written."

"I'm surprised. I never pictured you as a romance reader." She chuckled.

Kurt chuckled with her. "Only what you write."

"According to my publisher, many men are closet romance readers."

"I admit, I enjoyed them all, but I didn't like the similarity to our own situation."

"They say, 'write what you know.' Betrayal was something I'd experienced."

The sadness in his eyes caused her to look away. She finished reviewing the books on the shelves but found no journal.

With a groan, she pushed herself to her knees.

Kurt jumped up and offered a hand. His gesture produced memories of happier times. Being friends first, before any romantic inclination occurred, provided a good basis for their relationship. At least until everything fell apart.

They'd always had fun when they'd dated. She missed it. No one else she'd dated made her laugh as much as Kurt.

Their eyes met. His smile seemed bittersweet. If only she could read his thoughts, but she understood his sorrow.

She stepped back, turning her face, unsure what her own eyes revealed.

Chapter Nineteen

Liesl

Kurt excused himself to check on Ross. Once he left, Liesl chided herself for the sentimental journey to their past. The past had been happy until it imploded. Her mind needed to stay focused on *now*.

She mumbled as she scanned Aunt Suzanne's bedroom. "Where did you hide your journal and key?"

Kurt returned. "Ross is still asleep." He stopped and stood with hands on his hips. "Did you check under the bed?"

"Yes."

"What about between the mattress and the box spring?"

She walked to the side of the bed and slid her hands under the mattress, running the length of it. Touching something solid, she squealed. The journal. Its cover was a deep shade of purple leather, with a gold leaf edge.

She rushed to a nearby chair and opened it to the last entry. The familiar handwriting slanted toward the right and made her smile.

"Read it aloud," Kurt said. He took a seat on the side of the bed.

She turned on the lamp.

October 30. The meeting with George was so upsetting. Someone has spent the money. Stole the money. A thief. One of the board members is a thief. It's unimaginable.

I got the board's bank records and went through them. The money was not there. Then I pulled my copies of the financial records from past board meetings, but when I compared them, I couldn't make heads or tails of the figures.

I took the list to all the businesses. Cash refund for returned items. No one remembered who'd requested the refunds, or worse, the employee who'd made the transaction wasn't there. The forms for cash returns just showed 'Butterfly House' and an illegible scrawl for a signature. Months of this type of thing. Thousands of dollars. Why were we so blind?

When Liesl stopped reading, Kurt said, "There's nothing wrong with her mind. She sounds her usual self."

"Usual, but upset. George is Mr. Barnaby at the bank. What list is she referring to?"

"Maybe a list of checks or debits from the Butterfly House account?"

Liesl flipped to the entry from the previous day.

October 29. Last night was a nightmare. My mind in a whirl from the confrontation after the meeting. The thought of the missing money kept me pacing in the dark. I'm writing this in the faint light of dawn. Who pilfered

123

our money? With so many having access, how can I sort this?

I was tempted to see George about it last night after the meeting, but he needed to be at the bank to help me. Today, I'll call and make an appointment.

At the Circle, Doreen asked me if I was ill. How I wanted to blurt out my problems! But the thought of the other ladies listening to us kept me mum. How did I get into this quandary? Doreen was smart to resign from the board.

"Nothing shows she'd solved that old murder and confronted somebody about it," Kurt said. "That takes away a motive to poison her."

"Would someone poison her for discovering embezzlement?"

"It depends on the amount stolen and the reputation of the person who took it. Would they kill to keep it a secret?"

"If the board had a confrontation about it, there's no need to kill. The whole town would know within a few days."

"Read it again," Kurt said. "The confrontation part. I didn't get that it happened during the meeting."

She re-read the passage. "Last night was a nightmare. My mind in a whirl from the confrontation after the meeting."

"After the meeting," Kurt repeated.

"That's a big difference."

"It could have been a confrontation between her and one person or several people. Her words don't indicate who or how many."

"It's also possible the embezzlement isn't related to her poisoning. It could be related to Winnie's killer." Liesl's voice broke. "Maybe that's why she warned me about talking to people who'd been there. Perhaps she figured out the killer and realized she'd talked too much."

Kurt rose and snagged a tissue.

"Thanks." She dabbed her eyes. "Also, it's possible she was upset about the money and accidentally poisoned herself."

"Right," Kurt said, taking a seat again. "Anything's possible, but I don't believe it's likely she poisoned herself."

She blew her nose and then flipped back to the October 28 entry.

"The sunrise was beautiful this morning. Shades of pink and red, then the bright gold globe. I'll have a busy day today with my lunch date and the B. H. meeting."

Kurt rose and offered her a hand. "Time for us to go. When do you want me here tomorrow?"

"I'll be up by eight."

"Ross has a play date at nine. How about after I drop him off? I'll bring doughnuts and milk. Don't touch any food or drink in this house. That's an order."

She nodded, not bothering to bristle at Kurt's command. She was in no mood to joke about a cop's affection for doughnuts, either. "They better be Ralph's Donuts, or I won't let you in the house." That was not a joke, and Kurt knew it.

They returned to the sleeping boy sprawled on the couch. He'd partially kicked off his cover. Kurt shouldered him and took the stairs with cautious steps.

At the door, Kurt realized he needed to get his gun.

"You get him in the car, and I'll get it out," she said.

"Just unlock the cabinet. It's loaded. We can't have you accidentally shooting yourself."

The scenario was all too likely, so she didn't take offense.

In the study, she unlocked the cabinet and put away the

key. Out of curiosity, she opened her old desk and saw Aunt Suzanne had filled it with her own records. Flipping through the files, she snagged the one marked 'Butterfly House,' but the file was empty. Why were these missing? Without a doubt, she'd kept years of records here. The folder looked well used.

Kurt appeared and re-holstered his gun. "What do we have there?"

"Her Butterfly House file. It's empty. Isn't that odd?"

He strode toward her. "Her records are around here somewhere. You look tired, Liesl. Go to bed. We'll have tomorrow to search."

She avoided his eyes.

"You're going to stay up and read that journal, aren't you?"

With a smile at his psychic ability, she pointed toward the door. "Out. Get out. Don't come back until tomorrow."

He bowed, sweeping off an imaginary hat. "As you wish, my lady." Then he grinned. "That's the way they do it in your books, isn't it?"

She gave him a curtsy, holding her invisible skirt in her hands. "Until tomorrow, my lord."

* * *

Upstairs, she changed into pajamas and settled into bed with the purple journal. Although her eyelids were heavy, the excitement of reading the journal was too great to allow her to sleep, so she started at the beginning.

January 1. Liesl and I had a great day yesterday. We put the old year to bed by going to a romantic movie, Liesl called it a "chick flick" and made me laugh. We ate our weight in popcorn. Having her here keeps me young. When she's gone, I complain to Doreen and Patricia about my arthritis or other ailments. They keep me informed of their own aches and pains. I may be old, but spending time with Liesl makes me feel like a girl again.

Liesl smiled. Thanks to Aunt Suzanne's daily diligence, it was as if she was here, talking to her. How lucky she was. Most people who'd lost loved ones didn't have the luxury of reading their words and finding comfort in them.

By the March 3rd entry, she stopped fighting sleep and turned off the light.

Chapter Twenty

Suzanne
March 19, 1961

other fixed a pallet for Zest on the floor of Suzanne's bedroom. Then she helped Suzanne into her nightgown and poured her into bed.

Within seconds of her mother's departure, Suzanne slipped out and brought the dog into her bed. Even with Zest, she tossed and turned, fighting off nightmares until dawn broke. Why had this happened? Who was responsible?

At first light, she gave up trying to sleep and to understand why. She couldn't make sense of a senseless act. Winnie was with God. Those left behind had to grapple with acceptance. Her heart and prayers went to Winnie's family. Their only daughter, gone. Charlie, her older brother, had lost his only sister. How could any of them shake off the agony of their loss?

Never again would Suzanne experience a childlike belief in the world's goodness. She'd seen the devil's work and prayed for the power of God to help them recover.

Zest motivated her to get out of bed and dress to take her outside. When they cut through the kitchen to head out the back door, her mother surprised her. She was there, awake and dressed, drinking a cup of coffee.

Her mother tried to smile, but the effort failed. "Good morning, dear."

"Morning, Mother." She glanced at Zest, bundled in her arms. "I forgot to thank you last night for letting us keep the dog. I was proud when you didn't hesitate about it, even though no animal has graced our family home."

"Please don't make me regret it." Her mother eyed Zest with obvious suspicion. "I understood how Evelyn could blame Zest for Winnie being outside. Removing the dog was the least I could do for her. After all—" Her voice broke for a moment. "I was taking my daughter home. She will have to bury hers."

Tears filled Suzanne's eyes, and she couldn't get out of the kitchen fast enough. Normally her mother was like a smooth slab of granite in a world of sand. Now she was disintegrating, and Suzanne couldn't watch.

When she and Zest returned, her mother informed her of her plan.

"I'm contacting Pastor Bailey today and will schedule grief counseling sessions for all of us."

"Even Myron?"

"Yes, even Myron. At least one session."

One way her mother expressed love for the family was by planning and organizing their lives. They might not like it, but it was love, offered her way. Her interest in their well-being was sincere.

"Do you think Myron will agree?"

"I hope so. It's a horrible loss we're trying to understand. Grief can eat you up if you don't process it correctly. It would do us all good to have some help. Pastor Bailey was a chaplain in the war, dear. I believe he can help us all."

Suzanne stared at her mother. Had this horrible situation opened her eyes to the important things in life? They constantly wrestled with opposing views. Suzanne felt her mother's focus on social status was silly. Helping those who need help and making the world a better place was what Suzanne found important. Different values, yet they were eerily alike in pigheadedness, and this made for ugly confrontations.

"Thank you. I'd like to talk to him. I'm questioning how the Lord could let this happen."

"I hope Pastor Bailey can help us find peace."

When her father appeared, they made a list of items to buy for the dog. Although he mumbled about having to stop in two places to get everything they needed, she considered it lucky both the feed store and the hardware store were open on Saturdays. He surprised her by suggesting he build a small, fenced-in area for the dog to use.

"I know your Mother won't want a fence in her backyard, but she also won't want to step in ... anything left by the dog. If we can fence off an area, she won't see easily from the house and won't walk through, your dog will have an outside place to run."

Suzanne hugged him. She couldn't ask for a better father. He might not stand up to her mother when he should, but he would never act like poor Doreen's dad.

* * *

The phone rang when the whole family was pretending to eat breakfast. The sound made her jump. Mother pulled a sour face, which disappeared as quickly as it came.

Myron popped up from the table. "I'll get it."

Suzanne shot Myron a look of surprise. Then she realized he was using it as an excuse to run away from their silent table.

"Suzanne," Myron shouted from the pantry. "It's for you."

"Be right there." No way would she discuss last night with Patricia, Doreen, or other friends. Only Pastor Bailey would hear her thoughts and experiences.

She made her way to the pantry. Their house had two telephones, one for each floor, both located where servants worked because they'd handled calls in the olden days. In modern times, her mother refused to move something as crass as a telephone to the living areas of the house.

Myron passed the receiver to Suzanne without a clue who it was.

"Hello?"

"Suzanne, it's Max."

Her heart felt lighter in her chest.

"I wanted to make sure you were doing okay today."

"Thank you. I'm as well as you'd expect. How are you?"

"I've been upset about everything and worried about you. I didn't want to call too soon, but I'd like to see you. Just for a few minutes. Is that okay?"

She'd never had a guy ask to come visit before. She had no experience of what her parents would say or do. Unwilling to have them say no, she decided not to ask them. "That's fine, Max. I'd like that. I look awful, but I suppose you would expect that."

"I should be there in about fifteen minutes, give or take."

"Have you eaten breakfast?"

"I tried but couldn't manage it. Don't worry about food. I won't stay long, but I've got something for you."

"You do?"

"Just a little something. See you in a minute."

* * *

She grabbed Zest and waited for Max in the music room. That way, she could beat her mother to the door. Their doorbell was a little tricky to those unfamiliar with something that old. Most visitors stared at the handle until they figured out how it worked. It was almost ninety years old and had an elaborate brass plate with a center handle. Two brass bells hidden behind an ornate cover chimed when someone turned the exterior handle.

Listening for steps on the porch, she heard him approach and hurried to the door, so no bells were necessary. Zest gave a low bark but stopped when she recognized Max.

"Thank you for coming, Max." She stepped back to let him in. "Let me take your coat."

He tossed a small wrapped package from hand to hand as he pulled off his gloves. Then he handed the package to her. "This is for you."

She set the dog down to take the gift and admired the package. "This is a pleasant surprise."

Max crouched to pet Zest for a moment.

While he did, she hung his coat on the brass coat rack beside the door. "Come into the den, and I'll open it."

He followed her through the music room and into their den, which was currently uninhabited. It was Suzanne's greatest wish that her family would stay away during this visit by Max. Her mother's supervision could be nerve-racking at the best of times.

Suzanne led Max to the two wing-backed chairs near the fireplace. Her father had started a fire before he left, so the room was cozy.

"Open it," Max said. "I want to explain."

"A gift that needs explanation? You have my full attention."

She studied the lightweight and silent box. Clothing? A scarf? Neither. Instead, nestled inside were three handkerchiefs. One displayed the initial "S" embroidered in emerald green, another had a bunch of daisies embroidered in a corner, and the third was edged in a practical white lace. "These are beautiful, Max. Thank you."

Zest settled down onto Max's lap. He petted her as he launched into an explanation. "No matter what I wish for you, you're going to have some rough days ahead. I thought handkerchiefs would be practical for two reasons. They could dry your tears and remind you of me while you go through this."

"These are lovely." She had to fight back tears. "I don't think I've ever received a more thoughtful gift."

He smiled. "I'm glad you like them. It was an interesting experience trying to pick these out for you at Fredendall and Wilkins this morning. A sales clerk took pity on me. She helped me choose and then wrapped them."

She smiled. "I figured you didn't wrap it yourself."

"I've got sisters who would, but I'd have to find them and explain. Glad the clerk offered."

"A farmer shopping for a feminine gift. It proves you are a brave man."

Myron walked into the den. "Max is brave? I'm not so sure about that."

"Hey, there." Max turned toward Myron. "How are you doing?"

She swung toward Myron and gave him an icy stare. "Did I invite you to join us?"

He shrugged. "Sorry to interrupt. Max is my friend, too, Suzanne. I figured he'd want to see me."

Max smiled. "I want to see you, but I wanted to see her more."

This statement released her tension. "Oh, sit on the couch, Myron. Dad will be here in a minute, anyway." She turned to Max. "Get ready for Dad. Once he realizes you're here to see me, he may go 'protective father' on you."

"It's not your father I'm worried about. It's your mother."

She grinned at Myron. "Max is wise and brave."

"He didn't always used to be so smart," Myron teased.

The three of them enjoyed a magical conversation until her father broke the spell.

Chapter Twenty-One

Liesl
November 11

It surprised Liesl to find Patricia Sizemore on the porch, rather than Kurt.

"Good morning, Liesl." Patricia offered a Styrofoam plate filled with delectable sweets, covered in plastic wrap. "Thought you might enjoy these."

The plate of cookies looked pristine and above suspicion, but they were an unpleasant reminder of her aunt's demise.

"Thank you, Mrs. Sizemore." She hoped her voice portrayed some sincerity. "Won't you come in? I've made a fresh pot of coffee."

Patricia stepped into the house. Liesl admired her soft, brown leather jacket and multi-colored scarf. She'd styled her hair in an elegant swirl that survived the windy morning, thanks to her scarf. A delicate, diamond-encrusted Rolex twinkled on her wrist.

Although Aunt Suzanne could have afforded luxuries, she

hadn't indulged in such ostentation. This was a huge personality difference between the two old friends.

Liesl led Patricia into the kitchen, where she served coffee and gestured for Patricia to take a seat. "Care for your own cookie?"

"No, thank you." Patricia pulled out a chair and placed her purse on the chair beside it. "The nice thing about baking is, you smell the concoction so much it's easy to resist when cooked."

When Liesl sat down, Patricia studied her face. "How are you getting along?"

"It's been such a shock." She glanced around. "It seems strange Aunt Suzanne won't be coming down to join us."

"It's hard for me too. We did so many things together. As widows, we had dinner together frequently and acted as each other's 'plus one' at parties. Between church, the Butterfly House board, and the Historical Society board, it will be a daily mourning for me."

"I don't believe I've thanked you properly for taking care of her. It's a comfort to know her two best friends were here with her until I could arrive."

Patricia nodded. "It was the least I could do."

"When did you realize she was sick?"

She paused. "She was fine at the Butterfly House board meeting and at the church dinner. I didn't realize she was sick until I stopped by Thursday."

"Did she tell you what was wrong?"

"She said she'd spent most of the night with vomiting and diarrhea. In fact, Doreen answered the door and warned me about coming in, afraid I'd catch the flu from Suzanne, but I insisted. Later, I offered to stay so Doreen could get something from the drugstore."

Although tempted, Liesl didn't discuss the possibility of poisoning. "Did she eat anything?"

"No, I made her some tea, and she kept it down for a bit. Doreen returned with the medicine, which didn't seem to help. Then we took shifts to stay."

"I'm grateful you were here."

Patricia sipped her coffee. "She was like a sister. We've been friends since we were children."

"Were you a friend of Winifred Whitcomb, too?"

She stiffened. "Yes. Such a tragedy."

"Sorry, I didn't mean to upset you."

"You would think an event so old wouldn't bother me, but it does." Patricia's finger traced the pattern of the tablecloth. "Being an only child, I loved hanging with them. We would constantly play at each other's houses."

"It must have been nice to have such close friends."

Patricia smiled. "Parents opened our homes to dances and parties. We'd spend hours planning what to wear, shopping for something new, and talking about who might dance with us, or how we'd try to sneak a kiss. It was all innocent fun. At least until the night Winnie died."

"Wasn't it a birthday party for her?"

"Yes. She had our group over for a party and dancing. For several years, her house was the 'dancing house' because of the third floor."

"I don't understand."

"Her father owned a construction company. Although her house wasn't as wonderful as this," she gestured with both hands, "it was a beautiful Craftsman style home. Winnie talked her father into flooring the attic with smooth wood floors so we could use it for dancing. Dozens of us would crowd in there and dance to our hearts' content. We were careful not to slip. It was a polished floor."

Liesl couldn't imagine an entire floor of a house devoted to dancing, even if it was the attic.

"What happened that night?"

She sighed. "I'd rather not talk about it."

"I've been rude. It's still painful for you."

"It is. Life can be cruel."

"Yes." Liesl averted her eyes.

"It's my turn to apologize. I know you're upset, and a comment about life's cruelties is out of line." Patricia paused. "I assume Suzanne left you this home?"

"She did. It surprised me. I figured she would donate it to one of her charities."

"You were her immediate family, so why wouldn't you inherit? A charity would have a hard time affording the upkeep on it. Will that be a problem for you?"

Her nosiness caught Liesl off guard, and she groped for an appropriate response. "I can manage."

"Do you know when her donation will come through?"

"Her donation?"

"She made a bequest to the Butterfly House. Has that changed?"

"No, I understand that's one of her charitable donations. I have no clue when it'll happen."

Patricia frowned. "That money is important." She rose to her feet. "It will work out soon. I must fly now."

Liesl couldn't resist probing for information on the erratic Butterfly House funds a bit as they walked to the door. "Who is the treasurer? I'll speak with Mr. Van de Berg about handling the donation as soon as possible."

"Van de Berg."

Liesl blinked. Wait, the treasurer was Mr. Van de Berg? Was he responsible for the pilfered funds?

The doorbell snapped her from her reverie. When she opened the door, Kurt stepped across the threshold carrying an enormous stack of small cardboard boxes. He smiled at Patricia.

"Mrs. Sizemore, how are you?"

Her eyebrows reached the top of her forehead before she answered. "Fine, Kurt. What a surprise to see you here." She whirled on Liesl with a piercing look that demanded justification for Kurt's presence.

"He's helping me. Er—sort through Aunt Suzanne's things to donate to charity," Liesl said, looking away from Mrs. Sizemore's frosty blue eyes.

"I see," she replied, clearly not believing her.

Kurt placed the boxes on a nearby table while Liesl handed Mrs. Sizemore her jacket and scarf.

"Thanks again for the goodies."

Through a tight-lipped smile, Patricia said, "Enjoy," then disappeared out the door.

Kurt hung up his coat and said, "She wasn't happy to see me."

"She knows our history. It's logical she's shocked to see you here."

"What a terrible liar you are." He chuckled a bit. "She didn't fall for your excuse for me being here."

His words infuriated her. "I don't take many opportunities to lie, so I'm out of practice."

He pushed his palms toward her. "Whoa. I'm not trying to make you mad. I'm stating the obvious. You're not a good liar. She didn't believe a word you said about me helping clear out your aunt's things."

"I didn't know she'd be here. I had no time to fabricate a good reason for you. I couldn't rightly say you're here to find my aunt's killer."

"No, but we must agree on what we're telling people. The whole town will have the same reaction."

What would she tell people? They'd want to know why their seven-year feud had ended. She had to agree with him. "We need a plausible explanation, not a thinly disguised, poorly delivered lie."

* * *

In silence, they savored the culinary perfection of a Ralph's doughnut. Kurt reached for a second helping and chuckled when he caught her gazing at the selection in the box.

"Go on. Have another."

"I'll be as big as this house."

"No, you won't." He stood up, grabbed the carafe, and tipped the steaming coffee into their empty cups. "We're going to work hard today. You need those carbs for strength." When he'd replaced the pot, his oversized paw reached into the doughnut box, selected a devilish treat, and placed it in the center of her empty plate. "Hope you don't mind my fingers."

She surrendered and ate the second doughnut. "I missed these doughnuts more than I realized. No place in Houston comes anywhere close to this bit of heaven."

"It's because no one except Ralph Jones is silly enough to get up in the middle of the night to bake doughnuts, cakes and pies from scratch," Kurt proclaimed as he helped himself to a third doughnut. "I see him driving to his bakery in all kinds of weather. Makes you admire someone who enjoys his life's work that much."

"Why do you see him so often?"

"The hazard of being in law enforcement. Bad stuff mostly happens at night. Thieves prefer the dark."

"Ah. Makes sense. The ghastly hours associated with law enforcement."

"It wasn't so bad when I was on patrol, but being a detective means I respond to anything important when I'm on call. Poor Ross is getting used to being dragged from his bed at night and buckled into his booster seat in the back of my car."

"Poor thing. But he's such a jolly kid, he won't have bad memories about it. By the way, one good thing came from Mrs. Sizemore's visit this morning."

He licked his fingers and eyed another doughnut. "Really?"

"Yes. She told me Mr. Van de Berg is the Butterfly House's treasurer."

"No kidding?"

She nodded. "She ought to know. She's on the board."

"If he's been stealing money from the society, he'll lose his license to practice law. Quite a motive to stop someone who found out about it."

"There was an underlying tension between him and Mr. Barnaby when we were at the bank. With the account for the Butterfly House there, Mr. Barnaby could have realized something was wrong when Aunt Suzanne requested their financial records. He'd know who was acting treasurer."

"To look into the bank information, we'd need a subpoena. To get that, we need probable cause. Notes in your aunt's journal won't meet the standard. Not sure how we can use them, but we'll figure it out." He smiled. "One mystery at a time, okay?" He scooted back his chair. "We need to get started on our collections. I've got to pick up Ross after lunch, and we're burning daylight."

Without argument, she cleared their dishes. "You sound like a cowboy."

He smiled. "What's wrong with that, little lady?"

"Not a thing, John Wayne."

"My friends call me Duke."

She rinsed the plates and put them in the dishwasher, silently wondering whether Van de Berg could be an embezzler. If so, she needed to make sure he didn't help himself to any of Aunt Suzanne's estate. Was this why Aunt Suzanne was so upset about the money? Could her longtime friend be a thief?

Chapter Twenty-Two

Kurt

The morning passed quickly as Kurt and Liesl followed his list from the night before, taking samples and labeling the specimen jars, then placing the jars in the boxes for shipping.

When he put the last two boxes of samples in the trunk of his car, Kurt said, "We forgot about the garage!"

She glanced at the closed doors. "We sure did."

They went in and eyed the shelf of chemicals. Drain cleaner, bleach, and various cans of oil were there, separated by garden tools and old rags.

Kurt turned. "Any doubt these things are what they say? If so, why should we test them?"

She agreed with his logic. Dust and grime dotted the surfaces of the containers. "None of them look recently used."

"We're good to go." He shot several pictures of the shelves and their contents with his phone. "These will document everything is old and not recently used."

When they turned to leave, Liesl noticed the driver's door of her aunt's car was ajar.

She pointed. "Look. I'm sure that was closed yesterday."

Kurt stopped her as she approached the door. "Don't touch it. I have a fingerprint kit in my trunk. Maybe we can pull a print or two."

"Fingerprints? It's just an open door."

His voice became as hard as flint. "Look, the other night, someone grabbed your aunt's coat and burned it. Now we find her car's door open. The dome light's still working, so access was recent because the battery would be dead otherwise. Why would someone want to be in there?"

"Like they tried to steal it?"

"It's possible. But what if they were looking for something?"

"Like what?"

"Maybe someone thought your aunt had stuff in there related to the Butterfly House theft or Winnie Whitcomb's murder."

She paused. "Possible, but not likely. It's more plausible kids from the neighborhood were looking for money or valuables."

He spun to face her. "Have you seen any kids or adults wandering around?"

"The night of the burglary."

With a sigh, he said, "I'd rather check for prints now than regret it later. Wait here. It won't take long."

He'd done nothing halfway in his life. Why would this be any different?

He returned with a box and kneeled on the concrete floor. He pulled out a jar, opened it, and dipped a brush in the black powder. Then he applied the powder to the surface of the white door.

"There is a true skill in pulling up latent prints. I'm not sure I'm good enough. I just learned how to do this."

"At least you're trying."

He waited and then applied more powder. A few grunts later, he appeared satisfied and pulled tape and index cards from the kit. He pressed the tape over the black powder, then peeled it back and taped the results to the card.

"Did you get one?"

He shrugged. "A couple might be usable. We'll have to see. We compare them to prints on file in the AFIS database. That includes people booked for crimes and anyone who served in the military or the government or was employed in a hazardous industry."

"Okay."

"These could all belong to your aunt."

"When you're through there, I'd like to look inside the car. I haven't found her purse, and she always carried one. I'll bet that's where her car keys and possibly the lockbox key are."

Kurt didn't respond, his attention once again focused on his work.

She walked over to her Jeep.

"Don't touch that one either. It's next."

"Why? The doors are closed."

"The perp may have had time to close your door, but had to rush away from your aunt's car."

When he finished Suzanne's car, Liesl performed a thorough search. After peering under the seats, going through the papers in the glove box, and running her hand between the leather seats, all she had to show for it were two fuzz-covered breath mints, a receipt from Taco Bell, a rubber band, and a paper clip.

After he finished her Jeep, she stared at the black residue covering the doors. Terrific.

"Sorry. Both cars will need a wash now." Kurt packed up his gear. "I better be off. Time to pick up Ross from his play date."

"Thanks for doing this. Your help means a lot to me."

"I'm the law. It's my job. The question is whether we'll learn anything. It's frustrating to wait for lab results, then have to deal with the findings. Don't expect too much."

She followed him to his car.

He turned. "You'll need to run to the station and let them take your fingerprints."

"Why?"

"Elimination prints."

"At least we've done something and attempted to understand what happened. I've felt helpless since talking with Dr. Johnson."

"As far as the testing of the samples, do you pay the lab up front? I can go inside and write you a check."

"No, they'll send a bill." Kurt walked around to the driver's door. "See you later."

* * *

Liesl needed out. She'd had her fill of footsteps echoing around the empty house, so she went for a walk. Whether it was a sugar high from the doughnuts or a restless spirit, she needed to think. Although it was cold, the sun was shining, and she soon warmed. Her pace was brisk.

After thirty minutes, she realized she was within two blocks of Winnie Whitcomb's house, now the women's shelter.

She walked there huffing white puffs, evidence she was sadly out of shape. Other than her obvious lack of physical fitness, the long-needed exercise felt wonderful.

The Butterfly House stood at the corner of the street, a

three-story Craftsman-style structure with square columns and a wide front porch. Two dormers added additional charm. It was a popular style in the 1920s and '30s, so was likely built then. Other than the need for a coat of paint, it was in great shape, with no hint of the past tragedy.

Strange that a brutal murder over fifty years ago still affected the living. Was it because the killer got away with it? Or because such a grizzly horror seemed unthinkable in this quiet setting?

She rounded the corner, where a thick hedge encircled the side and back yard, effectively dividing it from the neighbor's property. This left her blind to the area where Winnie lost her life.

She turned around and established her former pace. Somewhere in the neighborhood, a dog barked. A rustle in bushes across the street caused her to spin toward the sound. A medium-sized dog, his teeth exposed, barreled toward her, barking with conviction. He appeared intent on taking a bite out of her leg. Or worse.

She vaulted over a low shrub and grabbed the branch of a nearby oak. With skills akin to those of an Olympic gymnast, she swung to safety, high above the snapping jaws.

The beast jumped at the base of her perch, its tan hair standing erect from neck to tail. She teetered on the limb, her arms and legs clamped around it in panic, and prayed it would hold her weight. How long could she do this? Already her muscles were cramping.

A tall, thin man burst through nearby bushes. "Stop, Al. Right now! Bad dog!" He scooped up the slobbering menace and stared at her with a horrified expression. "I'm so sorry. I didn't realize—" Disheveled blond hair and wide blue eyes added to his aura of surprise.

The man's dismay was almost comical. "Does he do this a lot?" she asked, with no move to lower herself.

"My apologies. I thought he was barking at a squirrel."

"Is his name Shylock? Seems he wanted a pound of my flesh."

He shook his head, and she couldn't tell if he understood her reference to Shakespeare's *The Merchant of Venice*. "His name is Al, for Al Capone. He's a great dog, but he attacks anything in motion. He's done it since he was a puppy, hence the name. Again, I'm terribly sorry."

She eyed the now docile creature. "Hard to imagine he's so ferocious over a pedestrian."

"Please come down. You're out of harm's way. I promise."

With much less grace than in her initial rise, Liesl dropped from the tree and realized her hand was injured. Blood oozed from where a patch of skin had peeled away from the palm. She held it up. "A battle wound."

His eyes widened. "Oh no. Does it need stitches?"

"No. Soap and water will take care of it."

"Please come to my house." He gestured across the street. "I'm just right there."

She hesitated.

"I'll put the dog in his pen. It'll be okay."

They crossed the street and passed through thick bushes lining the sidewalk. Then he strode across the yard and put the dog in a sturdy chain-link enclosure.

He secured the lock on the gate. "See? All's well."

She couldn't imagine the dog staring calmly at them through the fence as the same one who'd hungered to bite her lower limbs. Without a bark of protest out of him, they made their way across a wooden deck and in through the back door.

He waved his hand at the sink. "There's some anti-bacterial soap near the faucet." He opened a drawer and passed her a clean dishtowel. "You know, I don't even know your name."

"Liesl Schrader."

"Hi, Lisa. I would have preferred to meet you under better circumstances."

She smiled. This happened at every introduction. "It's Liesl, pronounced like Lisa, but adding an L. It's German. The oldest girl in *The Sound of Music* was Liesl."

"Ah. Sorry about that, Liesl. I'm Justin Frazier."

She, too, wished they'd met under better circumstances. Instead of commenting, she washed the wound.

Justin found a bandage and then realized she couldn't put it on without his help. With the tip of his tongue in the corner of his mouth, he gently applied it.

"Thank you," she said. "It's fine now."

"I can't say it enough. I'm so, so sorry."

"No problem, I'm fine." She leaned against the counter. "How long have you lived here?"

He smiled, revealing a row of even white teeth. "About three months. I'm the new manager of Lumber City. And you?"

"I grew up here and moved to Houston about seven years ago. My aunt was still here, but she, uh, recently passed away."

"My condolences."

She nodded, not trusting her voice.

"When will you go back?"

"I'm not sure. I'm here for some time to take care of my aunt's business interests."

"Would it be a gross breach of etiquette for me to ask you out for dinner one night?" He hesitated, and then added, "Assuming, of course, that you're available?"

She chuckled. "I am available and unaware of rules against asking out someone your dog recently attacked."

He blushed but seemed satisfied with her response. "Are

you busy tonight?"

The suddenness surprised her. What did she have to do tonight? Pace through an empty house and maybe search for Aunt Suzanne's purse? "I have nothing planned. Where do you want to go?"

He pushed his hands into his jeans pockets and shrugged. "I don't know. Being a single guy, I usually do drive-through fast food. You know of a good place?"

"Do you prefer steak, Mexican or Italian? In this town, those are the choices."

He studied her for a minute. "I'll bet you like Italian."

"I like everything but liver." Heat rose to her face. *Really? Must she over-share with this man?* "I'll bet you like steak."

"I do, but I'd rather talk to you over a plate of pasta."

"Italian it is, then." A man who wanted to sit and talk? Awesome.

"Do we need to make reservations? It's Saturday night."

She grinned. "You're a city guy, aren't you? We don't need reservations, I promise."

"You pegged me. I'm originally from Atlanta." He glanced at his watch. "If I pick you up around seven, would you give me directions to this bit of Italy?"

"I would, indeed, be so kind."

"May I take you home now? It's the least I can do, since my dog attacked you."

"No, I'd like to walk. Especially with pasta and cheese in my future. Assuming, of course, that you keep Al in his pen until I'm gone."

He smiled. "Done. But I need directions to your house before you go."

When she relayed them, he asked, "Am I going to have trouble finding it?"

"It's one of the big, old ones. Hard to miss."

Chapter Twenty-Three

Suzanne
March 19, 1961

Once Max left, Suzanne's spirits sagged. She searched for a distraction from the grief. Although she had many friends within the pages of books, it was Jo and her sisters who called to her. *Little Women* was sad in parts and included the death of a main character, but it also shone hope through hardship. She needed her old friends from Massachusetts to help her deal with the loss of her own friend.

Her visit with the March sisters paused when the doorbell signaled another visitor. The sound immediately made her think of Winnie. She always stopped by unannounced whenever it suited her. Life would no longer include her surprise visits.

Her mother called from downstairs. "Suzanne, please come down."

She tensed. Her mother wouldn't call her down for friends,

she'd send them up. "Be right there." She scrambled to locate shoes.

Officer Ziegler stood near the parlor entrance with another man she didn't recognize. He was shorter and thinner than Ziegler. She could tell they planned to stay awhile because her mother was taking their coats and hats.

"Officer Ziegler." When she neared, her heart went out to him. He looked exhausted.

She acknowledged the stranger by offering her hand. "I'm Suzanne. How do you do?" He was younger than Ziegler, but better dressed. Must be a city man. Maybe a big gun from some other agency? Columbia? St. Louis?

The man said, "Agent LaRue. I'm assisting Officer Ziegler."

He didn't mention his law enforcement association or his assignment location. She pegged him as FBI or state police.

Her mother returned. "Would you care for coffee or tea?"

Ziegler attempted a smile. "No, thank you, Olivia. We've had plenty today."

She gestured toward the small sofa. "Officer Ziegler has additional questions for you, Suzanne. I'm going to stay." She sat and patted the space next to her.

Suzanne wanted to help the police but resented her mother's imperious tone, which left no room for negotiation. She resigned herself to her fate.

Ziegler sat across from her and took out a small notebook. "I hope you're feeling better, Suzanne."

"Yes, sir. Thank you."

LaRue leaned into the high-backed chair and watched her from hooded eyes.

Ziegler continued. "I know last night was traumatic. However, we need more information. Information you can provide."

"Whatever you need." She gave her mother a look that she

hoped would keep her silent. Mother wouldn't hesitate to interrupt if she felt a question, or Suzanne's answer, was crass or uncouth.

"You were the victim's best friend."

"Yes, sir. Since we were very young."

"Are you aware of any problems she might have had with anyone?"

"Problems?"

"Was anyone mad at her?"

"No, sir. People didn't get mad at her. She is ... er, was the kind of person who bossed you around and did it so well you'd thank her for caring. Know what I mean?"

Ziegler nodded.

"What about at school? Anyone upset with her there?"

"Not that I know of."

"Edgar?"

She stared at him, confused. "I've never seen Edgar upset with anyone in my life. Has someone said he was upset with her?"

"How well do you know him?"

"I've known him since he and Myron began playing together as kids. I remember him being around here when I was five or six. He would have been eight or nine. He's always been nice to me."

"How has he been toward Winnie?"

"I can't imagine he's been anything but a gentleman."

"Have you ever witnessed him not being nice?"

"No."

"Did Winnie ever complain about him?"

"Never."

"Not even because he ignored her or made her mad?"

"As far as I know, they'd never had an argument. She didn't complain about him or anything he did."

"Would Winnie have told you if she had a complaint about him? Or, if they'd had a fight?"

"Of course. She tells, ah … told me everything. It's what best friends do."

"How long have they dated?"

She calculated. "Right at six months now."

Ziegler paused. "Why so precise?"

"Edgar asked her to Homecoming in September. They've been dating since."

"Did you ever go with them? Like on a double date?"

Her cheeks colored a bit. "I've never been on a double date." It was embarrassing to be a junior in high school and a dateless wonder. "I've been with them in group situations, like the party last night. We were all in a musical together last spring. They weren't dating then, but they interacted a lot."

"You saw nothing that concerned you? No pressure from him for her to … get more involved, shall we say … in the relationship?"

He wasn't asking how involved they were. He was asking if Edgar pressured Winnie for more. Suzanne wasn't going to rat out their "Secret Shed" if she didn't have to.

"She said nothing about being pressured or being uncomfortable about their relationship." After a pause, she added, "If you want firsthand information about them on a double date, you need to talk to Patricia Sizemore. Patricia and her old boyfriend, Cy Peterson, went out with them occasionally."

Ziegler scribbled on his notepad. "Is that Ben Peterson's son?"

"He's Ben's nephew," Mrs. Thatcher said. "Cy's father is Cyril Peterson."

Suzanne wasn't surprised she spoke up because her mother knew the relationship of all town citizens.

"You said 'old' boyfriend. Does that mean they used to date, or is he a lot older than the rest of you?"

"They broke up a few months ago. Why all these questions about Edgar? He would never have hurt Winnie."

Zeigler ignored her question. "Last night. When did you last see Edgar?"

"On the dance floor. The same time as I last saw Winnie."

"You didn't see either of them leave?"

"No."

"Did you see either of them separately after that?"

She sighed. "I just said the last time I saw them, they were together."

Her mother cleared her throat, a warning sign of unladylike or unacceptable behavior.

"Sorry. I didn't see them together or separately after that."

"Tell me about the last time you saw them. You said they were dancing."

She thought for a moment. "I'd been watching Billy for Edgar while he and Winnie danced. At least until Max arrived. Max asked me to dance, so I was going to call Edgar off the dance floor, but Doreen offered to watch Billy."

"Who is Billy?"

"Edgar's little brother. Billy Van de Berg. Their mom works nights at the newspaper, so Edgar has to watch Billy when she's working."

"How old is Billy?"

"Eight."

He nodded his understanding. "So he needed to be chaperoned."

"More like entertained and protected. Some of the older guys pick on him. He's a little boy, so an easy target. None of us wanted that to happen."

"Did you see anyone who seemed upset or angry?"

She hesitated. "Well, two senior guys picked on Billy on Saturday when we gathered to help clean and decorate for the party. Ray Thompson and Tom Hardesty."

Ziegler wrote their names and then looked up at her. "Anything else? Especially at the party?"

She paused again to think. "I didn't see any disagreements or anger at the actual party other than a quick, sarcastic argument between Doreen and Patricia."

Ziegler made another notation. "Anything else out of the ordinary?"

"No. Not sure if this is relevant, but on Saturday, when we decorated, I saw a man outside. He looked down on his luck and out of place. But that's all. He didn't seem threatening."

"Describe him."

"Middle-aged. Wearing a brown hat. Dark overcoat and pants. I didn't know him, so it made me wonder what he was doing there."

"He was walking?"

"Standing on the corner. Like he was waiting for a ride."

When the questioning ended, and Mrs. Thatcher closed the door behind them, she turned to Suzanne. "I hope you understand why he had to ask all those questions."

She shrugged.

"Suzanne, shrugging is crass."

"I'm sorry, Mother. Habit. It angers me to have him ask all those questions about Edgar. He's the sweetest fellow. He doesn't deserve someone thinking that way about him."

"You gave him an excellent character reference." She put her arm around Suzanne. "Poor boy. Everyone is looking at him with suspicion. The newspaper article made him a suspect, along with just about everyone who was there last night."

"Did that other man, Agent La Rue, say what agency he was with?"

"No."

"I bet he was a city man. Nice suit. Stranger to town."

Mother frowned. "Suzanne, a lady doesn't speculate on such things. Or, if she does, she doesn't talk about it."

Suzanne bit her tongue. Her mother analyzed everything and everyone around her. The mistake was telling her she'd done the same thing. Live and learn.

As she climbed the stairs, Suzanne vowed to keep evaluating. Only she'd keep her mouth shut about it.

Chapter Twenty-Four

Liesl
November 11

The heady aroma of freshly baked bread and Italian spices greeted their arrival at D'Angelo's restaurant. Justin inhaled and smiled his approval. "It smells heavenly. I'm glad you recommended this place."

"You won't be disappointed." The anticipation of tempting culinary delights made Liesl's stomach growl.

He grinned as he helped remove her coat. "My stomach is singing the same tune."

Josephine D'Angelo Conner, the eldest daughter of the owner, hugged Liesl and led them into the crowded dining area. Liesl spotted her cousin Gretchen seated across the room with her husband and waved. Gretchen's eyebrows rose—likely at the tall, blond Adonis on her heels. Liesl prayed her cousin would resist the temptation to run over and insist upon an introduction to her mystery man.

Justin showed his manners and pulled out her chair.

Although Josephine handed her a menu, Liesl didn't bother with it. She was going to order her favorite. A glance around the room caused a sudden pang of grief. Aunt Suzanne loved this restaurant. It hurt to be here without her.

Justin eyed the choices and quizzed her about selections that tantalized his interest. She studied him as he studied the menu. He was thin, but not scrawny. A longer version of an ordinary-sized man. Had he played sports?

She bit back a smirk when he lined up the silverware to his exact specifications. A perfectionist, was he? Maybe just nervous.

Once satisfied with his cutlery arrangement, he asked, "Do you know everyone in town?"

"The girl I waved to is one of my cousins. In our small community, family or friends are everywhere. I'm not exaggerating when I say I'm related to nearly half of the residents, if not directly by blood, then by marriage." She shifted in her chair and turned a question to him. "Have you always lived in cities?"

He nodded. "Pretty obvious, eh? I grew up in Atlanta. When I started working for Lumber City, I spent time in Memphis and St. Louis before coming here."

"It must be a shock to live in a small town."

"I've nearly broken the habit of leaving my house a half hour before I need to be at work. Commuting less than five minutes, with no traffic to speak of, is quite a perk. It took me nearly an hour to commute in Atlanta, and that was when I was lucky enough to avoid rush hour traffic."

"My reaction was the opposite. When I moved to Houston, the bottlenecks and traffic jams made me crazy. Thank the Lord for audiobooks. Without them, I'd be another ugly road rage statistic."

"Aren't you a writer? How'd you get into that?"

"I received an unexpected offer the spring of my senior year at Rice University. One of my English professors stopped me and asked whether I'd consider an assistant professorship for a free ride of tuition and books to pursue a master's degree. I was overjoyed."

"You must have impressed him if he came to you with that offer."

"Her," she corrected. "Dr. Sylvia Rockefeller, no kin to the wealthy Rockefellers. She knew novel writing was a dream of mine. I needed more education to make a go of it, and I'm grateful to her for providing that chance."

"What happened after that?"

She scanned his face to assess his interest. He appeared absorbed.

"By sharing digs with a friend working her way through med school, teaching as a part-time professor's assistant, and dabbling in some freelance writing, I supported myself and finished my master's. Freelancing paid little, but I got my foot in the door of a local magazine. That gave me real publishing credits."

She sipped her water. "I wrote at night and on weekends. Three bad manuscripts and hundreds of rejection letters later, I went to a writer's conference and met a publisher who liked the premise of my novel."

"Now you're on the New York Times Bestseller list?" His blue eyes sparkled with the tease.

She smiled. "It's just some minor oversight why I can't locate my name there. I've had three books published in paperback and digital. They've done well enough, but better in the digital realm. The fourth comes out in a few months. They're all romance novels, to the chagrin of my literary professors."

"Romances are Lumber City's second-best sellers," he said

with a crooked smile. "The bestsellers are DIY books. That's the extent of my knowledge of the publishing world."

"I didn't realize Lumber City carried paperbacks outside of DIY books."

"A few."

"The business side of publishing is the hardest part of the job. I love putting words on paper, not necessarily to market them, but it's an important aspect of a successful career."

"Do you still teach?"

"No. I have a part-time job in Houston, but my goal is to be a full-time writer now."

He cocked his head to one side. "No thought of marriage or children?"

She looked away. "I had a boyfriend in high school." She gestured toward the other diners. "Most people in this room can give you the gory details about our breakup. Let's just say it didn't work out." She sneaked a glance, to gauge his reaction to her evasion of the details. "I've dated since then, but nothing serious."

He fiddled with his glass. "I can relate. I was engaged until a few months ago. She broke it off when my work brought me here. She chose city life over traipsing to a small town."

"I'm sorry, Justin. Your hurt is fresher than mine."

He nodded.

The waiter returned and saved them from further discussion. Justin scrambled to re-scan the menu while she ordered.

He peered at her over the list of options. "You're positive I won't regret the manicotti?"

"You won't regret any food in this fine establishment."

She was right. The meal was a smashing success, as was their rapport with one another. If he had perfectionist tendencies, they were minuscule. What captivated her was his ability to listen without a hint of impatience. Catnip for women, yet most men seemed unable to provide it.

She tried not to drone on, but he seemed more comfortable as a listener. With direct questions, she discovered he was one of eight children of a residential builder, and he'd put himself through college working part-time at Lumber City.

"You must have liked Lumber City."

"I like the paychecks. When they offered a full-time job as a management trainee, I was simply too lazy to look somewhere else."

"Surely not. You don't seem like a sloth to me."

He laughed. "I love your words, Liesl. It's fun to listen to you."

Although they'd discussed dessert options before their meal was served, they both rolled their eyes at the waiter's query while he removed their plates and settled for coffee.

She probed further. "Do you play any sports?"

"I played basketball in high school, but I gave it up when one of my sisters could beat me with ease. The only reason I'm not totally ashamed is that she played professional basketball."

"No kidding? That's so cool."

"It was, actually. It's expected that a girl with athletic ability and a houseful of older brothers would develop into a skilled player. Sarah had a head start playing aggressively. Even when she was little, we wouldn't play with her if she whined about getting hurt and stuff." He smiled at her. "Typical big brother behavior, you know."

She reserved comment. As an only child, she didn't know such things.

"She learned to be quick and cunning, to compete against taller and stronger players. In high school, I had to get over the 'not holding a candle to your younger sister's abilities' thing.

She's retired from her professional career, and she's now a coach. I'm proud of her."

"Any other athletes in your family?"

"My dad was a standout in high school, but my mom was the bookish, quiet type. Two of my older brothers and Sarah received sports scholarships for college. The rest of us had to push for academic scholarships. There was no option for parental payments." He shrugged. "Paying my way through college helped me appreciate it more." He smiled. "In hindsight, of course. Going through it, I didn't find any silver linings."

He intrigued her. Was it his ability to listen? Or his sincerity? It was a nice, unexpected feeling.

* * *

Mother Nature's call had Liesl threading her way through tables filled with diners. She waved at a chum from her school days seated toward the back, who raised her fork in return, her mouth full of food.

Gretchen burst through the bathroom door. "Who's that handsome man you're with?" Her curly red hair bounced around her eager face.

"Ah, dear cousin, it's nice to see you too." Liesl hugged her. "His name is Justin, and he's the Lumber City manager."

"Gossip and details are much more fun in the ladies' room. Tell me all about him."

"I'm so glad you're related to me. I can chew you out for your impertinence, directly to your face, and you still have to send me a Christmas card."

Side by side, or rather stall by stall, she relayed the details of her introduction to Justin and smiled at Gretchen's delight with the description of the "attack dog."

163

"Only you would meet a man under such conditions."

Liesl eyed the bandage Justin had applied, still on her hand even after a shower. "If you don't believe me, I've got the scars to prove it."

"I can't wait to tell Cameron. He made me swear I wouldn't go over to your table and introduce myself."

Liesl said a tiny prayer of thanks that Gretchen's husband had the sense to corral her crazy cousin. She owed him one. "You can tell Cameron about it. No one else. I don't need this town to buzz about me picking up a man while adhered to a tree."

She tugged on her black wool slacks and decided the apple green sweater and pearl necklace had been a good choice for the evening. Her lipstick was long gone, so she reapplied it.

"Sometime, I have business to discuss," Gretchen said as she washed her hands. "I was going to call you this week, but I didn't want to upset you." She pulled a couple of paper towels. "A few days before Aunt Suzanne became sick, she brought me some financial papers. Said she wanted me to check for—er, irregularities. Does that ring a bell?"

Gretchen was a CPA and a partner in a local accounting firm. It would make sense for Aunt Suzanne to turn to her with the Butterfly House financial quandary. "If it's about a local non-profit organization, then yes, I'm aware." Liesl didn't say her knowledge came from their aunt's journal entries rather than discussion.

Gretchen frowned. "Even though she is no longer living, I can't breach client confidentiality." She threw the towels in the trashcan and met Liesl's gaze. "Let's *suppose* this paperwork involves a non-profit organization. It would be wrong to review my findings with someone who was neither my client nor a member of the organization."

Liesl thought for a second. "As someone who is to inherit

most of the estate of your client, would I become your client upon inheritance?"

"Not unless you agreed to continue the matter with me."

"What kind of paperwork would you need?"

"Something proving you are the estate's beneficiary."

Liesl pondered this while she formed a response. "What if the person who would handle that legal matter also happens to be the treasurer of a particular non-profit organization."

Gretchen's eyes widened in disbelief. "No."

"So, you understand why I would hesitate to approach this person if it would lead to tough questions about my request, right?"

"I see." She paused. "Perhaps if you provided a copy of the will. I could check to see if that works."

Liesl nodded. "That's a better option. I already have copies of the will."

"I'll research it first thing on Monday and call you, okay?"

"Sounds like a plan." Liesl moved to the door, then turned back. "May I assume what you've seen so far is more than a bookkeeping error?"

"It's not a simple error." Gretchen's face was grim. "It might even be a matter for law enforcement. I'd need more information to know for sure."

"Look into what you need from me to step into Aunt Suzanne's shoes. Then we can decide what to do."

"I'll call you."

"Do that. And give Cameron a special hug from me, okay?"

Gretchen flashed pearly white teeth and held open the door. "Not a word to anyone about this financial matter, okay?"

"Believe me, Gretchen, it's the last thing I want to discuss tonight."

She made her way back to their table and pushed thoughts of Van de Berg's possible embezzlement out of her mind.

She wanted to have fun and not worry about thieves, murderers, poison, and death. Just one night of fun.

Was that too much to ask?

Chapter Twenty-Five

Liesl

A pristine blanket of snow covered the ground on Sunday morning. The delightful surprise was enough to remind her she was back in Missouri. Although Texas was a great place to live, winter consisted mostly of rain or cloudy days and cool temperatures. This morning's vision of a pure white carpet soothed her soul and brought out a desire for warm blankets and a glowing fireplace.

Last night provided a warm beginning with Justin. Splendid dinner, great conversation, and a great kiss on the front porch. Thoughts about that kiss made her smile. She didn't need any romance in her life right now. It was complicated enough, but wasn't that the way it always happened?

Justin had been a gentleman the entire night, and they'd had fun. His ability to listen was endearing. After dinner, he'd walked her to the front door and pulled her into a hug with a short, but promising, kiss. He'd saved her contact information on his phone and promised a call to schedule another date. She pushed aside the fear of getting hurt again.

Today she was going to Nicole's church and then having lunch with her friend and her family. As children, they frequently attended each other's churches, so it was tradition. Sharing church families kept the relationship close.

Liesl wrestled to lock the front door while holding her purse and a "to go" coffee mug. She lost the match and spilled coffee on the porch. Typical.

After cleaning the spill, she abandoned the coffee and locked the front door. She cautiously descended the porch steps in her high heels, a poor choice on a snowy day, but she'd run out of time to find a pair of boots. When she turned the corner toward the garage, a line of footprints in the snow caught her attention.

They were small, yet larger than a child's shoe. There was an indentation of a narrow heel with each step. A woman's shoe. They led from behind the garage to the side of the house. She stopped, staring at the prints' configuration. Why had someone peered through her window?

Several footprints crisscrossed under the window, as if the intruder had stayed for a while. A single line of tracks led from the window to the backyard.

She stood stunned, and the smell of smoke invaded her thoughts. Black smoke bellowed from the margins of the garage doors. She spun back toward the house and scrambled up the front steps while trying to dig out her phone. She dialed 911 and reported the fire.

After noting her address, the male dispatcher said, "Don't hang up, miss. I need you to stay calm and answer some questions."

"Okay," she replied, panic clear in her tone as she paced across the wooden porch boards.

"Is your garage freestanding or attached to your house?"

"Freestanding."

"Is the fire localized to the garage structure?"

"It appears to be. I can only see the front."

"Any reason someone would be inside that structure?"

"No."

"Are you a safe distance from the fire?"

"I'm on my front porch. About six car lengths away."

"Are there other structures or trees close to it?"

"No. Look, I can't talk anymore. I've got to put some water on that fire."

"Ma'am, if there are cars, trucks, or other gas or diesel propelled equipment in that garage, it isn't safe for you to get near it."

"My car is in there, and my aunt's car too."

"Let the experts handle this. If there is an explosion, flying debris could hurt you. Since it's winter, you probably don't have a hose connected, anyway. Please be patient and let the fire department do their job."

She wanted to argue with him, but the faint wail of a siren heralded help approaching. "The truck's coming. I can hear it."

"The first responder is likely the chief. He lives close. Stay on the line until you confirm someone from the fire department has arrived. Can you see flames?"

"No. Only black smoke curling out of the doors. Or rather, around the edges of the doors."

"How many doors are there?"

"Two large garage doors. There's a regular-sized door on the north side, but I can't see it from here."

The sound of a siren intensified. It drowned out the voice of the dispatcher. She yelled that a pickup truck had arrived and hung up.

A middle-aged man dressed in fire gear hopped out of the truck. The bed of the pickup housed a large hose threaded around a wheel. He signaled Liesl to stay as he strapped on his helmet and strode toward the garage. He examined the front of the structure, and then walked around the side, disappearing behind the back of it.

The firefighter reappeared on the far side of the garage as another siren approached. He advanced toward the group of neighbors collecting on the sidewalk. Everyone who'd gathered to watch wore their Sunday best and stood in a row. He gestured for them to stay back.

Nicole! She'd be looking for Liesl at church. She called but got no answer, so she tried Kurt.

* * *

Kurt was helping Ross dress in his best clothes, getting ready for church, when his cell phone rang. Liesl.

"Good morning," he said.

"My garage is on fire!"

His stomach clenched. "What?"

"I think it was intentional. The fire department's just now getting here."

He turned to Ross and gave him the "let's go" signal. When he returned his attention to the phone, his cop voice replaced his former jolly tone. "Are you hurt?"

"No. I ran back to the porch as soon as I saw the smoke."

"You think the fire just started?"

"Yes."

"Go inside and don't come out. I'm on my way."

He hung up and rushed Ross into the car, choosing against

flipping on lights and sirens, hoping to catch the arsonist. "Buckle up, son. Miss Liesl has an emergency."

With trepidation in his voice, Ross asked, "What kind of emergency?"

"Her garage is on fire, son."

After backing up the car and heading toward Liesl's house, he called her back. "We're heading your way. Where are you now?"

"Downstairs, in the library."

He needed to keep her busy so she wouldn't panic. She could also help him investigate. "Can you run upstairs and look out those windows? Look for any people, cars or trucks parked on the street."

"Yes, but why?"

"People who set fires sometimes like to watch them burn. Why do you think someone set this fire?"

"I don't know, but I saw footprints. In the snow. It means the footprints are new. That leads me to guess they came to set the fire."

"We'll be there in a second."

"Please don't hang up."

There was a plea in her voice filled with obvious fear. Although she was strong, the situation was getting to her.

"I won't. When you get upstairs, tell me what you can see."

He heard a loud noise, a sound like stumbling or something falling. "You okay?"

"I tripped on these stupid high heels. I'm kicking them off."

"Good."

"The tracks I saw were small, with a narrow heel, like a woman's shoe." She described her location at a window at the mid-way landing of the stairs. "I'm looking at the boulevard, and there are no parked cars."

"Small prints, you say? Why do you say it's a woman's shoe?"

"Boots made these tracks, but the heel looked narrow, like a woman's. Kids don't wear narrow heels. I've reached the front window, and nothing's out there but fire trucks."

"See any tracks in the snow?"

"No."

"Go to the master bathroom. You should see the rest of the side yard there."

He waited with trepidation until she said, "No people, cars or footprints on the side. I can't see much of the backyard."

"I'm turning onto the boulevard now. We'll be there in a second. Go check the north side."

He turned the car onto a side street and drove up to the east side of the house.

"No sign of tracks, but bushes block my view near the street."

"I'm going to turn and circle back around to the front. Go check the windows in your room and the guest rooms." He turned to Ross. "I need you to stay in the car. Can you do that for me?"

Ross nodded, his eyes were wide with fear.

Liesl spoke up. "Kurt, don't leave him in the car. Drop him off on South Washington. He can run across the backyard and I'll let him in the back door."

Kurt considered that for a second. "I think he'd be more comfortable doing that."

"Then do it. I'll head downstairs right now."

"Before you go, tell me what you see."

"Sorry, I'm in the first guest bedroom and can see the tracks. Only the one set I told you about. The firefighters are going to eradicate them. Hold on a sec. I'm going to take some photos with my phone."

After a pause for picture taking, she added, "Whoever it was didn't leave by the same route. I'm going downstairs now."

Kurt circled the block and parked the car. He tapped on the window to his left and pointed toward Liesl's back door. "Do you see that door?"

Ross nodded.

"That's the back door of Miss Liesl's house. I want you to run there when I open the door."

"Is there a bad person out there?"

"Not between you and the house. You'll be fine." Kurt then asked Liesl, "Are you ready for Ross?"

"I'm ready."

Kurt got out of the vehicle and opened Ross's car door. "You'll be fine with Miss Liesl, okay? I'll be right back." To Liesl, he said, "He's on his way now."

"I see him."

Once Kurt saw Ross enter the house, he whispered to Liesl, "I'm going through backyards. I'll stay on the line, but I don't want to say anything, okay?"

"Got it."

He walked quickly, his breathing short and swift. His pistol was in its holster but easy to grab if he ran into trouble. He also had cuffs, if he lucked into detaining a suspect.

Then he spotted the outline of a shoe, similar to what Liesl described. In a hushed tone, he asked, "Square toe, narrow at the heel?"

"Yes."

"I see the tracks. They came up the street about three houses down from yours. I don't see any return tracks. Hold on, I'm gonna take some pics."

He bent and took some shots of the footprints, putting his foot alongside the track for a size reference. "I'm following them toward your garage." The sound of firefighting efforts reached him as he followed the tracks with his body hunched like a hound dog following a scent, intent on his mission. When he got close to the garage, he scanned the house to spot her at a window. "You should see me now."

Liesl waved at him and so did Ross. They appeared to be handling this situation as well as could be expected.

He walked as close to the garage as he could, then waved at a firefighter as he headed toward the side of the house.

"Liesl?"

"I'm here."

"Whoever it was walked around the kitchen windows and then walked along the side of your house to the boulevard. I'm going to follow the tracks down the sidewalk. They head north."

He followed the tracks until he lost them about two blocks north of the house. Whoever it was, they either disappeared or got in a vehicle at the intersection of the boulevard and South Clark. "I've come to the end of the tracks. I'm heading to the porch."

"Okay. We'll wait by the door."

"Don't open it until you see me."

When he made it to her front door, he heard her fumbling to unlock it. She swung the door wide as she stepped out, tears running down her face and her phone still clutched in her hand.

On instinct, Kurt gathered her into his arms. She began sobbing, her warm cheek pressed against his cold one. She hugged him tight.

"Ross, run and find some tissues for her."

Kurt patted her back and made soothing noises until Ross returned with his treasure.

Ross pulled several tissues from the box. "Here, Miss Liesl, blow hard."

Liesl relaxed and pulled away from him, taking the offered tissues from Ross.

"Thank you, Ross. You're a great help."

Kurt nodded. "The best."

Ross said, "I'm sorry you were scared. You're okay now. Daddy and I will take care of you."

Liesl nodded and reached for another tissue. "Your daddy was good to come help me."

Ross studied her face. "What's that black stuff under your eyes?"

Kurt felt his checks redden. "Ross," he admonished, "it's not nice to say that."

"He's right, Kurt." She leaned down to Ross. "It's mascara. Women put it on their eyelashes to make them look longer. It ran when I cried."

"It's okay, Miss Liesl. You're still pretty, even if you look like a raccoon."

Kurt frowned and considered launching into Ross, but Liesl held up her hand.

"Thank you, Ross. Even hysterical women like to hear they're pretty." She then turned to Kurt. "Let's sit while you tell me about the garage."

"Sure." He moved toward the couch. "I'm glad you're better. You've been through a lot."

"I'm not proud I collapsed in a heap of tears, but I've got to own it. I need to call Nicole and tell her what's happened. She was expecting me at her church and then to have lunch with them."

"I'll call her."

When he called Nicole, she again failed to answer. He left a message, calmly outlining the circumstances of the morning.

The three of them stood at the music room window and watched the firefighters extinguish the blaze. Kurt was glad he'd had an opportunity to help Liesl. His greatest wish was that someday she could forgive him and give their former romance another chance.

Standing by the window, with Ross and Liesl on either side, it felt natural to put his arms around both of them. He felt a deep sense of satisfaction, knowing the people he loved most were beside him and safe. That feeling lasted until someone rang the ancient doorbell.

Chapter Twenty-Six

Suzanne
March 25, 1961

M ax visited often. After braving the Inquisition, he won a place in her father's good favor. Her mother was different. Her interactions with Max walked a fine line between cool and rude, but he never wavered. He visited for a few minutes at a time and brought either Suzanne or Zest a little surprise.

He asked her on an honest-to-goodness date. Suzanne kept dodging the issue, but when her heart healed a bit, she'd say yes. She understood life must go on, even with tears that seemed to flow forever. All the while, she worked to understand the pain and the loss.

Winnie's funeral was delayed until the coroner released her body. Once it was scheduled, Winnie's mother attended but had to have help leaving the church after the funeral, almost carried by family members. Her father looked nearly as weak.

A procession followed the hearse through town to Oaklawn Cemetery. Citizens of Mexico showed their respect for Winnie and those left behind to grieve. People walking along the sidewalks immediately stopped as the cortege approached. Men took off their hats, and women bowed their heads. Drivers pulled their cars to the side of the road and resumed their journey after the whole convoy passed.

Tradition dictated that people brought food in times of crisis. Mrs. Whitcomb was too distraught to handle it, so Mrs. Thatcher opened their home for a gathering after the funeral. Suzanne imprisoned Zest in her room to keep Mrs. Whitcomb from seeing the dog.

Two days after the funeral, Suzanne walked into the den to say good night to her father. As an accountant, he spent evenings working at his desk and would watch television at the same time. This night, ledgers full of numbers and stacks of paper surrounded him. Yet, he paid no attention to work because of an episode of *Dragnet*. When he realized she was in the room, he tried to shoo her away.

"Honey, you don't need to watch this kind of show right now."

The officers in the show investigated crimes. The actors were playing cops from Los Angeles. The concept was an inspiration to Suzanne, and she hovered in the doorway. Perhaps she could learn basic investigative techniques and look into the circumstances of Winnie's murder. No one needed to know. It would give her something to do for Winnie, a positive action amid all this chaos.

Her father stared at her, perplexed by her inaction.

"Sorry, Dad, I'm leaving." She gave him a peck on the cheek and left, her mind tumbling with ideas and plans.

Suzanne vowed to collect everything pertaining to Winnie's death, big or small, significant or insignificant. The better record collected, the better chance she'd have to solve the murder. She'd need a notebook to store impressions, interview answers, and photographs. She'd also fill it with newspaper clippings related to the murder and all of her investigative notes.

After the difficult questions she'd received from Officer Ziegler and the silent glares from Agent LaRue, she knew people would be more comfortable talking to her. The police had a job to do, but she remained stung by how they'd questioned everything she'd said about Edgar. She could ask what the police had asked, but in a kind way. Offer sympathy for the ordeal of questioning, while having suffered the same experience.

Suzanne never had much interest in crime or criminals before, but now she felt a great desire to understand the subject. Terms like suspicion and motive were now part of her life. Perhaps research would explain why they were so suspicious of Edgar.

Finally, she had a goal. A goal to bring justice for Winnie. Research was an action she could take, a step in a positive direction.

* * *

The Carnegie Library's brown brick Georgian-style building was built in 1914. The smells of paper, furniture polish, and leather from the bindings of older books greeted her. In her youth, the stairs to reach the second-story children's library seemed endless, but everything she needed now was on the first floor.

She waved at Mrs. Sanderson, who carried herself with an air of nobility. As the head librarian, she served the reading public, and she took her profession to heart. She was the book queen, and she performed her "royal duties" admirably. No query went unanswered, no book was left mislaid.

Suzanne settled at a small table, trying to signal her desire to be alone. She left her jacket there, grabbed her list of reading topics, and headed to the middle of the floor. Wooden drawers, filled with row upon row of cards sorted under the Dewey Decimal System, awaited.

Investigations and forensic information were in the category of Applied Sciences. She fingered through the card descriptions and wrote down the numbers of books she might need.

In a moment, Mrs. Sanderson approached. "Are you finding everything you need?"

Suzanne shut the drawer she'd been thumbing through and picked up her list before Mrs. Sanderson could read it. "I'm doing fine. Thanks."

She compared books along the shelves. Two of them focused on investigations, so she decided she'd check them out now and come back later if others were needed.

Mrs. Sanderson would be suspicious if she checked out too many books on the same subject. Her mother might react the same. With this in mind, she pulled some civil procedure books too.

When she passed her orange library card with an embedded metal tag displaying her name to Mrs. Sanderson, she relaxed. In the past, the librarian had raised her eyebrows at some of her book choices. Today, with science books, she didn't glance twice at what Suzanne had chosen.

Chapter Twenty-Seven

Liesl
November 12

Liesl opened the door to a shivering, smoky-smelling fire chief. "The fire's out."

"Thank you. Please come in."

"No, miss. I'm too dirty and wet." He remained shivering on the porch.

She started to step out of the house but realized she was barefoot. "Is the garage still standing?"

"The rafters are scorched, but the overall structure of the garage appears stable. The vehicles are a different story. We'll know more when the fire cools."

"So they're both damaged?"

"Yes, though I'm not at liberty to discuss the specifics. Make plans for other transportation until we conclude our investigation."

"Okay." How confusing.

"My assistant chief is in there now, doing some

investigation. You need to come to the station and answer some questions."

"Sure." She glanced down at her bare feet. "I need to go upstairs and find my boots."

"There's no rush. I'm going to stop and clean up at my house. How about we meet at the station in thirty minutes?"

"Perfect. Oh, I'll need a ride to the station." She turned to Kurt.

He nodded. "I'll take you. I have business there, anyway."

The chief pierced him with a glance. "No discussing this." It was an order, not a request.

"Yes, sir," Kurt said.

When the chief left, they moved to the kitchen. Kurt made coffee and thrilled Ross with a doughnut left over from yesterday's batch. Then Kurt turned to her. "When is your alarm system being installed?"

"Wednesday. I'm supposed to travel to St. Louis tomorrow for a meeting."

"So you're leaving in the morning?"

"Not without a car. That was the plan before this fire. Now, no car, and it's a bad idea to leave the house unoccupied with a crazy fire starter out there."

"How about I call Donnie and see if he can install everything tomorrow? You need an alarm and heat sensors."

"Yes."

Kurt arranged for the installation while she emailed the St. Louis investment firm, asking to reschedule.

She grabbed her shoes from the front of the stairs and took a quick look outside. Crime tape encircled the garage. She stared at the ice-encrusted structure. From the ground, the roof appeared intact. Smoke damage marred the edges of the garage doors, but she couldn't see the interior. An acrid smell hung in the air. She felt sorry for any investigator still inside the structure and prayed it was safe for anyone working in there.

* * *

When she went upstairs for boots, Ross tagged along. Kurt tried to deter him, but she wanted him to come and won the point.

In her room, Ross sat on the bed and swung his feet while she dug in the closet for the boots she'd neglected to find earlier. While on hands and knees, not having any luck, she turned to Ross. "A monkey like you might help me find my boots back there."

Ross reacted with a deer-in-the-headlights look on his face, and he stopped swinging his legs. "Nope. It's too dark and scary." He shuddered.

She'd forgotten his claustrophobia. "It's okay. I can relate to being scared today, can't I?"

His small pink lips turned up in a smile. "Yep, you can." The legs went back to swinging again. "Daddy made you feel better."

"He did." She lunged into the blackness, returning from the shadows with one boot. "Got one." She held it aloft.

"That's a big closet."

"Because it is, it's easy to lose things." With another lunge, she burrowed until she found the match. "Victory!"

Ross clapped his hands and watched her put on the boots.

"Now, to remove the raccoon look." She headed into her adjacent bathroom to fix her makeup. To her surprise, Ross followed her and took a seat on the corner of the claw-foot tub.

After a moment, Ross said, "This is a big bathtub. Big closet, big bathtub, big house. Everything is bigger here."

"Not everything, just some things."

"And this bathroom looks old."

Liesl smiled. "It is old. Over a hundred years old. See those tiny tiles on the floor? Someone placed each one by hand to make that pretty pattern."

He flopped on the floor and studied it, running his finger around the boundaries of the tiles. "They're pretty cool. Like puzzle pieces."

After a moment, he watched her redo her makeup. This was a rare show for a motherless boy. Poor thing. They shared a similar loss. He didn't have a mother in his life, and she barely remembered hers.

* * *

At the police station, she chuckled at the greetings to Ross. Whether day or night shift, Ross must be their favorite visitor.

The reception area was deserted, but police and fire department personnel milled around in the back. The reception desk wasn't manned on this Sunday morning. When a firefighter spotted them, he led her to an interview room. He reported the chief was on his way. Kurt started to follow her, but the firefighter waved him off.

She shrugged at Kurt and sat down in the chair indicated. The room temperature was nippy. Thankfully, she still had her coat.

Her phone rang. It was Nicole.

"Are you okay?"

"I'm fine."

"I worried when you didn't show up at church until I got Kurt's message. How bad was the fire?"

"I'm not sure. The garage is still standing, but the vehicles may be toast. I'm at the police station, waiting for the fire chief to interview me. I believe the fire was set. On purpose. As the new owner, I'm the first suspect if it was arson."

"How horrible! They could have hurt you. Who knew you were heading to church this morning?"

"Almost anyone would expect me to go to church. They didn't know I was going to your church."

"Is there any reason someone would want to hurt you or scare you?"

She needed to tell Nicole about Aunt Suzanne's possible poisoning. Her help would be invaluable in unraveling the mystery. "When my questions are over, could we have some girl time?"

"Of course. When will you finish?"

"No clue. Keep your phone handy, and I'll text you."

"I'm sorry about this morning. I went early to church to help with the infants. Since I was in the baby room, I put my phone on silent. You never want to wake any sleeping kids. Not that any of them slept for me today." She paused. "Oh, man! I'm such an idiot. I'm complaining about crying babies, and you're dealing with a fire. I'm ashamed of myself."

"Thanks for making me smile, Nic. Crying babies are almost as terrible as a fire. I'll contact you when the inquisition is over."

"Inquisition? That bad?"

"Possibly, but I can handle it. The sooner they eliminate me, the sooner they'll look for the actual arsonist."

"You hang in there, girl. I'm glad Kurt was there."

"I called him, actually. Didn't have to ask him to come. As soon as I said fire, he and Ross came running."

"No surprise there, Liesl. That man still loves you."

"Give it a rest, girlfriend. My day's been tough enough. I'll call you when I'm through."

"Good luck."

"No worries. I've got this."

When she hung up, Liesl felt her false bravado seep away. This would be a nightmare. She hadn't started the fire, and her job was to convince the chief of that.

A clean-smelling chief, dressed in a jacket and tie, entered the room. He held a thin file folder in his right hand. Before taking a seat, he offered water or coffee.

Seeing he had neither, she declined both.

He pulled out the chair opposite of her and settled in, tossing the file folder onto the table. After he dug in his pocket, he pulled out his phone and said, "I'd like to record this session."

Although he hadn't officially asked a question, she responded as if he did. "Of course."

He stated her name, the date and time, then asked if she agreed to his recording this interview.

"Yes."

"Ms. Schrader, we're going to discuss a fire that occurred this morning in the garage structure at 1105 South Jefferson Street, Mexico, Missouri. Is that correct?"

"Yes."

"Who owns the property?"

"My aunt did, but recently passed away. According to her will, I've inherited it."

The chief remained silent and stared. Perhaps more information would remove the scowl on his face. "You can get all the legal documents from Mr. Van de Berg," she said. "I'll tell him to provide you with everything you request."

"Do you have insurance on the property?"

This question surprised her. She'd given no thought to insurance on the house or any of Aunt Suzanne's other property. "I don't know." She hesitated. "I assumed my aunt had insurance on the house and her other property and possessions. Whether that passes to me, I don't know." Why hadn't Mr. Van de Berg mentioned that?

"Do you know her insurance agent or what company she dealt with?"

"Paul Duck was her agent for as long as I lived with her. You can contact his office. If it's not him, I'll look through her finances to figure out what company or companies were being paid." Her leg was bouncing under the table, and she shifted to quiet it.

"So you don't live at this property?"

"I used to. About seven years ago, I went off to college. I got a job in Houston after I graduated." She gave him the address of her Houston apartment.

"What is your occupation?"

"I'm a writer. Freelance journalism and novels."

"When are you returning to Houston?"

"Right now, I'm staying in Mexico until we straighten out some legal things."

"How long will that be?"

"I don't know."

"When did you first realize there was a fire?"

"I was going to church. I walked down the front steps and turned toward the garage when I saw tracks in the snow."

"Tracks? What kind of tracks?"

"They appear to have been made by a woman's shoes." She described the details she'd noted about the prints. "Then I saw smoke coming from the edges of the big garage doors. I ran back onto the porch and called 911."

"What color was the smoke?"

"Ah, it was basically black." Really? How was that relevant?

"Be more specific, please."

"In my limited experience with campfires and such, smoke

is gray. This wasn't something I'd call gray. Not at all. More black or dark charcoal color."

"Are you wearing the same clothes you wore this morning?"

"Yes." She hesitated. "Well, except for the boots. I was wearing high-heeled shoes when I first went outside. I kicked them off inside because I couldn't run up the stairs in them. They made me fall."

"Why did you need to run?"

"Kurt asked me to go upstairs to see if I could spot anyone watching the fire."

"The Kurt you refer to is Detective Kurt Hunter with the Mexico Public Safety Department."

"Yes. We've known each other for many years. He's an old, well, he's a friend of mine."

"He's an old what?"

"He's a former boyfriend of mine. But that was years ago. He helped me when I witnessed a break-in across the street from my aunt's house a few nights ago."

"How did Kurt get involved today?"

"I called him."

"Why?"

"Because I was afraid. I didn't want to be alone."

"Did you see anyone watching the fire?"

"No, I checked all sides of the house from upstairs. Kurt found some footprints when he checked outside. He took pictures, or maybe video." That reminded her. "I took pictures of some tracks from an upstairs window." She pulled her phone out and showed him the pictures.

"May I look at your recent call list?"

"Of course." She flipped to the list, and he took a picture of the list with his phone.

"I'll get your phone records as part of my investigation. Do you have any other phones?"

"No, just this one." She gave him her number. "Do you want me to send these pictures of the tracks to you?"

He nodded and gave her a number to use.

"Describe the shoes you were wearing."

She did. He looked either unhappy or disappointed. They were nothing like the tracks she'd seen.

"The vehicles in the garage. Were both of them in good condition? As in running, regularly maintained?"

"Yes. I can get you my maintenance records from Houston for the Jeep. It works fine. I can find out where my aunt serviced her car. It was relatively new, so I'm sure it's well maintained."

"Just one more thing, Ms. Schrader. I'd like to take a few pictures of your arms, face and neck area, and your legs and feet. You can stay fully clothed. We just need to document the condition of your extremities."

Pictures of her? Why? Then it hit her. He's looking for evidence of burns from a fire. As if she set it. She grimaced at the thought of having photos taken in a police station. It seemed similar to booking photos.

"Ms. Schrader?"

"Fine," she stated in an abrupt tone. "Whatever you need. I didn't set that fire."

"I never said you did."

The chief had a female police officer step into the room so they wouldn't be alone as she exposed her arms and hands, ankles, and wrists.

She called Nicole from the lobby after the pictures. "I'm finished. Can you meet me at the house?" She cupped the phone when she saw Kurt and Ross. "Are we ready to leave?"

Kurt nodded, so she turned back to the call. "We're good to go."

"Good. See you in a minute."

"That would be great." Relief poured through her. "I'd rather not be there alone right now." She glanced at Kurt as she said to Nicole, "We need to talk."

"Of course we'll talk. What are best friends for?"

"They're for coming over and hearing all about my troubles. What are you going to do with Claudia?"

"That's what fathers are for," Nicole said in a tone that wouldn't allow argument. "Lee planned a big evening of football watching in his man cave since you were going to be here, so he can just keep her with him."

"He now has a man cave?"

She chuckled. "No female, except for Claudia, would want to go down there. She's too young to have discriminating taste just yet."

"I see. Because of this, your living room stays nice?"

"I highly recommend it for anyone married to a sports fan."

"I'll keep that in mind." She frowned. As if she needed such advice. She spotted Kurt shifting his weight from side to side. Years ago, she'd learned that meant action. "We're leaving now."

"Great. Are you hungry?"

At the mention of food, a pang of hunger she hadn't previously noted coursed through her midsection. "Starving."

"I'll swing by our favorite food truck and get us a couple of kwikis and fries. I might even spring for lemonade too. Overall, I'll see you in twenty minutes. Be ready to talk."

"Just like old times." She hung up and turned to Kurt. "Nicole's on her way to my house. We're having some girl time."

His relief at this news was visible. "Good. You don't need to be alone after this."

She frowned. "I don't need a babysitter. But time with my best friend should make me feel a lot better."

He nodded. "Nicole's at her best when she's riding rescue for someone. I'm sure you'll both benefit."

She squatted to Ross's eye level. "Your daddy really helped me today. I hope my being upset about the fire didn't scare you."

"Nah," he said with a shrug. "Everybody gets scared. There are lots of spooky things."

"Yes, there are."

* * *

When Kurt pulled into the driveway, no firefighters were around the garage. Although there was crime scene tape around the structure, the investigator must have left.

Kurt said, "They've gone. I'll check the outside again and then walk you to the door. You stay in the car."

She glanced into the back seat. "I've got Ross to protect me."

Ross seemed pleased that she'd dubbed him her protector, straightening in the back seat. "This car has a radio, and Daddy's taught me how to use it. We can call for backup if we need it."

"That's very good to know, sir."

Kurt returned and escorted her to the door, taking the key from her to unlock it.

"Sure you're okay?"

"I'm disappointed in myself, but okay. Seeing smoke billowing out of the garage terrified me."

Kurt squeezed her arm and returned the key. "Don't be hard on yourself. You've gone through a lot in a short period.

Now you need to tell Nicole everything. She can keep her mouth shut, and she's a great source of information. She knows everyone in town and can ask questions without causing a stir."

"You know everyone in town."

"I do. But I'm a cop. When I ask questions, people clam up, worried they might get in trouble. No one wants to testify in a criminal case, so people become guarded. Nicole won't have those problems. People love her, and they'll tell her everything. Also, she has a great brain. Cops bounce theories off each other all the time. She could be a real asset."

Liesl waved her hand in the air. "I'd already planned to tell her everything. No need to convince me."

"I can come back and stay here tonight, if you want."

She looked away. "Thanks, but I'll be fine." No matter how scared she was, she didn't want Kurt in the house overnight. People would say something was going on between them.

He pushed open the front door. "Wait here. I want to check the house." Without waiting for her permission, he walked from room to room, downstairs and upstairs. When he'd descended the stairs, he asked, "Want me to stay until Nicole gets here?"

"No, that won't be necessary. Thanks anyway."

"Whoever set this fire is enraged. Angry. Call me if you notice anything out of the ordinary. It takes two minutes to get here using the siren."

"Could it have been the guys who broke in across the street? Paying me back for ratting them out to the police?"

"Doubtful. Both of them accepted a plea deal. They'll be serving six months behind bars and three years' probation when their jail time is over. And it appeared to be a woman's shoes, right?"

"Right."

Chapter Twenty-Eight

Liesl

Nicole raced up the stairs of Liesl's porch, her hands full of drinks and a bag of food.

Liesl prayed Nicole would ignore her tear-streaked face, but still clinging to the food packages, Nicole wrapped Liesl in a mama bear hug. She was always a comfort in crisis. "No worries. Dr. Nicole is here to medicate you properly."

"Let's go to the couch upstairs," Liesl said. She took the drinks and food from Nicole so she could remove her coat. "I'll light the fireplace. We can stretch our legs and relax."

"I wish I could take away your pain," Nicole said. "You've been through so much."

"You don't even know the half of it. Yet. Come on, I'll give you an earful."

Upstairs, warmed by the dancing gas flames, they stuffed their faces with kwikis, barbeque-sauced handmade corn dogs, a staple in town. Back in high school, this had been their meal of choice. All romance quandaries, school issues, and part-time-job woes were cured through food and girl talk.

Liesl enjoyed every bite of the corn dog. She moaned in frustration as the last of it disappeared. "These are one of the best things in life."

Nicole smiled. "Your love for food is unparalleled."

After a few minutes, Liesl opened with, "Someone may have poisoned Aunt Suzanne."

"What?" Nicole shook her head, as if to dispel the sinister information. "No, that's unbelievable."

Liesl nodded. "I've been living a nightmare since Dr. Johnson called me to his office on Friday. He thought she accidentally poisoned herself."

Liesl explained about his evaluation of her aunt's blood work. "Kurt helped me scour the house and garage for anything she could have hurt herself with."

"Kurt has come to your rescue a lot lately."

Liesl thought about that. "The fact that he betrayed me will never change. There's nothing between us but an investigation. He stopped by after I'd been to Dr. Johnson's office and realized something devastated me. I had to tell him." Tears spilled over her eyes and ran down her cheeks. "It's too much for me to handle alone. When he materialized in front of me, a trained police officer, I trusted him with what Dr. Johnson suspected."

"I'm glad. He is trustworthy."

Liesl snorted. "With everything but my heart."

"Oh, Liesl." Nicole's eyes also filled with tears. "He hurt you deeply. But you've had years to heal from that horrible betrayal. You've got to move past it."

"You're right." Liesl wiped her nose with a tissue. "There are so many other problems to deal with. We found nothing obvious, like rat poison in the cabinet mixed in with food or spices. I refuse to believe her mind was foggy enough to poison herself. Kurt took a sample of nearly everything and will send them off to a private lab for analysis."

Nicole wiped her own tears. "How could such a thing be possible? Why would anyone want to kill a sweet lady?"

"How can anyone make sense of any murder? Maybe she solved Winnie's murder, and the killer acted to silence her. Or it could be a financial inquiry she made a few days before she ... got sick. She'd discovered money was embezzled from the Butterfly House."

Nicole stared at her. "But I know the people there. They're honest, aren't they?"

Liesl shrugged. "Last night I went to D'Angelo's and bumped into Gretchen."

"You went to D'Angelo's without me?"

She held up a hand. "Well. I had a date."

Nicole squealed with delight. "A date? A real live date?"

Liesl shoved her friend. "It's not that big of a deal."

"It is to me. Spill!"

Liesl talked about the unusual way she met Justin, and Nicole soaked it up.

"How do I meet him?'

"Look for the tallest guy working at Lumber City."

Nicole chuckled. "I'm there all the time with business. Blond?"

Liesl nodded. "Yeah."

"So what's this financial information you mentioned?"

"At D'Angelo's, Gretchen said Aunt Suzanne asked her to review stuff she'd gathered on the Butterfly House. She said there's something wrong with it. She couldn't get into specifics because I'm not officially a client of hers yet, but she's working on a solution. When I find out more, we'll know whether it was a large theft and a plausible motive for murder."

"So money *was* stolen?"

"She called it embezzlement. Someone siphoned off their assets, or they were tricked out of money or something."

"Do they have suspects?"

"I'm not sure, but Mr. Van de Berg's the treasurer."

Nicole pondered this information. "That's unbelievable. Why would a man with an excellent reputation and plenty of income want to pilfer funds?"

"He may not be involved. We don't know yet. But I noticed strain between him and Mr. Barnaby the other day. Mr. Barnaby knows Aunt Suzanne was interested in the Butterfly House accounts because she went to him and got copies of the records."

"She told you about that?"

"Well, her journal did. I've only read the most recent one so far." Liesl took a sip of her drink. "There should be more in the 'missing key' lockbox."

Nicole leaned back against the couch, trying to take in all the information. "How soon can you read the journals you have?"

"I was supposed to go to St. Louis tomorrow to handle some estate business, but I canceled that appointment. Donnie is coming to install the alarm first thing in the morning. I may read some while they do the installation."

Nicole pushed her hair off her shoulder. "Isn't Mr. Van de Berg handling your aunt's estate?"

"Yes. How do I trust him with her money if he's embezzled funds from a non-profit organization?"

"You don't know that. But you're right to be cautious until he's not a viable suspect anymore."

"Exactly. I've got to maintain a true vigilance of the estate's issues he's handling. Some of it may be handled by an investment firm in St. Louis. That's why I had a meeting scheduled with them tomorrow. I'll make sure they hold off any fund transfers through the estate until we know about Mr. Van de Berg."

"Perfect." Nicole pierced Liesl with her eyes. "What does Kurt say about all this?"

"He wanted me to tell you everything. Kurt thinks you'd be able to find out a lot of information from people without causing concern. He said if he asks, they'll clam up because he's a cop."

"They will. But people will talk to you too. Especially if you pretend you're doing it for research on a new book." She sipped her drink and frowned. "Isn't Kurt helping?"

"He is, but we have that history between us. It bubbles under the surface of everything we do and say. You and I don't have those issues, and we make a great team."

"That we do, sister." Nicole sighed. "So, where do I start?"

"Priority one is finding out who stole the money from the Butterfly House and if they could be responsible for Aunt Suzanne's death. Her journal mentioned some type of blowup or exchange she had with someone after the last board meeting. That's what started her on a search for the finances."

"What if I ask board members what happened at the last meeting? I can comb the town and 'bump into' them over the next few days."

"Great idea. But remember, Aunt Suzanne's altercation or confrontation happened after the meeting. I'll keep you posted about what Gretchen can tell me once she's figured out how I can become her client." Liesl rose and paced the room. "I need to know if Aunt Suzanne fingered the killer, or got close enough to put her in danger. Right now, all we have are suppositions."

Nicole frowned. "Your aunt's burned coat is not supposition, and neither is that burned garage out there. With the possible poisoning and embezzlement, these take on a wicked meaning. I'm glad you're putting in an alarm system."

"While Kurt was here taking samples, I noticed the door to Aunt Suzanne's car was open. He tested for prints."

"Did he get any results?"

"Not yet."

"All this is too much. It makes me shiver." Nicole dug in her purse. "I'm calling Lee right now and telling him I'm spending the night. I don't want you alone in this house."

"Oh, Nicole, you don't have to do that."

"I don't have to, but I'm going to. No arguments."

Liesl's shoulders sagged with relief. Nicole had just lifted a heavy burden.

"Thank you."

"It's what best friends are for."

After her call, Nicole said, "All is well there. Lee seemed excited to watch football games this evening too. Claudia has a play area in the basement, so she won't miss me at all. He said he'd order pizza for them tonight."

Liesl was grateful at how understanding Lee was about Nicole's plan. She hugged her friend. "You're the best."

Nicole flung her hair behind her shoulders in a mock attempt at theatrics. "It's because I'm a perfect friend. And modest too."

"Ri-ight."

"I promise to hunt down the board members this week and pump them for information."

"Can you do the same with anyone who knows about Winnie's death? Talk to those who were there? Or heard gossip about it?"

Nicole nodded. "It's hard to bring up a subject that's so old. But if I told them you might use the murder for a book, they'd talk. The real estate business is slow right now, so I have lots of time to devote to this. What can we do right now? This very evening."

"I've started a spreadsheet to log what was in the diaries and the newspaper clippings she kept. Let me run and get my laptop."

Nicole rolled her eyes as Liesl raced away, "A spreadsheet, eh?"

Liesl returned with her computer and newspaper clippings.

Nicole reviewed the clippings and scribbled notes while Liesl worked on the spreadsheet. Together, they created a list of current town residents who might have been at Winnie's birthday party.

After they'd worked for a while, Liesl asked, "Don't you think it's odd I can't find the key to the lockbox she'd recently used?"

"Yes, considering your aunt was acutely organized. Dare I say painstakingly orderly?"

Liesl chuckled. "She had exacting ways. But that's what's causing me concern. Where are her keys? She always hung them by the back door. Why aren't they there?"

"Are they in her purse?"

Liesl heaved an exasperated sigh. "What purse was she using? You know how she was with accessories. It could be in so many of her purses."

Nicole stood up. "Let's check her bedroom."

"Kurt and I went over it, looking for her journal. She kept her current purse right on her bedside dresser, but nothing was there. Did someone steal her purse and keys?"

"Maybe. What about her phone?"

"No phone found either."

"Let's look for all of them."

Liesl moved toward the bedroom with the energy of

someone on a scavenger hunt with another team on her heels, but stopped at the doorway. "Going in there makes me sad."

"Of course it does." Nicole looked at the mussed bed. "Tell you what. When we finish this search, why don't we put clean sheets on the bed? I'll bet you could use some help to do laundry too."

"I haven't touched the laundry since I've been home. Good idea."

God, thank you for Nicole and giving me peace tonight.

Chapter Twenty-Nine

Suzanne
April 1, 1961

Nearly every school day, Suzanne rode home with Myron, much to his chagrin, since they attended the same high school. Suzanne was in Concert Choir, her nose buried in a difficult measure of music, when their director surprised her with an office note. It said her mother would pick her up after school.

The note instantly made her anxious. Anything outside her usual routine caused anxiety now. She worried through the rest of the class. What was wrong? What else had changed in her world?

Once she slid into the passenger seat of her mother's car, she realized she'd overblown her anxiety. Her mother's face was serene.

"This is a surprise," Suzanne said. "I'll take you over Myron any day."

Her mother smiled. "I can't make a habit of it, but today is special. How was school?"

"Okay." She turned to her. "So, what's up?"

"You mean, why am I picking you up today?"

"Yes."

"Well, I received a call from Florence this afternoon."

"Doreen's mom?"

"Yes. She's worried about Doreen. Really worried. Doreen's been hiding in her room a lot and not talking. Her mother wants to divert her behavior toward a better path."

"We've all been upset. I've seen more of Patricia than Doreen since that night. Now I feel bad. Like I haven't been a good friend."

"Not to worry. Florence and I decided Doreen needed some time away from home. She needs a chance to do something fun."

"I'd like that too."

"So the plan is for me to take you home to drop off your books, then you'll take the car over to Doreen's house and ask to take her shopping. Don't let her know it was our idea to do this."

"Okay. This kind of secrecy is easy. The lack of funds is the hard part. Doreen's never been a shopper. Now, even less so because their money is tight."

"I convinced Florence that this shopping adventure would be my treat. If something like this can help cheer you up, then that's marvelous."

"Thanks, Mother. It's a nice thing to do."

"Is it okay that I told Florence you're seeing Pastor Bailey? I thought he might help Doreen too."

"Sure. Doreen knows he's counseling me. I already told her."

Her mom nodded. "I encouraged Florence to see if Doreen would talk to him. Will you support the idea?"

"Of course. Doreen doesn't talk much about her feelings to adults. She's not so fearful opening up around us."

"She seems to be afraid of me."

Suzanne chuckled. "She's petrified of you."

Her mother frowned. "That girl needs some gumption. Some courage. She can be such a wet rag."

Suzanne stared at her mother over her rare use of slang. "You've taught me to have some gumption, haven't you?"

"Life can roll all over you, Suzanne. A woman must be strong to handle everything God throws at us. Standing up to me is your first lesson in standing up for yourself in life."

"Really?" She smiled. "I'll remind you of that the next time we disagree about something."

* * *

Suzanne arrived at Doreen's door, and her mother played off her "surprise" visit with as much talent as an Academy Award-winning actress. Doreen seemed delighted Suzanne had permission from her mother to buy both of them an addition to their wardrobe, like a skirt or shirt.

Suzanne drove them to the town square, and they made their way from one shop to another. The plan was to examine everything available within their price range, and then, and only then, would they return to the specific store which held the perfect item to purchase.

They found fashion contenders at Weiss Dress Shop, Blattners' Shop, and Fredendall and Wilkins Department Store. Once winners were chosen, Suzanne was grateful her Mother had charge accounts they could use.

Glowing with happiness, they returned to the car with

their purchases. Their day would not be complete without a stop at Dairy Pride for a chocolate malt and a kwiki, so that was their next stop.

Dairy Pride required you to walk to the window to order, but they delivered the food to your car. A friend named Chris took their order. When he also delivered their food, Suzanne teased Doreen.

"You saw his smiles were only for you, right?"

"Because of Max." She shook her head. "Everyone in town knows Max is interested in you. Chris realizes he doesn't have a chance with you anymore."

"Are you kidding me? He's had my whole life to show an interest in me. There's been nothing. *Nothing*! It's all about you, my friend."

The lightness of their mood remained while they consumed their food. The way Suzanne ate would have horrified her mother, and knowing that made her feel rebellious.

"I hope you've enjoyed our afternoon," she said.

"I have. Please thank your mother for me."

"I will. I think she feels sorry for me about Winnie. So much that she's inventing ways to cheer me up." She patted her mouth with a napkin.

"I've been depressed since that night," Doreen admitted. "I've had so much to handle. First, my parents are divorcing. That was bad enough. No one gets divorced, yet my parents are leading the way. Then, losing Winnie."

Suzanne studied her for a moment. "I'm sorry both things happened. They are tragedies."

"Yes. One is still ongoing, and I'm stuck in the middle."

"I support your mother in this divorce, you know. Marriage is supposed to be forever. God said, 'Let no man put asunder.' But the Ten Commandments also say, 'Thou shall not commit adultery.' With your father in love with someone else, she deserves to be happy too. God wouldn't want your mother to be miserable, actually, just to stay married."

"What about my dad? My feelings for him are all confused."

"Once you have time to get used to things, you might feel better about your father. Loving him and supporting his decision to fall in love with someone else are two different things."

"What about all the gossips in town? They're talking about him and his girlfriend."

Suzanne shrugged. "You can't change that. Eventually, another juicy bit of gossip will emerge. It'll turn attention away from your parents. It's not your fault, you know."

Doreen nodded. "I know, but it could take forever for the scandal to die down. I want to get out of town. Get away. Be free of all this."

"Do you have a relative you could visit this summer?"

She thought for a moment. "Not that I can think of."

"What about camp? You know, we're both old enough to be counselors at Camp Pin Oak."

Doreen sipped her malt and nodded. "That might work. Actually, it's a fantastic idea. I could make some money doing that, and I wouldn't if I stayed with a relative."

"That's true."

"I'd be canoeing, swimming, making lanyards." Doreen's face perked up, along with her tone. "We would spend nights in front of a fire making s'mores and singing songs. It would be fun."

"You'd be away from your parents, pulling you in two directions."

"I'd be gone for most of the summer too. Mom's been talking about her getting a job to help with our expenses. She might feel better about working if I'm out of the house. And she wouldn't have to feed me, so her expenses would be less."

Suzanne smiled. "I think spending weeks at a camp at the Lake of the Ozarks would be really keen." She vowed not to tell her mother about Doreen's desire to leave town to become a camp counselor. She was still stinging from her comment about keeping her speculations to herself. Doreen becoming a camp counselor was pure speculation, wasn't it?

Doreen said, "With my luck, they'll probably put me in charge of a cabin full of bedwetters." She frowned. "I have experience with that."

They shared a smile. Doreen couldn't stay overnight at Suzanne's house when she was young because of her bedwetting.

"All the better for you to be assigned to them. You could provide proof they can outgrow it."

"Maybe. What about you being a counselor, too? Could you do it?"

"Do you honestly think my mother would let me?"

She grimaced. "Nope. I don't see your mother letting you out of her sight for several years."

For whatever reason, this made both of them giggle.

"You're right. She couldn't tolerate not having me under her thumb."

"Speaking of your mother, I can't believe she hasn't scared Max off yet."

"It's a surprise to me too."

"He's more resilient than I imagined. Your mother is formidable."

"Yet, he smiles and acts as if the cool treatment she's giving him is warm. I'm afraid it will be something I do or say, rather than what she does, that will scare him away."

"Why do you say that?"

"I can't figure out why he likes me."

Doreen scrunched her face in anger. "I blame your mother for taking away all of your self-confidence. Ugh! It makes me mad." She set down her malt. "You're pretty in your own way. It may not be the typical way, but so what? He likes that you're smart and funny. Faithful to your friends. Reliable, and on and on. You dismiss so many of your fine qualities because of your mother's unreasonable expectations."

"Thank you, Doreen. That's nice to hear."

"It's all true. I'm glad Max is smart enough to see your great qualities. Guys are pigs, as you told me. He seems to be above the rest."

"I think it's because he's out of high school. He's matured even more since his graduation last year."

"He knows the meaning of hard work. After all, he's running a farm with his brothers and pitches in to help his father and older brother with the old farm. He's cute too. I need to fall for one of his brothers."

Suzanne laughed. "When I get to know them all better, I'll introduce you to the best ones."

"Pinky swear!"

After they confirmed the promise, Suzanne changed the subject. "I think I told you about talking to Pastor Bailey, didn't I?"

Doreen nodded.

"I felt better after the first session. So much so, I'm seeing him once a week until I decide I don't need to talk anymore. He's helped me rejoice in my friendship with Winnie and not to focus on the negative."

"Is your mother pushing you into this?"

"She suggested it, but I'm glad she did. It's helped me. Might help you if you need someone to talk to."

"Is he real preachy?"

"Not at all."

Doreen looked out the side window. "I don't enjoy talking about what happened that night."

"I get it. I don't either. It's hard to explain, but Pastor Bailey does a lot of listening, and he's not judgmental. It's like talking to yourself, with an occasional suggestion from him on how to uplift the sorrow. Make sense?"

"I guess so."

The roar of a souped-up engine caused both of them to look around. A bright red jalopy, a mechanical miracle owned by Ray Thompson, caused the noise. He was one of the two who'd picked on Billy the day they'd decorated. He pulled himself out of the car over the door, without opening it. Typical. Either he was showing off or the door didn't work. He waved at them.

Suzanne ignored him and turned back to Doreen. "I can't stand that guy. He's a bully."

Doreen eyed him through the window as he made his way to the order window. "He sure has a temper. I saw him beating up one of the freshman boys earlier this year, until Mr. Willer broke up the fight. I wonder if he was anywhere near Winnie's house that night."

"Think he had something to do with her murder?"

"He could have. He certainly has the temperament."

Suzanne shuddered. Doreen had a point. She would look into Ray's history and determine where he was before Winnie was killed. "Did I tell you Officer Ziegler questioned me again?"

Doreen turned in surprise. "Really? Why?"

"I was so upset that night. He came back to ask me more questions the following day. Mostly about Edgar. Some about Winnie, but he kept asking about Edgar's temperament and where I last saw him. It was pretty awful."

"Edgar would never have hurt her." Doreen frowned. "We

used to play together as kids, when we lived on the same street. He's always been a nice guy. The nicest I've ever known."

"That's what I told them. Mother sat in on their questioning, and she told me I did a good job defending his character. There was another agent with him—a man from out of town. He never said a word. Just watched and listened. He was pretty scary."

Doreen nervously twirled one of her home perm curls with her index finger. "Do you think they'll question me again?"

Suzanne threw up her hands. "Who knows? I never thought it would happen to me. Then, here they come, ringing the doorbell."

"I hope they leave me alone. Once was enough."

Suzanne eyed Doreen. "I never saw you after they found Winnie. Probably because they divided us in the aftermath. Where did they make you wait?"

"In the attic. There were a bunch of us who stayed up there and didn't go outside. They questioned us first."

"Was Edgar up there?"

Doreen shook her head. "I didn't see him." Her finger twirled her curls at an even faster rate.

"But what about Billy? You had Billy, didn't you?"

"Just for a minute. When the police spotted him, they asked me about him. Once they found out we weren't related, the officer took him away."

"Poor Billy. Was he upset?"

"Didn't seem so. I figured they made his mother come get him."

Suzanne nodded. "He's so much younger than everyone else. I'm sure they had to consider his well-being. Any idea where Edgar was?"

"I saw him and Winnie line dancing with you and Max. That's the last time I saw either of them."

Suzanne thought for a moment. "He wouldn't have left the attic without Billy, would he?"

"Maybe he went to the bathroom or something. He knew I had Billy, so maybe he didn't want him tagging along."

"When I was watching Billy, Edgar was good about checking in on him. Why would he go downstairs without letting you or Billy know?"

Doreen shrugged. "Who knows? But Edgar wouldn't have hurt Winnie."

"I agree."

Chapter Thirty

Liesl
November 12

Liesl turned from the open wardrobe and declared with waving hands, "I give up. We've looked everywhere, and there's nothing here."

"There's plenty here." Nicole swept her hand across the room. "The problem is that it's not what we're looking for." She grimaced. "How about we change the linens and do some laundry? Maybe we'll find more places to search if we're doing something else."

"Sure." Liesl stretched her stiff muscles.

Nicole moved to the bed and reached to yank off the sheets.

"Stop! Wait, just a second."

The harshness of Liesl's tone made Nicole jump. "What? You're scaring me."

"Sorry. Something's occurred to me. If we fold the bed linens and comforter into a ball, we can keep the fibers and hairs for testing. I'll run and get some paper bags. We can have them tested for traces of poison, hair, fibers, and things."

"Sort of like CSI, but you're bringing the stuff to the technicians."

"Exactly. If someone poisoned her with food or drink, they could have spilled some. We took samples of the food and medicines in the house. What if someone put something in her water or food and took it away or destroyed the container? We might never find it."

Nicole nodded. "But if they spilled it, the evidence could be here. Great job."

Liesl snagged paper bags, plastic gloves, and a permanent marker. They wrote the date, time, and description of the item on each bag. Starting with pillowcases, they peeled them off the pillows, rolled them into themselves to keep any hairs and fibers, and put them in a bag. The process was repeated for all the linens.

Nicole turned to her. "If this turns out to be important evidence, I may end up having to testify." She gestured to the bed, and the bags lined up beside it.

Liesl blew her a kiss. "You're already involved in this, no matter what. You'll make an impressive witness. Right after you finish being a brilliant investigator."

"Ready to do your bed?"

"Sure," Liesl said. "We'd better put clean sheets on one of the guestroom beds as well, if you're staying here tonight.."

When they'd finished making both of the beds, Nicole gathered the sheets and started out the door.

"Where are you going?"

"Downstairs to throw these in the washer."

"Let's throw them in the laundry chute, so we don't have to carry them down two flights of stairs."

"Of course," Nicole grinned. "I forgot about it."

Liesl led the way into the short hallway between Aunt Suzanne's bedroom and bathroom. The wall had a built-in door for the chute, which she held open.

Nicole began feeding sheets through the opening. "More two- and three-story houses should have these things. They're really handy."

"Aunt Suzanne's mother insisted this be in the plans for the house. Too bad she didn't put one in my room."

"Doesn't it go through the kitchen?"

"No. On the first floor, the chute's door is in the butler's pantry. The laundry chute and the dumbwaiter run side-by-side, with the dumbwaiter only running between the first and second floors. The laundry chute runs from up here to the basement."

"Oh, that's right. Didn't we get in trouble once for dropping stuff in there?"

"Yep. Not one of our brightest ideas."

When they'd passed everything down the chute, they headed to the basement.

* * *

A dank smell rose as they descended the stairs, and Liesl wrinkled her nose. "Whew. This basement needs some airing out. If it weren't so cold, I'd open a window."

The windows were located high on one wall, close to the ceiling. In a remodel several years earlier, the basement was equipped with egress windows and wall ladders. Aunt Suzanne made these improvements because of nagging by Liesl and the insurance agent. In case of an emergency, like a tornado, Aunt Suzanne could go to the basement. If she needed to escape, she could climb out, using the ladder-window combinations.

Nicole turned to her with exasperation on her face. "Hello? You had someone trolling around outside this morning. Now you want to invite them in?"

"Don't worry, I won't open anything."

The sound of rattling metal made Nicole jump. "What's that?"

"Just the giant."

"I'm jumpy, I guess. It's been a long time since I've been near your giant." She eyed the huge old furnace malevolently, slid her hands into the pockets of her jeans, and shrugged. "Honestly, I'm not much of a protector, but at least you're not alone. As far as the damp smell goes, there are products that take dampness out of the air. Probably where Justin works."

"An excuse to see him."

"Exactly." Nicole strode over to the large canvas laundry bin and pointed. Dirty laundry exploded from the top and dribbled onto the floor. "You weren't kidding when you said you haven't touched it." She grabbed an armload from the basket and dropped it in front of the washer.

"Nope. I need to do some of my own laundry too." Liesl filled her arms, and they began sorting Aunt Suzanne's accumulation into piles for washing. She dug out her phone and started some music, and the two harmonized with an oldie while they worked.

"Are you going out with Justin again?"

"He's supposed to call me."

"Good. When can I meet him?"

"He'll have to call me first."

"Has he bought a house?"

"I believe he's renting." Laughing, Liesl tossed her hands in the air. "That's it! You can sell him a house."

Nicole sniffed in mock offense. "Gotta make a living, you know." She returned to the basket for more laundry, then dumped her armload of clothes in front of Liesl. When she did, there was a clunking sound.

"What was that?"

Together, they bent down and pawed through the pile.

Liesl's hand hit a solid object. She untangled it from the clothes and pulled free a medium-sized gray leather purse. "This is Aunt Suzanne's."

"Why is it down the laundry chute?"

"No clue." It showed no exterior damage. She unzipped the main compartment and spotted a wallet and key ring. "Well, here's her car keys." She fished around and came up with her aunt's checkbook and a single lockbox key on a separate ring.

"Bingo," Nicole said.

Liesl took the purse over to the laundry-folding table. Everything you'd expect to see in a well-organized bag was there, save one item: no cell phone.

She met Nicole's gaze. "Did she drop her purse down the chute on purpose? To hide it from someone?"

"Makes more sense than dropping it accidentally while she tossed down laundry."

Liesl chewed her lip. "What better place to hide it? No one would look for it here. But why would someone want her purse? For the car keys, her wallet, or the lockbox key? Maybe all of them?"

Thumbing the wallet, she found two twenties and some change. "This isn't enough money to tempt a robber. And only Aunt Suzanne could use the lockbox key because of the signature requirement. Maybe the Butterfly House thief was looking for the financial documents she got from Mr. Barnaby?"

"But she gave them to Gretchen."

"We know that, but the thief wouldn't know that. It might

explain why someone opened her car. To get the proof of the embezzlement and then silence Aunt Suzanne."

"But Mr. Barnaby knows about the money problem, and possibly, so do other board members. I don't believe that's motive to kill your aunt."

"Good point. Well, no matter what, we'd better tell Kurt." Liesl stopped the music and hit his contact icon. "The laundry can wait."

Kurt didn't answer his cell, so Liesl left a vague message about a discovery. "That's odd. He's been so responsive. I hope nothing's wrong."

Chapter Thirty-One

Kurt

That night, Kurt telephoned Liesl to ask if he and Ross could stop by, as they were only a few blocks away.

"Perfect," she said. "Meet you at the front door."

When they arrived, Ross hopped out of the car and ran up to Liesl. He gave her a hug and then threw off his gloves and coat in obvious excitement.

"Ross, pick up your things," Kurt said. His tone was harsher than normal, and he regretted it immediately.

Liesl frowned. "It's okay. He's just enthusiastic."

Ross scurried to gather his errant gloves and handed them and his coat to Liesl. "I'm sorry, Daddy. Miss Liesl."

"I'm sorry, bud. I've had a tough day. But that's no excuse to take it out on you." Kurt ruffled Ross's hair.

Liesl chimed in. "It's fine, sweetie. I'll hang your coat right behind the door, and we'll put your gloves in your pockets. You'll find Nicole in the basement if you want to run down there."

Ross looked at her with trepidation. "It's scary down there."

"I need to lock up my pistol." Kurt pointed to his shoulder harness.

Liesl glanced at the two of them and said, "The library it is." They trooped there and stowed the weapon.

As they walked toward the basement door, Liesl asked, "Why a tough day?"

Kurt frowned. "After I dropped you off, the chief called me back in for questioning about your fire."

"Did you get in trouble because I called you here?"

"Not really. It's expected he would question me. I didn't know how unpleasant it is to be a witness."

"I'm sorry. It's my fault."

"I've been on the other side of interrogations since I started my career. Everyone in law enforcement needs to experience being questioned as a witness. Call it a 'career development exercise' I've been through today. Not fun, but definitely educational."

"Did the chief believe you?"

"He believes both of us. For now. I emphasized that the tracks you and I saw appeared to originate west on Jefferson. Who lives west from you?"

"You suspect it was a neighbor?"

"It could be anyone. I'm curious if any of your aunt's friends live nearby."

"Mrs. Detmeier is about two blocks down, near the Green Estate. Doreen lives about three blocks down and a couple of streets over. I'll do some thinking about who else might be close."

"They could have parked close and then walked."

"True."

"If you come up with more names, I'll pass them to the chief."

"Any idea about the garage?" she asked. "I can't get to my car, let alone look at it, with the crime tape. I may need a rental car."

He nodded. "It'll take two weeks for the samples to process at the State Crime Lab. They won't let you walk around in there until the samples are tested."

"Rental car it is. Speaking of lab processing, Nicole and I carefully marked, gathered, and bagged the linens on Aunt Suzanne's bed. If someone was actually feeding her poison in her food or drink, they might have spilled some on her sheets."

"Good thinking."

"The bags are still upstairs. Don't leave without them."

"I won't. What did you bag them in?"

"Those old-fashioned brown paper bags. Aunt Suzanne has a collection of them."

"Perfect. I'll drive everything to the lab in Jefferson City. Speed the process."

"Wonderful."

"Did the hospital give you any clothing your aunt was wearing?" he asked.

"No. When they brought her out of the ER and into intensive care, she had on a hospital gown. They probably cut her dress off and threw it away."

He nodded. "I'll check to see if discarded clothing goes to a special disposal area."

At the steps, Liesl held out her hand to Ross. "Come, and I'll give you the guided basement tour. We can examine the giant from a distance. If you're not comfortable with that, we'll run back up here. Okay?"

"Okay."

Kurt followed them down the steps. "So, what did you find in the basement?"

She waved off the question. "Wait until we get down there."

The stairs bottomed out in a large room Liesl had used as a recreation room when she was younger. It was a vast space with a banquette table in one corner that could seat about twelve teenagers, a fireplace in the center of the exterior wall, and old couches with an enormous coffee table arranged facing the fireplace. A swinging double door led into the combination boiler room and laundry room.

Ross danced around the rec area for a minute. "You could almost play soccer down here."

"Yes, buddy. If we cleared out the couches, you could."

Kurt remembered all the fun times they'd had here. This was the place to congregate as teenagers, a place to sneak a kiss. A stab of sorrow pierced him. He was the one who'd blown their relationship. And he had no idea how to fix it.

Liesl led Ross to the door of the boiler room. "Come on, buddy. You need a proper introduction to the giant."

"Is it a real giant?"

She bent down and whispered, "It's not really a giant. It's a machine that makes steam to heat this ancient house. When I was young, the sounds convinced me there was a giant. I imagined he worked hard to blow steam up the pipes and keep the house warm."

They pushed through the swinging doors and found Nicole sorting laundry.

"Miss Nicole!" Ross ran, and they shared a hug. Then he turned and studied the enormous, cylindrical metal boiler with multiple pipes reaching into the ceiling. "It's huge."

"Yes, it is. I'd say he takes up most of this room."

Kurt enjoyed watching Liesl and Ross. It made him happy

to see how comfortable they were together. "It's old," he said. "One of these days, Liesl will buy a new, efficient boiler, and it will be half this size." He turned to her. "Right?"

She nodded. "One day. It might be half the size of this fella, but it won't have the personality." She walked over and patted the tank. "In the winter, he sings to me at night. Sometimes, during the day, if I listen carefully."

"He also makes other sounds." Kurt rolled his eyes at her.

They shared a smile at his reference to the gassy noises.

Ross didn't approach the boiler. Instead, he turned and trotted to the ladders and the egress windows lining the exterior wall. He climbed one of the ladders.

Kurt stopped him. "No, buddy, those are for emergencies. Those windows are like doors. You climb the ladder, hit the red button that unlocks the window, then push it open and climb out to the grass outside. We don't have a reason to climb up there this afternoon."

Ross descended the ladder with reluctance.

Kurt turned to Liesl. "What did you discover?"

She walked to the laundry-folding table and held up the purse. "This has to be the purse Aunt Suzanne was using at the end. Inside are her car keys and the missing lockbox key. We found it in the laundry basket. We believe she purposely threw it down the laundry chute."

Kurt looked across the room. "I'd forgotten about the chute."

"What, Daddy?" Ross pulled on Kurt's sweater. "Did Liesl shoot something?"

They all smiled.

Nicole explained to Ross what the laundry chute was and held him aloft for a closer examination of the opening.

Kurt unfastened the purse, extracted all the contents, and placed them on the table. "Does anything seem missing?"

"I haven't found her cell phone. I didn't miss it until recently. Other than that, I'd say everything she'd normally carry in her purse is still in there."

"Speaking of her phone, I'm going to request her records and cell tower report if you'll give me the name of her cellular service provider."

"I can find out."

He turned the empty purse inside out and followed the stitching along the edges of the bag. "It doesn't appear the lining was separated or a false bottom or side installed. It seems to be a normal leather purse." He returned it to the proper shape and set it on the table.

Liesl watched him examine it, then asked, "Don't you find it odd she threw it down the chute? Like she was hiding it from someone?"

"She may have been keeping it from someone." He paused. "Or maybe she threw it down the chute to signal something was off. She felt bad, growing weak, and maybe became suspicious. No phone access for whatever reason. No way to leave a written message if someone was watching her. She knew you'd come home and eventually do the laundry. I think it was a sign for you."

The look on Liesl's face told him she believed her aunt would have done exactly that.

Chapter Thirty-Two

Suzanne
April 8, 1961

It was hard to catch her mother in the right mood for a quiz about the night of Winnie's murder. If her thoughts were elsewhere, Mother would dismiss any question as an interruption. On the other hand, she might discover Suzanne's investigation if she focused on the questions. Suzanne needed her distracted, but not by something important.

For three days, Suzanne busied herself in the kitchen, helping her mother with preparing dinner or clean up. Friday night, she'd set the dining room table for three instead of four because Myron was attending a basketball game. She was making a salad when her father walked in the back door with the newspaper in hand. He bolted the door, which was unusual for him.

"Hello, Suz. Where's your mother?"

"Hey, Dad. She's in the pantry. What's up?"

"There's an article about Winnie's cause of death in *The Colonel*." He tossed the newspaper onto the kitchen table. "It's horrendous. I'm going to talk to your mother. It's simply not safe for either of you to be out by yourself until they catch this killer."

He stalked off toward the pantry, and it unnerved her a bit. Her dad was calm, with a soothing temperament. His agitation made her uncomfortable.

She scanned the article. It was unsettling to read that Winnie had suffered multiple blows from a cylindrical object. They speculated it was a log from the nearby stacked firewood. Cause of death was blunt force trauma. Gossips from town had speculated, but it hit hard to see, in print, a gruesome cause of death.

She was wiping tears from her cheeks when her parents returned to the kitchen. Her dad put his arm around her. "Did you read it?"

She nodded.

"I shouldn't have left it here. I'm sorry."

"It's not your fault. She was my friend. I wanted to know what happened." With a sniff, she added, "I wasn't ready for it." She used one of Max's handkerchiefs to wipe her face. She'd add this newspaper edition to her collection once her parents discarded it.

Her mother gestured to a chair. "Sit down. Your dad wants to discuss this."

They gathered around the table.

"This news has upset all of us. We can't allow you to be by yourself right now, day or night. You understand?"

She nodded. "It scares me too. What kind of monster hurt Winnie?"

Dad sighed. "Until the police solve this, I want both you

and your mother to be extra careful. Neither of you goes anywhere alone."

Mother spoke up. "Tomorrow, I'll call around and see if I can find a man to be here when your father's at work. Someone trustworthy. I'd feel better if I'm not alone here all day."

Suzanne hadn't thought about her mother being alone in this big, creaky house. "Great idea, Mother. You've been talking about getting the yard and garden fixed for spring. Why don't you see about a gardener?"

Her father nodded. "A permanent gardener. One to take care of the yard and flower beds, unlike this husband of yours."

Her mother raised an eyebrow at him. "Using this as an excuse to eliminate your outside duties? You, sir, are a very poor gardener. A permanent addition will be just the ticket." She stood. "Now, that's settled. Give Suzanne and me about fifteen minutes, and we'll serve dinner."

Her dad left, and her mother returned to the pantry for the serving dish she'd never retrieved. Perfect time to ask Mother some questions.

"Any idea who this gardener might be?"

"No, but my first call will be to the courthouse," Mother said. "They have many people who work their property, full time and part time. I can get a recommendation from them. If not, there are always my gardening friends. They use handymen a lot for big jobs."

Suzanne peered through the kitchen window at their backyard. "We have a big job for him, whoever he may be. Can we have him improve the space Dad set aside for Zest? Make it a bigger run?"

Mother was dishing up the spaghetti. "I'm sure we can work something out."

"I appreciate you letting me keep her. She's actually been a comfort to me." Suzanne pushed forward. "Did you see Winnie take her out that night?"

"No, dear."

"Where were you?"

"Most of us who cleaned up after the downstairs part of the party stayed in the kitchen visiting. Mrs. Whitcomb was there. No one went out that back door."

"Could you see the stairs or the front door?"

"No."

"What about the dining room table? I passed some adults sitting there but didn't get a good look at them."

"Some of the church women gathered around the dining room table. They didn't want to play cards, so they just talked there." She picked up the serving dish. "Bring that salad, please. Most of the men were watching television. Some game was on. Wait. Why were you going past the dining room?"

"Billy and I took Zest out earlier in the evening."

Her mother turned to her with horror. "You went outside that night?"

"Yes, with Billy. To walk Zest."

"You could have been killed!"

"I didn't see anyone out there. Before Winnie was hurt, I never gave it a thought."

Mother frowned. "No more walking the dog alone until they catch the killer. We can expand her run, as you suggested."

"Of course, Mother. Sorry." Suzanne stopped the questions. Her mother had provided enough information to prove she hadn't seen anything.

* * *

It was easy to catch her dad alone, to ask him some questions. The perfect time came a day later, after dinner. They usually ate around 6:30 p.m. After that, he'd sit at his desk in the den, pretending to work. Actually, he watched television.

"Are you busy?"

He glanced at her and smiled. "Not for you, Suz. I'm always available when you need me."

"I don't want to interrupt if you're working."

He waved at the stacks of paper on his desk. "This can wait."

She walked over and turned down the volume on the television. Then she moved the large wingback chair over to his desk. When she plopped into the seat, her skirt floated down around her. They chuckled about it.

"That is some skirt, kiddo."

"It's the fashion."

"That's your mother talking, not you. What can I help you with?"

"Officer Ziegler and his shadow came and talked to me the day after the murder."

A worried look came over his face. "Are you upset about that?"

"No, Pops. I'm not. I just didn't understand why they asked so many questions about Edgar. Do they think he hurt Winnie?"

"I don't know." He shifted in his seat. "They have to talk to everyone she associated with. I don't know much about crimes, but they're just trying to do their job."

"He drilled me about who I saw, when I saw them, where they were. Stuff like that."

"They did the same to me."

"So, did you see Winnie leave the house?"

"No. Didn't see Edgar leave either. Last time I saw them, they'd come down for the cake."

"Did you see anyone come or go?"

"When we were in the dining room, kids ran up and down like crazy. After the festivities, the men moved to the living room to watch basketball. We couldn't see the front door from there."

She nodded. She'd spotted him in the crowd of fathers when she and Billy took Zest for a walk. "Did you notice when I went outside? Earlier in the evening."

A panicked look crossed his face. "Tell me that isn't true."

"I'm sorry to upset you, but it's true. Mother was upset, too, when I told her."

"Why would you do such a thing?"

"I didn't think anything of it, Dad. Sorry. I was watching Billy for Edgar while he and Winnie were dancing. We were bored. I figured getting Zest out of Winnie's room was a good thing. Billy and I enjoyed the walk."

He frowned. "I'm sorry, Suz. We're concerned because someone hurt Winnie." He stood, walked to her chair, and bent down to give her a hug. "I couldn't bear it if something happened to you."

She smiled up at him. "I promise to be more careful in the future."

He went back to his desk. "Do you have a minute to talk with me about something else?" he asked.

"Of course."

"We've been trying to get Myron interested in studying accounting in college so he can take over my business." Dad sighed. "It's not going well."

She studied him for a moment. "If you want my honest opinion, it's the way you and Mother approach him. You've pushed and pushed. He's been pushing back, away from your plans, twice as hard."

"I hadn't thought of it that way."

"I'd do the same if you did that to me. Why don't you let him pick other courses, as well as one accounting course, for his first year? Let him see if he likes any of them. No point in holding the business for him if he doesn't want it."

"Good point."

"He really is a good guy, Dad. If you and Mother will back off the pressure, I think he'll come around. If he doesn't, let him get an actual job one summer. One that requires physical labor and not his brain. I don't think he'd like that much."

He smiled. "That's a great idea. Are you going to help me convince your mother if it comes to that?"

"Yes. You'll need my support because she won't want her boy doing physical labor. It might be a great experience, though. Life changing."

"What about you? What are you interested in?"

She grinned. "If you're waiting for me to say accounting, it won't happen."

"You have the personality for it. You're precise."

"I don't like numbers and still hesitate on my multiplication tables."

"It's more about operating an adding machine, but never mind. You have a great brain. Your mother thinks that women should stay at home, be married, and have children. I'm not sure that's what you want."

She pushed a lock of hair behind her ear. "It's not that I don't want those things. I'd like to apply that brain you mentioned to something besides party planning, bridge, charitable works, and child care."

He turned and shuffled through his stacks. "Here we go." He freed a single piece of paper and passed it to her. "That is a line graph of a stock one of my customers owns. She's made a generous profit from the investment working with a company out of St. Louis. They researched similar stocks in that market and recommended this one."

She looked at him, baffled. "What does this have to do with me?"

"You have patience and a curious mind. Investments in stocks and bonds require research, monitoring the markets, calculating possible future returns, and a lot more variables. Why don't you consider taking economics next year?"

"I don't know, Dad."

"If you like it, you can take more classes in college. There are so many related fields to pursue to find what you love. If you don't like it, you've earned another credit toward graduation, and you've learned about money. That's always a good thing, even if you don't want to handle investments."

She'd never considered this career, but she wouldn't dismiss her dad's recommendation out of hand. He was smart and had her best interests at heart. "I'll think about it."

"I'll take you to that investment company in St. Louis one day to look around and talk to some of them. There is more to St. Louis than shopping, art galleries, and museums. But don't tell your mother I said that."

She grinned at him. "You take me there, and I promise not to tell Mother what you said."

"Deal."

Chapter Thirty-Three

Liesl
November 13

When Nicole left the following morning, Liesl wrapped her in a hug and tried not to cry. They'd passed the evening in girl talk and even some giggling. It had been too long since they'd giggled. They also had a lengthy discussion about Aunt Suzanne's purse discovery. If Aunt Suzanne ditched her purse as a signal, then the three of them needed to get busy.

Donnie and his security company crew arrived an hour later. He and Liesl walked through the house once again and, with all the trouble she'd encountered since his last inspection, she upgraded from an acceptable system to his top-of-the-line offering and tripled the number of heat and carbon monoxide sensors.

Liesl accepted several changes he suggested, such as heat sensors to the ceiling of the screened-in porch at the back of the house. Also, she agreed that he equip the egress windows in the basement to be armed at all times, outside of the control of the main system. In an emergency escape from the cellar, authorities would automatically be alerted. With the upgrade, he pledged to return and add all his bells and whistles to the garage for free once it was released for repairs.

When the crew started work, she excused herself to the dining room. They needed a full-fledged investigation area, and the huge dining room table lent itself to spreading out.

The room was spacious, yet cozy, with wainscoting and a corner fireplace. A plate rail lined the upper walls. The enormous oak table, polished to a glossy sheen, dominated the room. Twelve people could comfortably dine there. If they needed more space, two leaves stowed under the table fitted into the top and added four feet.

When Liesl joined the family, Aunt Suzanne had table pads custom-made so little hands dragging toys across its surface wouldn't scratch it. She pulled out those same pads and a tablecloth, so their group wouldn't have to worry about scratching this beautiful relic.

After adding her laptop and newspaper clipping bundles, she stepped back to admire her handiwork. This would pass as "the workspace for new book research" to anyone who asked.

She made a quick call to Mr. Barnaby and sent the information about Aunt Suzanne's cell phone provider to Kurt.

A search engine review for women's shoes resembling the tracks in the snow elicited too many possibilities. She returned to entering information from the clippings and journals into her spreadsheet.

When her cell rang, she fumbled around for it. It was Kurt.

"I drove those samples and the bags with the linens to the lab in Jeff City this morning."

"Already? It's …" she glanced at her phone. "Oh, it's almost one o'clock!"

"Did you get lost in a book? You used to be so good at that."

"Nope, I'm working hard on research for my new book idea."

"Ah, so you have people around you?"

"Yes, the alarm installation is underway." Their presence was a continuous symphony of hammering, drilling, and construction noises.

"Good." He paused. "I wish I could get work done that quickly. The lab said it would be three weeks before we'd have the results."

Three weeks? "I thought you said they'd be quicker than ... the other option."

"I did. And they are. But I forgot about the Thanksgiving holiday. As far as samples from your garage, I'll bet it's a month or more before the fire chief gets his results."

"Speaking of the fire, I didn't call for a rental car."

"Better get to it, then. Any luck with what you're working on?"

"I've set aside some things to discuss later with you and Nicole. I figure she needs a night home with her family."

"Thanks for the cell provider. I sent a request for information. Anything else you need?"

She whispered, "Any way you could review the Winnie Whitcomb investigative file?" In a normal voice, she added, "I'd like to compare their information with all the info I have here."

"I'll have to have the chief's blessing. Additional evidence would be the key to reopening that file, especially one so old."

Fresh evidence? She glanced at the information spread across the dining room table. "Perhaps it's already here."

Chapter Thirty-Four

Liesl

The lobby of Barston Investments in St. Louis was amazing. Reminiscent of an old bank, likely its former life, it now held plush carpets atop the gray marble floor, and honey-colored wood paneling stretched to an eighteen- or twenty-foot tin ceiling.

She ogled the décor for a few seconds before a receptionist pointed to the brass elevator doors and advised her that the fourth floor was her objective. The woman seemed surprised her appointment was with Mr. Samuel Apple.

Her attitude caused Liesl to speculate about him as she rode the ancient, but charming, elevator. Either the man had many appointments with people who looked more impressive, or he rarely had appointments.

The fourth floor continued the lobby's charm, but darker wainscoting covered three-quarters of the walls. The ceilings were high but stopped around twelve feet. More marble floors here, with tan and gold rugs.

A woman with silver hair slicked into a tight bun approached. "You must be Miss Schrader."

"Yes, ma'am."

"Pleasure to meet you. I'm Colette, Mr. Apple's executive assistant."

"Nice to meet you, Colette. Please call me Liesl."

Colette opened an unmarked wooden door. Inside, a dark-haired man stood by a wall of windows. He turned and walked toward them, his youthfulness a surprise.

"You must be Miss Schrader," Mr. Apple said. "I'm Sam. So glad to meet you."

"Call me Liesl, please." She stepped forward and shook his offered hand, noting his expensive suit and a shirt with real cufflinks.

"Please, have a seat." He waved a hand at one of the leather chairs in front of his desk.

"Would you like coffee or tea?" asked Colette.

"Coffee, please." Anticipating her next question, Liesl added, "I'll take it black."

"I'll have coffee," Mr. Apple said.

With a nod, Colette swept out of the room.

Mr. Apple sat in the chair opposite Liesl, rather than behind his desk. "We're here to discuss business matters, but first, let me express my sincerest condolences to you on the passing of Suzanne."

"Thank you."

"I've known her since I was a boy."

"Really?"

"This is a family business. When I was old enough to do chores, my father made me work here in the summers. I met her and your Uncle Max when I'd graduated from cleaning crew to file clerk."

He had an interesting, almost lilting, speech pattern, as if he spoke English as a second language.

"I never would have guessed you rose to such heights from housekeeping duties."

He chuckled. "If you'll indulge me, I'll take a moment to tell you about our firm."

After a knock on the door, Colette entered with a silver tray. She turned to Sam. "Is there anything else?"

"No. Thanks, Colette." He gestured for Liesl to help herself to coffee. "My great-grandfather started this business. He ran it out of the home of a friend after he moved here from Germany. He was Jewish, and his parents were afraid for him to remain there. This was when the Nazi Party began identifying Jews."

Liesl nodded. "I'm German by heritage and familiar with the atrocities of the Nazis."

"In Germany, he'd helped his father by keeping the books for their manufacturing plant. Once in the States, speaking little English, he realized he didn't need to speak the language to handle money. He studied the stock market and began handling small investments for German friends. After several years, he was able to move into a building and hire part-time employees. The business has grown since that time."

"A success story. Were you engrossed in investments at a young age?"

"Never. I remain indifferent to that side of the business. I'd much rather meet with our clients and explain the markets to them, rather than study and handle stock market sales and bond yields. We employ people much better than I could ever be for that."

"Your job is to explain this to me?"

He nodded.

"What a refreshing change, since neither Aunt Suzanne nor Uncle Max saw fit to do so." She heard the bitterness in her tone, and her face colored. "Sorry. I'm still shocked at my large inheritance, when I had no prior knowledge of it."

He leaned back in his chair. "My father may have influenced your aunt and uncle to do that. For years, he saw kids here with their parents. Most had bad attitudes. Later, some got into drugs or killed themselves driving a Ferrari as wild teenagers. Dad cautioned all parents to downplay their money. Too much, too soon, can ruin or kill a child."

"But here I am, a multi-millionaire, with no clue how to handle it."

He spread his hands in the air. "Would you rather figure it out as an adult, or as a hormone-infested teenager?"

He had a point.

With a smile, he shifted to pour himself coffee. "I have a packet to give to you, and we'll walk through it, step by step. Stop me whenever you have questions, okay?"

Nearly three hours and two bathroom breaks later, they finished the overhaul of Aunt Suzanne's entire investment portfolio. Liesl had made two discoveries while they worked. First, she'd never want to handle investments alone, and second, she'd never fathom the amount of money now under her control.

They discussed the necessity of her making a will. She didn't want to ask Mr. Van de Berg to do it. At least, not until she and Gretchen resolved the "financial irregularity" issue. Giving no details to Sam, she asked for an attorney recommendation. He responded with several names of attorneys their firm used with expertise in tax planning.

"Have you given any thought to how you'd like to spend this money?"

"No. It's too much, too soon."

"That's fine. When you leave here, you'll have all of my

contact information, including my private cell phone. Call me anytime, day or night."

"Do you offer this service to all of your clients?"

"Actually, we do. Our clients must have several million to invest before we accept them. As a result, we pride ourselves on being the best that investors' money can buy."

"My aunt kept her wealth a secret in our small town, and I'd like to do the same. Is that a problem?"

"Not at all. Either Colette or I will be your contact when you want money transferred into your local bank account. Otherwise, we'll keep to the established investment plan, unless you want to change it."

"I don't want to change anything right now. But if I decide to buy something large, like a car or a vacation home, would I contact you or Colette?"

"Either of us can take care of you, but you should download our app. That will let you move money into various accounts without having to contact anyone. Does that appeal to you?"

"Absolutely. If I can add my local bank to it, you know, checking and saving account, that would be fantastic."

"Not a problem. In fact, we'll do it right now."

Twenty minutes later, she stood to leave. "Thank you for your time. I appreciate what you've done with these investments and look forward to working with you in the future."

He gathered the contents of her portfolio from his desk. "You can count on your money being safe here. My great-grandfather's family lost their wealth and their lives in Nazi Germany. Not only is it our mission to invest the money of our clients and provide a fair return, it's our purpose to make sure no government or market correction leaves our people penniless."

"That's reassuring, Sam. Thank you." They shook hands.

She walked to the elevator, her brain a mush of figures and stock analysis. Would she ever get her mind around this inheritance?

Burdened with financial papers, she hiked the great distance to the inexpensive parking lot she'd used. By the time she arrived, she was laughing at herself. For the first time in her life, it was time to consider valet parking.

Chapter Thirty-Five

Suzanne
April 16, 1961

Patricia called and invited Suzanne to her house. Because Patricia had the groovy car, Suzanne made her pick her up. It was a windy morning, so Patricia suggested she bundle up because she was coming with the top down. Suzanne chose to wear a scarf and jacket to enjoy the sunny day.

When Patricia drove away from her house, music blasting from the radio set on KXEO, Suzanne felt released from bondage. Patricia's convertible was every girl's dream. She didn't want to leave it. "Do we have to go to your house today?"

Patricia glanced at her. Suzanne couldn't read her reaction with her eyes hidden behind dark sunglasses. "Why?"

"It's wonderful to have escaped my house. Couldn't we just drive around town and show off this car to everyone?"

Patricia smiled. "It is a fabulous car."

"The best. How did you talk your dad into buying it?"

"I told him I'd drive it to Vassar. He's the one who wants me to go there. Mother wants me somewhere closer, like Washington University in St. Louis, or William Woods in Fulton."

Suzanne sighed. "I have my suspicions about where Mother wants me to go, and it doesn't involve my opinion."

"Don't fight it. Go wherever your mother wants, and consider yourself lucky to get out of town. If you don't like it, tell her you want to transfer after a year."

"You're brilliant!"

"I've learned to make the most of my situation. With crazy parents, it's a finely honed survival instinct that keeps me functioning."

Patricia was born to a wealthy family, but their family dynamic was so strange. Suzanne realized her own mother was intense, but she was well-intentioned. The jury was out as to whether Patricia's mother had a heart or good intentions. Her father tried to buy Patricia's love with expensive gifts, like this car.

"Where do you want to take me?" Suzanne asked.

"Let's drive by MMA. Maybe some of the soldier boys are out on this beautiful but windy day."

"How long has Missouri Military Academy been around?"

"Almost seventy-five years, I think. They have a big celebration planned for 1964."

"How do you know so much?"

"I've dated some guys there," Patricia said. "Have you dated any cadets?"

"Are you kidding? I haven't dated anyone, much less a cadet."

"Well, I dated one who treated me like a princess."

"What happened to him?"

"Our fine young men of Mexico don't appreciate the 'town girls' dating anyone from the academy. I didn't want to be ostracized by the local guys, so I broke up with him after their Spring Ball. I really wanted to go to a ball. It was terrific."

"Why didn't I know about this?"

"It was almost two years ago. Before I dated Edgar."

Patricia had previously admitted Edgar had been her first love. Suzanne believed Patricia had never quite left him behind. Bringing up Edgar gave her the excuse to ask about the night of horror. "Did you see Edgar before they found Winnie?"

Patricia made a face. "I was dancing when the screaming started. In fact, when I saw you and Max head downstairs, I followed."

Suzanne shuddered. Terrible memories always pushed feelings of fear and confusion to the surface. "Did you see Edgar up there around that time?"

"The last time I saw him, he was with Winnie, and you and Max. When we were line dancing."

Suzanne hung her arm out of the car and enjoyed the sound of the wind. "That's the last time I remember seeing him too. You think he was with Winnie when she got hurt?"

"Heavens, no. Edgar would never allow anyone to hurt her, and he'd never hurt her himself."

"Where was he then?"

"I don't know. That's a police matter. Didn't you get enough questions from them? I sure did." Patricia rounded a street corner and pulled to the curb at the MMA parade field. The field was deserted. "No marching today, I guess." She glanced at her watch. "They should be out here by now."

"Probably too windy." Suzanne took in the view. "This spot allows for a good view of the parade field and the lake. Speaking of the lake, we need to come skating, if the weather stays cold enough."

"You won't get me on ice skates. I've never learned." Patricia sighed. "I can't say I'll miss this view, or anything else, once I'm free."

Suzanne straightened in her seat. "You're joshing me, right? You'll miss all of this at college. Think of the fun people you won't have around. Like me."

She pulled down her sunglasses and peered at Suzanne. "I will miss you, but I can't wait to go to New York this summer and then have a fresh start at a nifty college." She leaned over, opened the glove box, and started digging around in it.

Patricia's seat was so far from the glove box, she couldn't see inside. Suzanne asked, "What are you looking for? I'll find it."

"My cigarettes. And don't you say a word to anyone."

Suzanne turned to her, stunned. "When did you start that disgusting habit?"

Patricia frowned. "You're such a square! Both my parents smoke. I was curious about it. Can't say I like the smell or taste of them, but it seems to calm me down."

"Stop." Suzanne pulled Patricia's hand from the glove box, and a book of matches fell onto the floor. The matches were from Air Park Restaurant, a popular eating place east of town, at the airport.

"You'll have to take me home if you do that. Someone will see us, and Mother will never let me out of the house with you again."

Patricia raised an eyebrow above her sunglasses. "Even if I'm the one smoking?"

"Yes."

"Really?"

Suzanne held up three fingers in a Girl Scout salute. "Scout's honor."

Patricia sighed and closed the glove box.

Suzanne opened it and returned the matches. "Being my friend is hard."

Patricia started the car. "It's not you, it's your mother. I can wait until I get home for a smoke."

"You smoke in front of your parents?"

"No, I wait for them to be busy in one part of the house, and then I smoke somewhere else. They both smoke, so they never smell it or notice the blue haze in a room I've left."

Although Patricia acted like getting away with smoking was fun, it made Suzanne sad that neither of Patricia's parents cared enough to monitor her activities.

"Tell me about Max. Have you been on a proper date yet?" Patricia pulled away from the curb.

Suzanne grinned at her. "He wants to ask me for a dinner date Friday night."

"Think that'll be acceptable with the prison warden you call 'mother'?"

"That's harsh. The plan is for Max to invite me out in front of both of them. Even if Mother objects, Dad should agree to it because he likes Max."

"I'm glad at least one of your parents has some sense. Max is a nice guy."

An hour later, filled with windblown laughter and singing with the radio, Patricia rounded the street toward Suzanne's home.

"Thanks for breaking me out of jail," Suzanne said. "I appreciated the tour."

"We went north, south, east, and west. Because of that, we left town four times today. You don't have to tell anyone we turned around when we passed the city limits."

"You're right. It's the first time I've been out of town since that horrible night. Thank you."

They passed Joey Bauer riding his bike home from work,

and Suzanne waved at him. Joey was damaged during his birth. Physicians recommended he go to a home for those with low mental capabilities, but his parents refused. Instead, they kept him at home, and he functioned relatively well in the world. He could not drive a car, so he rode a bicycle everywhere. He wasn't much older than Suzanne. Everyone loved him because of his sweet disposition. He also observed things and remembered them.

His home was in the same neighborhood as Winnie's house. Could he have been out when Winnie was murdered? If so, maybe he noticed something. Suzanne realized she needed to ask him.

She couldn't ask Patricia to take her there. She'd question Suzanne's motivation. Her father would blow a gasket if she tried to walk there by herself. If Myron was home, maybe she could get him to take her.

* * *

When Patricia took her home, Suzanne walked to the garage to see if Myron's car was there. It was.

After about twenty minutes of pleading and a hefty five-dollar bribe, Suzanne convinced Myron to drop her off at the Bauer house. He would leave her there for thirty minutes and then circle back. The bribe was for him to get a malted or a kwiki at Dairy Pride while she tried to accomplish her mission. It was also to ensure he didn't rat her out to their parents.

Joey's mother answered the door and was gracious to Suzanne's request to visit. Suzanne waved off Myron and entered to the sumptuous smell of food being prepared for dinner. Joey must get his sweetness from his mother, who never let on that Suzanne's visit was a bother.

"Mrs. Bauer, do you think Joey would join us? I'd like to talk to him about something."

Mrs. Bauer smiled and shrugged. "I can ask. He just got home from work, and he usually holes up in his room until supper. No harm in trying."

Mrs. Bauer moved to the bottom of the stairs. "Joey, we have a guest who'd like to see you."

"Who is it?"

"It's Miss Suzanne."

"Miss Suzanne from the spooky house?"

Suzanne and Mrs. Bauer smiled. "Yes, but it's nicer if you don't comment on her home. I'm sure Miss Suzanne loves it."

"Be right there."

Suzanne said, "My house is spooky looking. One of the charming things about Joey is that he speaks the truth."

In a moment, Joey came downstairs. His mother gestured for him to take a seat. They exchanged pleasantries for a moment until the opportunity presented itself for questions.

"I was at Winnie's house when she was hurt," Suzanne said. "It was a terrible thing."

Joey nodded. "It made me sad. She was always nice to me. Some people aren't."

"I'm sorry to ask, but I'm doing it because Winnie was my best friend in the entire world." Suzanne studied his face, not wanting to go too far. "You notice a lot of things around town. I wondered if you saw something that night."

Mrs. Bauer reached out and patted Joey's hand. "Poor guy. The police came here and asked him questions. It upset him."

"Oh no, Joey. I'm so sorry. I didn't know. I won't upset you again. I'll just go."

"Don't leave, Suzanne," Mrs. Bauer said. "Joey understands they're trying to catch the bad guy. When they heard Joey's alibi, they stopped questioning him. He's okay now, aren't you, son?"

He nodded.

Suzanne smiled. "They asked me questions too."

His eyebrows rose. "Did it upset you?"

"A bit. When it happened, I was in shock, I guess. But when they came back with more questions the day after—now, that bothered me."

"I was home when it happened. Lots of people saw me come out of the house when the police cars went down the street."

Mrs. Bauer sighed. "Thank goodness the neighbors saw him watch the police cars run by. The police wouldn't have taken my word for his activities that night, but they believed them. There were so many police cars, weren't there?"

Joey nodded. "There were seven police, four fire trucks, and six county sheriff cars."

Mrs. Bauer and Suzanne exchanged a look.

"See, Joey, that's why I wanted to talk to you," Suzanne said. "I saw all those cars that night but didn't count them in my head. You make note of the best things."

He ducked his head with a sheepish grin. "Thanks."

"I'm going to write that down, Joey. So I don't forget." Suzanne reached into her satchel and pulled out a small notebook and a pen.

Joey watched her write. "I'm not good at writing. So I keep everything in my head."

After she noted the vehicle information, Suzanne leaned back in her chair. "Where were you when you heard the first siren?"

"In my room."

"Did you hear anything else that night? Before or after the sirens?"

Joey looked at his mother. "The police didn't ask me that. They asked me what I saw."

Mrs. Bauer set down her teacup. "It's okay to answer Suzanne's questions."

"Okay." He hesitated, then said, "I heard someone running between our house and the Fishers' house before the sirens."

"Any idea what time it was?"

He stared over Suzanne's shoulder for a moment. "Maybe five or ten minutes. Before the sirens."

"You didn't see anyone?"

He shook his head. "Didn't see. Just running steps in the crunchy snow."

"Did it sound like just one person, or could it have been more?"

He tilted his head for a moment in thought. "Just one."

"Mrs. Bauer, you might share this with the police. Someone running between the houses around that time is suspicious. Joey's information might be important."

Mrs. Bauer nodded at Suzanne, then turned and smiled at Joey. "Good job, son."

Suzanne stood. "Thank you, Joey, for talking."

Mrs. Bauer walked her to the door. When she opened it, Suzanne turned to her. "If you don't mind, I'd appreciate it if you didn't mention this visit to my mother. She wants me to forget that night. Yet, I've found it's the only thing that makes me feel like I'm doing something for Winnie."

With a sweet smile, Mrs. Bauer said, "I understand, dear. I won't mention it. Joey would, if someone asked him about it, but no one will hear it from me."

Chapter Thirty-Six

Liesl
November 15

The following day, Liesl popped into the bank to talk to Mr. Barnaby. As usual, he wore a suit and tie and was intent on paperwork at his desk. He stood and waved a welcome.

"Are you doing okay? I read about your garage fire in *The Colonel.*"

"They're still trying to figure out what happened. No one was hurt, and that's the important thing."

He motioned toward a chair. "I'm glad you stopped by." He plucked a piece of paper off the credenza behind him, sat down at his desk, and passed it to her. "Here's the estimate of those coins from Suzanne's lockbox."

It revealed surprising values. She'd figured they were worth a few hundred dollars, but not thousands. "Is this correct?"

"It is, according to the expert. There were several Civil War-era coins, and one gold piece was from the nineteenth century. It's a collector's item."

"Were these coins of sentimental value? I don't know what to do with them."

He thought for a moment, absently brushing his mustache with a finger. "I don't remember Suzanne saying anything about them. I don't recall your aunt and uncle ever buying any coins. They certainly weren't collectors."

"I don't remember any discussions about coins, either," Liesl said. "Well, right now, I'll just hold them. Does the dealer have them?"

Mr. Barnaby shook his head. "He gave them back to me, and I've put them in the safe." He rose. "Let me get them."

She waved him back to his seat. "No, there's no point in you giving them to me right now. I found the missing lockbox key, so we'll have to meet with Mr. Van de Berg and make an inventory of its contents. Why don't you just give them to me then? I have more errands to run, and I'd rather not spend the rest of the day carrying around valuable coins."

He settled back in his chair. "Fine. Care for coffee or a soft drink?"

"Coffee would be great. There's a bit of bank business I'd like to discuss."

His eyebrows rose slightly in surprise. "My pleasure." He went to get their drinks and returned with two steaming cups on a tray.

She relished the smell of java on this November morning. "Thank you."

He took a sip of coffee. "I'm glad you found that last key. I was afraid if Van de Berg lost it, it wouldn't see the light of day again. Have you told him you found it?"

"No. But I have a meeting scheduled with him later today.

Should we call him now or have him call you when I'm at his office?"

"Let's do it now." He dialed the office number, then turned to Liesl. "Do you have the key with you?"

"I do."

He smiled. After talking a moment, he hung up. "He said you'll both come here to the bank when you finish your business at his office today."

"Excellent. I'm excited to see what may be in that last box."

"She was in it recently, so it may be things you need."

Liesl nodded. "The other day, I got the impression you're not overly fond of Mr. Van de Berg."

He flushed red and frowned. "I apologize for being so obvious. I'm a businessman, and my personal feelings should not be apparent to customers."

She hadn't expected this reaction. "Mr. Barnaby, I'm the one who should apologize. I didn't mean to offend you."

He waved away her apology, but she continued. "It's not that your feelings are obvious. It's because I know you so well. You've been a trusted friend and advisor for years, always kind. In the vault the other day, I could tell Van de Berg gets under your skin." She shifted in her chair. "See it from my perspective, if you will. With Aunt Suzanne gone, I'm alone now. I have to trust the people handling her estate. He's involved, and I'm not sure I can trust him."

Mr. Barnaby cleared his throat. "Van de Berg aggravates me for various reasons. The most annoying is, he's always late, rushing away to be late to something else, and poorly organized during the short time he's around. I've never seen him in court, but I've been told he has the same problems there. That said, I've never known or heard about any illegal or immoral behavior."

"You are aware there are considerable assets involved with Aunt Suzanne's estate?"

He nodded. "Yes. As your banker, as well as a family friend, I have no reason to assume your association with Van de Berg would be a problem. He's been a trusted man in this town for generations. As for your inheritance, your aunt and uncle preferred to keep their assets quiet. To ensure this, I've handled all of their bank business personally. I believe Van de Berg has been a party to the extent of their assets for many years, and I don't believe he's leaked any of that knowledge."

"I'd like you to continue the privacy about my business. I've been to the St. Louis advisers and educated in the estate's value. Aunt Suzanne and Uncle Max never told me about it, so it was a surprise."

His brown eyes became liquid. "It was a matter of honor to assist them when they were customers, and I promise to continue my best efforts." He gazed out the window. "There is another, entirely different reason I dislike Van de Berg. Nothing to do with business. A personal reason."

She waited for him to explain, but he remained facing the window. With that, she gave up the hunt for more specific information. "Thank you, Mr. Barnaby. It's an honor to have your help. Now, what do I owe you for this appraisal?"

He turned back to her and relaxed at the change of subject. "Nothing. I told the dealer to send the bill to Van de Berg. He'll pay it out of estate expenses."

"That's great. Thanks." After another sip of coffee, she switched to the real reason for her visit. "I'm searching for a housekeeper. I'd like to open a special account with a debit card. That way, the person I hire can use it to buy groceries and household items without having to come to me for money."

"Of course. Delighted to help you." Several minutes later,

they'd completed the paperwork for the household account. He excused himself and returned with a new debit card for her.

"For years, I tried to convince Suzanne she needed help to take care of the house. It is entirely too much for one person to handle. I worried she'd hurt herself by cleaning it. She had a handyman to help with the big jobs, but no matter what I told her about getting some inside help, she'd brush off the suggestion. I'm delighted you're doing what she should have done a long time ago."

"I told her the same thing for years. I'm not the cooking or domestic goddess type she was, so unless I want to be surrounded by dust balls and microwavable food, help is required."

"Do you have someone in mind? I have a woman who cleans my house once a week and does a marvelous job. She might consider working for you or know someone who would be interested."

"I'd love that information."

With the housekeeper's contact details in hand, she stood to leave then sat down again. "One more thing. I believe Aunt Suzanne spoke to you the day before she got sick."

He paused. "It was early that week. I can't tell you exactly what day it was."

"Did she appear sick when she was here?"

"No. She was upset with the business we discussed, but not ill." He held up his hands. "Please don't let me give you the wrong impression. It was not her own business that upset her."

"It was the Butterfly House business, wasn't it?"

He shifted in his chair. "I'm not free to discuss the nature of the business, but I'm surprised you know about this. Did she tell you?"

"In a roundabout way, yes. Did she say who was responsible for the problem?"

"No. She requested any paperwork I could supply. She'd been the treasurer several years before, and her name was still on their account. Nothing prevented me from providing her with the records she wanted." He shook his head. "She was quite distressed with what I copied for her."

"So, you gave her copies? A lot?"

"Yes, at least twenty pages of various account records. I'm afraid I can't get into the specifics."

"Has anyone else asked for these records?"

"Not to my knowledge. If someone made such a request to one of my employees, they would have mentioned it, but I'll check."

"I've been told that Van de Berg is the treasurer."

Barnaby shrugged. "I don't know what office he holds, if any. But legally, I can't discuss the finances with you." He studied her face for a moment. "What's happened?"

"My garage fire might have been random, but it could be related to the problem Aunt Suzanne was exploring."

He stiffened. "Are you okay? I hope this hasn't caused you any concern."

"Well, it's nothing I can't handle." She stood to leave. "As always, Mr. Barnaby, it's been a pleasure."

Chapter Thirty-Seven

Liesl

In Houston, Liesl had slogged for miles in blazing heat and humidity from distant parking lots. The relative ease of parking along Mexico's streets was one of the first things she'd missed. What she *didn't* miss from Mexico was parallel parking.

She held her breath, wedging her rental car into an empty slot bracketed by a massive, mud-splattered pickup truck and a gleaming white Lexus. Her success left her steps from Gretchen's office.

Inside, a young receptionist wearing too much makeup announced her arrival. Gretchen appeared, looking like a redheaded Taylor Swift with flowing curls surrounding her smiling face.

"So good to see you," she said. "Let's grab a soft drink before we get down to business."

In a small kitchen where the smell of popcorn hung in the air, Gretchen retrieved two glasses from a cabinet and dug in the freezer for ice. "So tell me about the cause of your garage fire."

"The fire department hasn't filled me in yet."

Gretchen grabbed two soft drink cans. "Patience. Such an ugly word. There's not an ounce of patience between the two of us. Must be a family trait."

They shared a grin.

"What about Mr. Handsome Guy from the other night? Have you seen him since?"

"Nope. Nothing. I thought we had a great time, but maybe I fooled myself."

"Not according to what I saw. He looked interested and ... charmed to use an ancient word. He seemed really into you."

Liesl shrugged. "I've heard nothing from him."

She frowned. "His loss."

In Gretchen's office, she waved her arms toward the desk and the credenza stacked with various files and papers "Sorry for the mess."

"I'm glad you could see me." Liesl fished in her purse for a copy of the will. "You said you needed this?"

"Yes. And you need to sign a contract of employment."

Gretchen pushed the document and a pen toward her. It was short and to the point. Liesl signed it, and then Gretchen added her signature.

"We're official now. I'll make you a copy, and we'll begin." She pointed to a table surrounded by chairs in the room's corner. "Let's sit where we can spread out."

Liesl grabbed their drinks and moved them to the table. Gretchen returned with the copies and a large manila folder.

"I'll walk through this, as Aunt Suzanne did to me. How she initially discovered that the Butterfly House records were a problem, I can't explain."

Gretchen related how Aunt Suzanne had visited all the

merchants. She told Liesl about the cash refunds and the financial documents from the bank. Everything as it was in the journal.

Gretchen pulled the contents from the folder. "Some of my clients are almost accountants themselves. Others, not so much."

Liesl squirmed and felt the need to confess. "I'm one of the 'not so much.' More of a remedial math kind of girl."

Gretchen handed her a bank statement. "This is a copy of the checking account activity for October. When Aunt Suzanne went to the bank, it was the most recent information available."

Liesl reviewed the numbers and saw immediately that debits were much higher than deposits. The second page listed various checks, reducing the balance by over $7,500. Pages three and four were copies of the fronts of the checks, most written to local businesses, the signature line illegible. "That's a lot of money in one month."

Gretchen nodded. "Aunt Suzanne said she'd gone to nearly every business where transactions occurred. Most purchases were returned for a cash reimbursement."

"There were no records of the cash being re-deposited?"

"No." Gretchen pushed curls from her forehead. "Aunt Suzanne brought this to me after hours. Cameron was at a Jaycees meeting that night, so I stayed to do paperwork. She called my cell phone and said she had a financial problem. I had her meet me here."

"So, no one else knew about the meeting."

"Right. After we discussed it a bit, I promised to review it and get back to her. She signed a client agreement, left the bank information, and explained that the recent purchases were returned for cash." Her voice broke, but she continued. "The next time I saw her was at the hospital. She was so sick, I didn't bring up this issue. What exactly did she tell you?"

Truth time. Liesl took a sip of her drink, then looked Gretchen in her eyes. "This is going to sound strange, so I apologize upfront. I learned about this situation from Aunt Suzanne's last journal entry, not directly from her."

Gretchen started to speak. Liesl brought up her hand to stop any thought of interruption. "Remember all of those date books and journals she kept around the house?"

"Yes."

"She had bank boxes filled with them. Her most recent journal was in the house, and the last two entries concerned the Butterfly House mess. Nothing specific, just that a problem surfaced after their meeting. Then she went to the bank. She was still allowed access to their bank account, so Mr. Barnaby gave her what she requested."

Gretchen listened, her lips pressed in a thin line.

"Armed with the bank information," Liesl went on, "she went to several businesses and verified purchased items returned for cash. I didn't know of your involvement until we talked in the restroom at D'Angelo's."

Gretchen blew out a breath of air. "I shouldn't have said anything."

Liesl patted her hand. "It made perfect sense that Aunt Suzanne came running to a favorite great-niece who happens to be an accountant. You didn't tell me about it, I guessed. With her death, it was also reasonable for you to mention you had outstanding business with Aunt Suzanne. This search was important to her and might develop into a criminal matter. Now that we're knee-deep in it, shouldn't we continue?"

Gretchen nodded and waved her hand over the paperwork. "There's something terribly wrong here."

"Since Aunt Suzanne died, I've had two instances of vandalism plus the garage fire," Liesl said flatly.

"Why on earth would someone do those things?"

"Kurt said whoever did it was angry."

"Kurt? You're speaking to Kurt again?"

"He's helped me with the vandalism and fire. When I mentioned this problem, he asked to be informed if it was a criminal matter. If it's worthy of an investigation, he'll act on it."

"Good, considering he's able to investigate. It's not a complicated Ponzi scheme like what Bernie Madoff created, it's a simple theft."

"If this thief was stealing money from the Butterfly House and felt someone was trying to close the treasure trove, they'd be mad. Whoever burned Aunt Suzanne's coat went into the house to steal it—possibly got in with a key because I'm sure I locked the house. They might have searched for this paperwork, come up empty because you had it, and expressed their rage with fire. It's a reasonable explanation. As far as the garage, I'd guess they're still enraged over the circumstances."

"That's frightening. Are you okay in that big house alone?"

"I've installed an alarm system. With all the high-tech gadgets, I'm technically not alone anymore."

"Good. Call if you need anything or want to stay with me." Gretchen tapped the papers. "Whoever is responsible should go to jail. Will Kurt pursue criminal charges?"

"We're supposed to talk about it. He'd like copies, if you think something criminal has happened."

"I'm happy to copy it, as long as you're the one giving it to law enforcement." She gathered another set of papers. "These are annual financial statements of the Butterfly House board meetings from last year, back to six years ago. As you well know, our aunt was one organized little lady. She didn't throw anything away."

Liesl laughed. "I know. There's a houseful of stuff to go through."

"When she was treasurer, she said they had a checking account, several long-term certificates of deposit, a regular savings account, and a few stocks. Their major assets are the house and surrounding property. Their financial investments are to keep it standing because they don't make enough on donations to cover upkeep. When Aunt Suzanne became the vice president, she gave all the treasurer documents to the incoming treasurer but saved the annual board reports in her own records."

"Who was the incoming treasurer then?"

"Doreen Martin."

Liesl's stomach lurched. "Please tell me Doreen had nothing to do with this. I adore her."

Gretchen shook her head. "No, everything was fine until about two years ago." She shuffled through the board reports, found something, and handed it to Liesl. "Doreen's reports to the board regarding funds are accurate when compared to the older bank statements. They didn't spend much when she was treasurer."

Liesl reviewed the papers. "About a week ago, Doreen told me she resigned from the board because she was tired of fighting over money with Patricia Sizemore."

"Interesting. Because Mrs. Sizemore became the treasurer after Doreen." Gretchen handed over more paperwork. "Look at the recent annual reports. The minutes are vague, but they list some of the larger purchases and improvements allowed. Spending began in earnest when Mrs. Sizemore was treasurer."

The board allowed a new roof, several new furniture purchases, and curtains for various rooms the previous year.

In the current year, they approved a new carpet and some repairs. Liesl looked at Gretchen. "Was this work actually done?"

She shrugged. "No idea. I haven't been inside Butterfly House. It would be good to verify these things. Like a physical audit. But since it's a women's shelter, the public is not welcome."

"We can't ask anyone on the board to verify it, in case that person turns out to be our thief," Liesl mused. "Maybe Kurt can get in."

"A female officer would be better for a women's shelter."

"I'll talk to Kurt about that."

Gretchen sat back in her chair. "Looking inside could help us. Aunt Suzanne's investigation related to recent, mostly small purchases. Purchases and returns for cash are a current problem. If the police verify what's been done in the last two years, it would show us when it started."

"Aunt Suzanne didn't give you any idea who was responsible?"

"No. Just that she was devastated. You're the one who told me Van de Berg was the current treasurer. After you said that, I looked through the board reports again. There was no change from Mrs. Sizemore to anyone else. We're missing the latest board report, but it may not be out yet. It's possible Van de Berg became the treasurer in the final meeting Aunt Suzanne attended."

"So, either Mrs. Sizemore or Mr. Van de Berg is our thief?"

Gretchen nodded. "I'd say yes. Doreen had stepped down before the money disappeared. We don't know when the last change of treasurer occurred at the bank. Until we do, both remain suspects."

"Mrs. Sizemore told me Mr. Van de Berg was treasurer when she pressured me to rush Aunt Suzanne's donation. Sort of like, 'He's the treasurer, and he's handling her estate, so what's the hold-up?' kind of thing."

"Do everything you can to keep that donation from happening until we have answers." Gretchen waved toward the papers on the table. "Until the large purchases are verified, we're grasping at straws to know the size of the embezzlement." She flicked through some papers and pulled one. "Here's the paperwork on their certificates of deposits. They were cashed out about six months ago and put in the checking account. They were valued at over fifteen thousand each. The most recent checking account statement shows about two thousand remained in the account."

"Could they have moved the money to a different bank?"

"It's possible. If so, there should be a notation in the minutes about the new bank account or cashing the CDs. I didn't find one. I believe it's all been spent. You can see the accounts draining month by month." She pointed to the recent statements. "All there in black and white. No payments to a different account."

"Why didn't the board stop it?"

"The best I can tell, the board didn't know. Whether anyone audited the books against the treasurer's reports is unknown. They could have caught the scent of a problem, if they'd audited regularly."

"Aren't boards supposed to do stuff like that?"

"At least annually." Gretchen flung her hands skyward. "They may have fallen into a relaxed attitude. No organization should be lackadaisical about money. Yet, many are."

"Anyone else know about this? Here at the office, I mean."

"Not the staff. I mentioned to Cameron that Aunt Suzanne brought me a project, but it would have been unprofessional to talk specifics."

"Good. Keep it that way. If you'll make a copy of all this for me, I'll give it to Kurt, and he can review."

Gretchen gathered the papers off the table. "It's the right thing to do. I'll put all of it on a zip drive for him too." She rose and patted Liesl on the shoulder. "Sorry to add to your burdens."

She returned a few minutes later with hard copies and a zip drive for Kurt. "Let me know what he says. I hope we're wrong."

"Doubtful."

"We can always hope, can't we?"

"How much do I owe you?" Liesl asked.

She smiled. "With the family discount, my services will cost you a steak dinner."

Liesl hugged her. "A bargain."

Outside, temperatures were low enough that remnants of snow and ice crunched beneath her boots. As she approached her rental car, the gleaming white Lexus was still parked in front of it. That Lexus was Mrs. Sizemore's car. With a glance around, Liesl spotted her leaving Mr. Van de Berg's office.

Liesl didn't want another encounter with Mrs. Sizemore. Her face would give away too much if she was the Butterfly House thief. Liesl pulled her coat up around her shoulders and jumped into the driver's seat. Thank goodness she was in an unrecognizable rental car.

Before either Mrs. Sizemore or Mr. Van de Berg realized they were suspects in the Butterfly House embezzlement, she needed to go over this financial information with Nicole and Kurt. Among the three of them, they had to figure out who did this before her face gave it away.

Chapter Thirty-Eight

Suzanne
April 16, 1961

When Myron returned to pick up Suzanne at the Bauers' house, he asked why she'd wanted to go.

"Now you're curious? But not when I wanted you to take me? I don't understand you."

He grinned. "Blame my lack of curiosity on an obsession with a chocolate malt. Now that I've polished one off, tell me what's going on."

She eyed him, then trusted him with the truth. "Joey bikes all over this town, and he sees and remembers everything. I asked him questions about the night Winnie died."

"The police considered him a suspect for a time."

She nodded. "He was, but he had an alibi. An alibi provided by people outside of his family."

"Did he see anything?"

"No." Technically, Joey didn't see anything, he heard something. Myron didn't need to know all the details.

"Actually, I don't remember seeing you when all the screaming started. Where were you?"

An embarrassed look crossed his face. "I was in a dark corner with a girl, and no, I'm not saying which one."

"When was the last time you saw Edgar?"

"I don't know. Why?"

"The police quizzed me about him. I believe he's their prime suspect. Have you seen him since the funeral?"

"No," Myron sighed. "He's finishing school from home, after what happened. I figured he needed some time to himself. I should go see him. He's got to be having a tough time."

"Yes, you should see him. You want me to come with you?"

He frowned. "I doubt he'd appreciate Winnie's best friend visiting."

"You're right. I didn't think about that."

He turned the corner toward their road and cleared his throat. "I've been meaning to apologize. I'm sorry about the fight with Mother about taking you to the party. To make amends, I'll drive you wherever you want to go, whenever you want to do it. No questions asked."

She evaluated his offer with suspicion. "What's this about?"

"It could have been you at that party." He shifted in his seat. "I'll deny I ever said this, but I love you and couldn't cope if something happened to you."

She chuckled. "I love you too, Dogface."

He grinned at the use of her childhood nickname for him, and their sappy endearment time ended.

* * *

Edgar. The only interview Suzanne had left. She'd give him some time and then try to find him. He hadn't been to their house since the funeral.

She organized her collection of clues. She'd typed notes from her interviews, including what she'd written in her notebook and details from the conversations. These pages landed in an expandable file folder from her father's desk.

Newspaper articles went into a shoebox until she started a scrapbook of clippings, placing them in order of the date reported. *The Colonel's* reporters covered a tremendous amount of specifics, even though law enforcement didn't offer details. Reporters interviewed people soon after the police walked out their door. With freedom of the press, law enforcement couldn't stop the information from going public.

The articles related the use of tracking dogs with inconclusive results. Travelers using buses and trains had been detained and questioned, to no avail. Roadblocks of the major roads leading out of town found no strangers or odd hitchhikers. An early theory had been that a vagabond caught Winnie alone and vulnerable, then killed her. This speculation was dropped when no vagrant was located.

Because local law enforcement didn't have experience with murder investigations, state police officers were called in to advise and test evidence. Suzanne surmised the state police was the organization associated with Agent La Rue. No newspaper report specifically mentioned him. He was like a ghost investigator.

When she added the newspaper photos of the police investigating outside Winnie's house to her scrapbook, she averted her eyes. She had taken her own pictures of Winnie's house and the area of her murder when her mother dropped off a pie. Forced to stay outside because seeing her might upset

Winnie's parents, Suzanne had taken the opportunity to photograph the murder scene.

It was hard to return to the place of her worst nightmare. Yet, spring was painting its magic colors in the sad location. Instead of a snow-filled yard with the ominous stack of firewood, the area was now void of firewood and filled with signs of God's promise of new life. When she completed taking her pictures, she said a prayer for Winnie, and her spirit felt lighter.

Later that night, Max asked her out for a date. They'd planned for him to ask in front of her parents, so they were "on the spot" about the matter. Sadly, it wasn't a brilliant plan.

Her mother's face burned bright red when he asked if they would allow him to take Suzanne to dinner. Her dad shuffled in his chair, glancing back and forth from her mother's scarlet face to Suzanne's pleading one, until he gave his consent.

Suzanne hugged her father and nodded to her mother, who averted her eyes. Max all but ran out the door after saying good night.

The minute he was gone, her mother began to rant. "Really, Thomas. I can't believe you consented to this."

Her father pierced her mother with a look. "You may not want to face the truth, but it's high time your daughter started dating. A fine young man has asked her out, and I wasn't about to deny him."

Father standing up to Mother was a surprise.

"Of course she's old enough to date," Mother said. "That's not what I'm worried about. She needs to date someone with a future. Someone with class and polish."

Suzanne turned on her mother. "Say it, Mother. He's not good enough for me because he hasn't been to college? Or because he doesn't come from money?"

Her mother's lips became a thin line. "Twenty years ago,

we fought the second of two World Wars because of the Germans. Now you want to date one?"

Suzanne stared, wounded by her prejudice. "His father was born in the United States a lot longer than twenty years ago. That makes his family Americans long before the war."

"What's next? Maybe you'd like to date a Japanese? They bombed us in a sneak attack at Pearl Harbor. Another great choice to consider for a life partner."

Suzanne looked at her father for support, but he remained mute. She turned again to her mother. "The Italians were part of the Axis during the war. Do we now quit dining at the D'Angelo family restaurant because of their Italian heritage?"

"Patronizing a restaurant differs from dating someone."

"This is crazy! The war ended. Times have moved on. Max wasn't involved in the war, and his father fought in the war. For the United States."

Her mother studied her hands.

Suzanne stood. "How can you call yourself a Christian when you forget all of your Christian teachings when it suits your purposes?" She exited the room with as much dignity as she could muster.

* * *

A big house has its advantages when you want to avoid someone. Suzanne stayed out of her mother's way after the confrontation. Once Myron came home, she knocked on his door and related the ugly details.

He seemed equally shocked at their mother's behavior. "I can't believe she thinks that."

"I didn't know she was prejudiced against Germans. Half of this state is of German heritage. Probably half of the citizens of this town."

Myron shook his head. "That's just her excuse. Her true prejudice is against his bank balance. She thinks because he's a farmer, he doesn't have any money."

She pondered this. Grandmummy had raised their mother to be a snob. It was a deep part of the English class system in which she'd been raised. Grandmummy's family didn't have a title, but they'd had money. "At least Grandmummy would have been honest about his lack of money, if that's Mother's real objection."

"Trust me, it is." He patted her shoulder. "Dad taking a stand against Mother is a miracle."

"You're right. I owe him. But I'm so furious with Mother. I don't know when I'll get over it."

"No rush. She needs to think about this. It's not a Christian way to act."

"Since you're on my side tonight, will you take Zest out to do her business? I don't want to bump into Mother."

He winked at her. "Now you owe both me and Dad."

* * *

When Suzanne came down the stairs after her father announced Max's arrival, Max grinned up at her. His reaction gave her an unexpected feeling of confidence.

He held out his hand when she reached the bottom step. "You look so pretty."

She waved at the dress. "Mother knows how to shop. You look nice, too, Mr. Schrader."

Max had dressed up for this night. He looked older, somehow, in a suit and tie. "Farmers can go shopping too." He cleared his throat. "Especially if they have two older sisters to go with them."

His admission made her laugh. She glanced at her father

but couldn't interpret the look on his face. He seemed happy and sad, all rolled into one.

"I'll have her home before eleven, sir."

Her father nodded. "Fine, fine. Have fun."

Max smiled down at her. "Shall we?"

She nodded and walked toward her coat hanging by the door. Max helped her shrug into it, and this simple act of manners made her feel like a proper lady. It promised to be a wonderful night.

Chapter Thirty-Nine

Suzanne
April 29, 1961

When Doreen called to invite Suzanne out to Woolworth's for an afternoon treat with her mother driving, she jumped to accept. Suzanne's heart was happy for the first time in a long time. Last night, her date with Max had been magical. Now she left the house and could enjoy the sun, which glowed with a warmth promising spring had arrived.

At the store, the aroma of hamburgers filled the air. Stools at the counter held a full row of people eating and drinking. Mrs. Winston eyed the crowd and turned to them. "You girls wait here for a seat. I'll be back in a minute. I'll use this time to get some things."

Doreen turned to Suzanne. "Good. I wanted to talk to you in private."

"What's new?"

"I've sent in the application to be a counselor at Camp Pin Oak."

"What did your mother say about it?"

Doreen reached up and began twirling a curl. "I haven't told her yet."

Suzanne frowned. "Why not?"

"I mean, what's the point of upsetting her if I don't get a job? I'd rather she not even know. If they hire me, then I can talk to her about it."

"My mother would be furious if I applied for a job without her permission."

"If I use the excuse of making money and her being able to save a little money by not having to feed me for almost three months, she'll forgive me for doing it this way."

Suzanne shrugged. "Well—" Someone entering the store caught her attention. It was a younger guy, lanky like Edgar. Once he made his way inside, she was certain it *was* Edgar.

Doreen squeaked. "Oh, look."

"Doreen, hush. I see him." A few people in the store turned to see who entered. Some people showed no reaction, others displayed anger or disgust. The less-than-pleasant reactions angered Suzanne. "Let's go say hello. Some people are being uncharitable."

Another guy pushed through the door behind Edgar. Myron. After witnessing those reactions, Suzanne was relieved that Edgar wasn't alone.

When the girls approached, something flickered through Edgar's face. Sadness? Surprise?

Suzanne reached him first and smiled. "It's been so long since I've seen you. I hope you're doing as well as circumstances allow."

He nodded, and a partial smile flashed. "Good to see you, Suzanne." He glanced at Doreen. "How are you ladies doing?"

Doreen reached out and patted his arm. "Hello, Edgar. I hope the police haven't been giving you a hard time."

He shrugged. "They've dropped me as a suspect. Now I'm trying to get back to a somewhat normal life."

"Isn't that good news?"

He nodded, yet sadness crossed his face.

An uncomfortable silence occurred, so Suzanne changed the subject. "How's Billy? He doing okay?"

"Mom and I were worried about him, but he's fine. He saw none of the tragedy. Being a little kid, his biggest problem has been improving his baseball skills."

Suzanne nodded. "Good."

Myron pointed toward the counter area. "Some seats opened up. Are you getting something at the grill?"

"Yes, thanks," Suzanne replied. "Come on, Doreen. Let's grab those stools before we lose them to someone else." She turned to Edgar. "Come to the house some time and visit Zest, if you'd like. Mother let me take her home."

Edgar nodded. "Take care of her."

Doreen hesitated, then waved to Edgar.

At the counter, they sat down and requested vanilla phosphates and an order of French fries to share.

Doreen whispered, "Edgar looks fine, doesn't he?"

"Sad, but better than I'd imagined," Suzanne whispered back.

"Think he'll come back to school now that the fuzz have stopped questioning him?"

"I doubt it. Too many memories for him there. He's still heartbroken."

"I suppose so." Doreen sighed. "Now, tell me all the details about your date last night."

* * *

Later that night, someone knocked on Suzanne's bedroom door.

She was lying in bed reading a recent novel, *To Kill a Mockingbird*, which was getting more exciting with every turn of the page. "Come in." She expected it to be her mother, so when Myron popped his head around the door, she smiled.

He saw her book and made a mock surprised face. "What? Not studying calculus?"

She chuckled. "Saving it for next year."

"Do you like the book?"

"It starts off a tad slow, but now it's almost impossible to put down. I really like the relationship between the kids. I remember when you and I were as inseparable as Scout and her brother."

"It's possible for siblings to grow up and become adult friends."

"You're right." She placed her bookmark between the pages and patted the bed. "Come sit. I'm glad you spent time with Edgar today."

He strolled over and collapsed across the length of the bed. She scrambled to make room for him.

"We had a pretty good time together. However, it's odd to see some of the looks people give him."

She shuddered. "That's terrible. I've been so worried about him. It never dawned on me that people would be so mean."

"Everywhere we went today, there a few ugly glances."

"The police were rough on me about him, so I can only imagine how they treated him. Poor guy."

"It's over for him now. The newspaper should soon print that he's no longer a suspect. Edgar's mother went there to insist they report it because of how people have treated him."

"Did he say where he was when Winnie was killed?"

Myron pulled upright, and his face turned red. "It's not your job to know what he was doing. You leave that to the cops."

"Don't flip your wig, I just wondered."

"They've cleared him from the investigation. That's all you need to know. I will not share the details he shared with me. It's none of your business. What should concern you is that there's still a killer out there." He rose and moved toward the door, then turned back to her. "Leave it alone. Your life might depend on it."

Chapter Forty

Liesl
November 15

Liesl's luck had not changed. Mrs. Sizemore spotted her scrunched in the car and knocked on the driver's window of Liesl's car. Liesl feigned surprise and hopped out of her rental.

"Mrs. Sizemore. How are you doing today?"

She frowned. "Feeling old. I just left Bill's office after revamping my will and charitable bequests. With Suzanne's sudden death, it was time to update things."

"I understand that."

"As president of several charities, I've spent an abundance of money updating them inside and out. Once I'm gone, I've set it up so they receive from my estate an equal amount of money I directed be spent from their assets for those improvements. It's time for me to give back. Like Suzanne did."

"That's a nice thing to do. I'm headed to see Mr. Van de Berg right now myself. More estate business."

Mrs. Sizemore scrutinized her. "Are you doing all right? We should lunch one day soon."

"Yes, let's do that."

They parted. Liesl walked away surprised by Mrs. Sizemore's warmth and believing she had been sincere about giving back. She doubted the woman was a thief or a killer.

Once face-to-face with Mr. Van de Berg, Liesl tried to keep her expression neutral as she announced, "I've learned a lot about Aunt Suzanne's financial situation since I was last here."

He stopped shuffling papers. "Really?"

"Yes. I met with some of her St. Louis advisers, and that clarified many things, including why she and Uncle Max kept me in the dark."

He cocked his head. "I'm delighted to hear that. She should have told you, herself, of her net worth. You understand?"

"I do. And I understand why you were loath to tell me yourself. However, the advisers brought a new perspective on why she raised me without that knowledge."

"Excellent. Any questions for me before we move on with today's items?"

"Just one. You mentioned one of her bequests was for the Butterfly House. Both Mrs. Sizemore and Doreen Martin were aware of Aunt Suzanne's plans for such a donation. Do you know why she mentioned it to them?"

He frowned. "She announced the bequest years ago. During a board meeting. We were discussing an estate bequest by one of our long-time supporters. Your aunt mentioned she'd made a donation in her will. Of course, I already knew about it. I wasn't surprised when she announced it. The board members were all her close friends. Is there a problem?"

She shook her head. "No, but Mrs. Sizemore has pressured me to make the bequest quickly. Almost as if the Butterfly House needs it. Do you know anything about that?"

"I've filed the estate paperwork and should be able to start the process of your aunt's bequest today, if you'd like. Most of her assets aren't liquid, so I'll need to request the sale of some stock to facilitate the payment. Then I'll write the check to the Butterfly House."

"No. Don't pay anything now. Not until you absolutely have to do it. Understand?"

"Not really, but it's your call."

"Aren't you the treasurer of Butterfly House?"

He blinked at her in surprise. "Well, yes, they voted me as treasurer at the last meeting. I haven't signed any paperwork to make those changes yet. Patricia is still the acting treasurer until we get everything transferred. With your aunt's passing, neither one of us had the heart to proceed."

He pulled off his glasses, plucked a handkerchief from his suit pocket, and cleaned them. "Are you aware your aunt purchased the Whitcomb house and created the charity called The Butterfly House Foundation, so she could donate the house to the foundation?"

She stared at him. "No."

He frowned. "Another example of your aunt keeping you in the dark."

"Why'd she buy the house in the first place?"

"It was my suggestion, actually. The property had become a sideshow for the curious. Like a circus. People, teenagers mostly, were making it a place of pilgrimage. Like a 'coming of age' spot to show their bravery or dwell on the gore." He replaced his glasses and tucked away the handkerchief.

This made her skin crawl. "That's horrible."

"It was. Your aunt was fit to be tied when she heard about it. She came marching into this very office. Mind you, I had a client in here. She insisted she speak to me 'on a matter of great urgency.'

So I apologized to my client, and we had a consultation in the hall that scorched my skin. She was fuming. I begged her to give me a night to develop a solution. She stomped off, still furious."

As awful as his description was, she couldn't help but chuckle. On the rare occasions when Aunt Suzanne lost her temper, she was like a flamethrower, incinerating everyone and everything in her path. "Did you arrive at a solution that satisfied her?"

"Not immediately, but I'm still alive, aren't I? I'd never seen her so angry. I tossed and turned all night until it came to me. If she bought the house, she could build a fence around it and keep people off the grounds. They'd still drive by, but not track through the scene of the crime."

"She didn't like that idea?"

"It wasn't enough. She's the one who made it a home for women and children who needed a fresh start or protection. Your aunt transformed that lemon of a crime scene and made lemonade for those who needed a haven."

"A lot of women and families have benefitted from the Butterfly House."

"After what we experienced the night Winnie died, I never thought something good could come from that house. She made it happen."

Liesl stared at him. "You mean you were *there*?"

"I was. I was a boy. My mother worked nights, and my older brother was dating Winnie. He convinced our mother to let him bring me to the party so he could attend. Otherwise, he'd have to stay at home with me."

She shook her head in disbelief. Why didn't she know this? "Wasn't your brother a suspect?"

He nodded. "Eventually, the police verified his alibi. After that, Edgar couldn't get out of town fast enough. He left for college at the end of summer. Since then, he's only come back to Mexico for a few days."

With a glance at his watch, he stood. "Let's walk to the bank. George will never forgive me if I cause us to be late for our appointment."

* * *

When they'd wrapped up at the bank, and she was on her way home, Liesl spotted a missed call from Kurt.

"You rang, sir?"

"I have information."

"Good. I have plenty for you too. You busy tonight?"

"Not really."

"My productive day included a meeting with Gretchen, and she confirmed a serious financial problem with the books for Butterfly House. Then we opened the last lockbox at the bank."

"What was there?"

"I think you call it a murder book. It's a three-inch deep, three-ring binder full of information about Winnie's murder."

He paused, then exclaimed, "Are you kidding me?"

"I'm talking pictures, diagrams and interview statements."

"Wow. I can't believe it."

"With Mr. Van de Berg there, I rushed the book into a shopping bag I'd brought. I didn't want him to figure out what it was. I told him it was a scrapbook."

"Why keep that from him?"

"He told me today that he was *there* the night of Winnie's murder."

Silence. Kurt was trying to do the math, so she helped him. "He was eight years old. Couldn't possibly be a suspect."

"But he's a witness. I need to take his statement."

"Does that mean you got the case reopened?"

"I'll explain tonight."

She clenched her teeth. Patience. Wished she had some. "What kind of food do you want for an evening session at my house?"

"Burgers or pizza."

"Got it. I'll call Nicole."

"What time do you want us?"

"Give me thirty minutes to pick up food."

"I haven't left work, and I need to get Ross. It'll be more like forty-five minutes."

"Even better."

When she explained the situation to Nicole, her friend jumped on the dinner idea. Liesl let her choose the food, and she went with burgers.

"See you in thirty. If I'm not there, let yourself in."

"Not a chance, sister," Nicole said. "You have a new alarm system."

"I forgot. We don't need you setting off the alarm. The authorities would freak out, after the fire last weekend."

"Exactly. If I beat you, I'll wait patiently in the car."

At the house, crime scene tape still encircled the garage. It was a depressing sight. The status of the cars inside and the overall structure remained a mystery. Kurt had said these things take time. He wasn't lying.

Nicole arrived and joined her on the front porch, where Liesl gave her a short course on the house alarm. Nicole took the food inside while Liesl grabbed the sack with the murder book, two journals, and the expensive gold coins she'd picked up on her second trip to Mr. Barnaby's office.

Liesl put the murder book and journals on the dining-room table but hid the coins in an old pair of boots in her closet. They were safe there until she figured out what to do with them.

Nicole bypassed the stacks of papers on the dining room table and suggested they eat in the kitchen. While she arranged the aromatic treasures, her husband Lee arrived with Claudia in tow.

Claudia was younger than Ross, but mature for a five-year-old. She was beautiful. She'd inherited Lee's enormous eyes and her mother's intelligence and outspokenness. Liesl couldn't get enough of her and her big hugs.

Like many small-town married couples, Nicole and Lee had dated during high school. Liesl had spent a lot of time pushing Nicole to consider a date with one tall, good-looking guy in a class two years ahead of them. Lee was a standout athlete with huge brown eyes and a soft-spoken demeanor. Eventually, Nicole realized he was perfect for her.

Liesl gave Lee a hug. "Thank you for letting me borrow your wife repeatedly. I've been monopolizing her time."

Lee took her hands in his. "She's your best friend, and you need her. I'm glad she can help you deal with everything. Now, tell her you're moving home, and she'll be thrilled."

She winked at him. "I'm almost there."

"Good." Then he moved off to kiss his wife.

Chapter Forty-One

Suzanne
June 4, 1961

It was a breezy day, making the summer temperature pleasant at the Schrader farmland. Max labored to repair the siding of an outbuilding for the cattle. Suzanne watched him from her perch on the fence. The only thing warmer than this day were the feelings she experienced being with Max.

She eyed him as he hammered nails into the replacement siding harder than seemed necessary.

"You know I don't want to go," she said.

The hammering continued. The bellow of a nearby steer added to the mix.

She sighed and tried a different tack. "It's only for two months. In that amount of time, you might forget about me. Why, you might fall for one of the exotic D'Angelo girls. Imagine how exciting that might be for you."

More hammering, still no words.

"Do you honestly think I can stop my mother from making me leave? If you do, you don't appreciate what a force of nature she is."

The hammering stopped. "I know what a force of nature you are," Max said. "You could stop her if you wanted to."

She winced at the accuracy of his statement and slid off the fence. "You're right. You're absolutely right." She paced the fence line. "I want to stay here, but the idea of getting away from all reminders of that night appeals to me. Maybe it's selfish, but in some ways, I think mother's right about getting away from all of this anguish."

He dug for another tool in his nearby toolbox. "She means to separate us."

Suzanne stopped pacing and strode to him. "So what? Are you worried I'll fall for some exotic guy in New York? Maybe a male D'Angelo that lives in Little Italy?"

He turned a cool pair of eyes toward her. "I resent the fact that she thinks I'm not good enough for you. Her plan, this trip, has two purposes. To distract you from me and from Winnie's death."

She studied his green eyes for a moment, one of his best features. There was truth in those eyes. All her life she'd been surrounded by half-truths and white lies spoken "for her own good." She wasn't about to lose a man who told the truth with every word uttered. His character was irresistible.

Articles in *Seventeen* magazine about good qualities in a boyfriend rarely mentioned that a candidate needed to be honest. Max was trustworthy. He made factual pronouncements, even if the truth stung. She wasn't interested in having someone pat her head and dismiss her opinions. She craved a debate partner to wrangle over a situation until they reached a compromise.

Suzanne sighed. "All right, let's address these issues. First, you're not a distraction to me. You're someone I trust, and there are few of you on this planet. Like Patricia. Both of you always tell the truth, even when it hurts. I appreciate there are no deceptions."

He eyed her balefully but said nothing.

"Second, I won't think any less of you after a few weeks apart. I'm also not worried you'll think any less of me. You seem pleased to have a girlfriend who is 'too smart for her own good' and a 'good catch' because of her chances of inheriting some money. Her reflection in the mirror is a bit lacking, but pots of money could make up for that."

He was scowling now. "I like your reflection just fine and couldn't care less about your money."

She nodded. "Duly noted. Now, on to the third issue. My very best friend was bludgeoned to death in her own backyard. My outpouring of grief has failed to lift my crushed heart. I've even questioned my faith. How could God take such a wonderful, kind spirit from us?"

Max took off his cap and wiped his forehead with his sleeve. "I can't answer that. I'm grieving too."

"Her mother and father suffered that incredible loss. A ripping, searing break of their heart, known only to parents who have lost a child."

"I wish we could help them."

"All of us who loved her have a pain that will never go away. Forever part of our lives. Now I understand why my dad won't talk about his service during the war. Too much pain to dredge up."

"So, we all go off in separate ways?"

"Sort of, but not forever. Myron will be here all summer working for Dad, then he'll head off to Westminster College in the fall. I mean, it's less than forty-five minutes away, so he should be home pretty often. Patricia and her mother are meeting Mother and me in New York. We might travel up to Boston and Maine too. Patricia is off to Vassar in the fall. I think she wants to major in finding a rich man to marry."

"Suzanne." Max struggled to hide his grin.

"You know I'm right. Now, where was I? Edgar is supposed to go to the University of Missouri, and Doreen and I have to finish high school."

"So, I'm stuck working the farms, and when I'm not working, left to wonder what you're doing while on your trip?"

She smiled. "Just remember, when I'm gone, I'll be chaperoned by my mother. No way for me to act out."

He chuckled. "You have a point." He hammered another place on the siding, then he sat back on his heels to review his repair. "Looking good, I think."

"Can we discuss the circumstances of that night again? I'd feel better if I could figure out why this happened."

"I wish you'd leave it to the cops."

She ignored his statement. "Night after night, I've wrestled with questions. We knew everyone at that party except for some adults, and the police have eliminated all of them. What have I missed, Max?"

He shrugged. "I don't know."

"It's hard to even comprehend, but the answer is obvious. The answer lies in a place we don't want to go. It was someone who was upstairs dancing, singing, laughing, and eating until they cornered Winnie in the backyard and beat her until she was dead. It was one of us!"

Max picked up his toolbox. "Come here. Let's saddle up some horses and take a ride. Almost any problem in life seems easier when you're in a saddle, out in the fresh air."

She joined him and took his outstretched hand, warm and

rough from his chores. "I don't believe I could stand it if it's one of us."

He threw his arm around her and they walked to the barn with her words echoing in their minds. *It's one of us!*

Chapter Forty-Two

Kurt
November 15

Kurt watched the tall, blond man get out of the truck and make his way to Liesl's porch. Who was this guy? What was he doing here?

"Hurry, Ross. I need to see who this man is." Kurt leaned over to the passenger floorboard and grabbed his briefcase.

Ross scurried out of the car and ran to the porch. He approached the man. "Hi. My name is Ross."

The stranger turned and looked down at Ross. He crouched and stuck out a hand. "Pleased to meet you. I'm Justin."

Kurt made it to the porch as Justin stood up.

"I'm Kurt. Father of this 'shy' boy right here." He cut his eyes to Ross.

"Justin. I've been trying to contact Liesl, but I lost her phone number. Do you know if she's home?"

"She should be. We're having dinner here."

Kurt took pleasure in the confused look Justin gave him. *What business does this guy have with Liesl?*

* * *

Liesl opened the door to find Justin, Kurt, and Ross on the porch. The men were both frowning. Ross ran to her and hugged her leg. She chose to deal with the smiling boy first.

"Hey, buddy. Put your coat and gloves on the couch and run to the kitchen. Miss Nicole has your hamburger ready to go."

"Yay!" He brushed past her and hustled into the house.

Her smile fell flat. What was Justin doing here?

"Liesl." Justin gestured toward the burned structure. "Your garage. I had no idea."

"An arson fire. Still waiting for information about that." She stepped out onto the porch. "You met Kurt?"

Justin nodded. "We introduced ourselves. I've been trying to catch you. Is this a bad time? I stopped by yesterday, but you weren't home. I wanted to explain why I haven't called you."

Kurt stood, briefcase in hand, glancing back and forth from her to Justin, as if their conversation was public entertainment. She shot Kurt the stink eye.

It took a moment, but Kurt got the hint. "I'd better check on Ross." He stomped past her.

As he disappeared into the house, she called, "Put your pistol in the safe place before you sit at the table."

She turned back to Justin. "Sorry. He's a cop. There are two children in there." Now she created a genuine smile. "It's good to see you again."

"I accidentally washed my phone. Washing away your phone number." He grinned and pulled a shiny new phone out of his pocket. "Don't worry. I backed up my new phone on the cloud."

She chuckled. "That sounds exactly like something I'd do."

"So you're not mad? Mad that I didn't call you after our date?"

"Heavens, no. Give me that phone."

He handed it over, and she entered all her information. "You can always reach me through my author's website if you ever feel the need to wash this phone."

He chuckled. "I didn't think about your website. But hey, I've got the cloud now. This won't happen again."

"Good." She returned his phone. "Sorry to have to be short, but there's a dinner meeting here tonight. Can you call me tomorrow?"

"Sure." He leaned in and gave her a quick hug. "Talk to you soon."

When she returned to the dining room, everyone but Kurt was eating. He frowned at her, either jealous or angry or both.

He sulked through dinner while the others ignored him. When dinner was consumed, Lee volunteered to take both kids to his house to let the others work. That allowed Kurt, Nicole, and Liesl to move to the dining room and settle in for investigation updates.

It took almost an hour of discussion about Gretchen's financial information for Kurt to stop sulking. By the time they'd finished, and she passed him his copies, he was almost back to normal.

He pulled his briefcase onto the table and stowed the bundle inside. "Even though it's a simple theft, it's still a crime. Why didn't Miss Suzanne report it to me?"

Liesl said, "Remember, these were her friends."

Nicole nodded. "I wouldn't go to the police until I had proof in my hands."

"When I bumped into Mrs. Sizemore today, she seemed sincere in her gift-giving," Liesl added. "She didn't strike me as a thief trying to cover her tracks."

Kurt grunted. "Any sign the theft relates to Suzanne's suspicious death?"

Nicole and Liesl exchanged a glance, then both shrugged.

"Okay, now for my information." He grinned. "I spoke to the chief about Winnie's murder. He's willing to reactivate the case with any new investigative leads. It's gone cold because they ran out of lines to pursue."

Liesl asked, "Doesn't the discovery that Mr. Van de Berg was at the party count as a new lead?"

"Good question." Kurt pulled a thick accordion file out of his briefcase. "Here is a list of statements taken and evidence gathered when it happened. Mind you, this is just a list. I'll need to review each statement individually and also verify that all the evidence they've itemized is where it should be, sixty years after the event. I looked for a statement from Bill Van de Berg. Nothing. Several statements from his brother, Edgar, but nothing from Bill."

"He was eight," Liesl said. "Doubtful they thought kids could be good witnesses in those days."

Nicole asked, "Any statements from his parents?"

Liesl turned to her. "Their mother was a widow. Bill said today that Edgar took him to the party. After the murder, the police contacted their mother and had her come get him."

Kurt nodded. "That's why a statement from Bill, even now, is what we need."

They shared a smile.

"My second bit of news involves a partial laboratory report. They haven't finished with all the samples, but they found something interesting on one of your aunt's pillowcases. They found apple juice and the ingredients for an over-the-counter stomach upset medication. Both were reported as having been given to your aunt to relieve her distress. But they also found traces of a prescription drug called colchicine."

"What?" Liesl asked. "We didn't find a prescription for that."

Kurt rifled through a notebook. "And it's not any drug Dr. Johnson listed that he'd prescribed for your aunt."

Liesl searched her laptop. "Let me double-check. I've got the names of her prescriptions in my spreadsheet." After a pause, she said, "No colchicine."

Nicole spoke up. "What does this drug do? What's it used for?"

"It's usually used as a treatment for gout." Kurt handed them a printout of the pharmaceutical information on colchicine. "In pill form, it can be ground into a powder that's tasteless in food or drink. Ten or more capsules or pills can be lethal. An overdose starts with gastrointestinal pain and mimics gastroenteritis. Later on, it causes multi-organ dysfunction and a rapid, progressive multi-organ failure."

"Wow. Those were Aunt Suzanne's symptoms."

He consulted the pharmaceutical information. "Know anyone who suffers from gout?"

Liesl considered for a moment. "No one has specifically mentioned a gout condition." Liesl looked at Nicole. "You know of anyone?"

"Not a soul," she replied. "Many people who were at Winnie's party now limp. They're all old."

"Doreen certainly limps. I haven't seen Mrs. Sizemore have any trouble walking, but doesn't gout come and go? Is it an old person's disease, like arthritis?"

Kurt stowed his pharmaceutical reference. "I'll check on that and update my chief on the lab findings, but I wanted to tell you guys first. This should be enough to open an investigation into Suzanne's death. No promises, but I'm hopeful."

Liesl shot a look at Nicole. They both knew the professionals needed to handle this.

"There is one thing," Kurt said. "Because of my closeness to this, they may relegate me to paperwork." He looked from Liesl to Nicole. "It's standard procedure. I'll accept it, and both of you need to as well."

Liesl frowned at Nicole.

Nicole raised her eyebrows at Liesl. "I'll make sure she follows the rules, Kurt," she said, never losing eye contact with Liesl. "I'll sit on her if need be."

"You do that." Kurt pulled out another piece of paper. "This is the report on Suzanne's cell phone. Either the battery ran out, or someone turned it off the night before Doreen called you home, Liesl. It's never been activated again. The last call she made was earlier that day. To Mrs. Sizemore."

Nicole asked, "You still haven't found Suzanne's phone?"

Liesl shook her head. "No. Someone must have taken it and turned it off. She was never without her phone."

Kurt asked, "Who was at this house, besides Doreen and Patricia, when she fell sick?"

Nicole shrugged. "I asked everyone I could hunt down, and no one admitted coming here. Before she was sick? Yes. During or after? No."

Kurt turned to Liesl. "Any of the neighbors see anything?"

She held up her hand. "I'm sorry, but I let the ball drop. I'll go door-to-door tomorrow."

Nicole stared daggers at her. "With some crazy person out there burning your stuff?"

"My best friend's going with me." Liesl stared daggers back at her. "We start at ten in the morning."

Nicole nodded. "Deal."

"We need to determine if there were any fires around the time Winnie was killed," Kurt said.

Liesl was surprised. "Really?"

"Arsonists are angry people who burn things, and it can lead to murder. Not always, but it's possible. Check Suzanne's journals, and I'll review this monster of a murder book for any references to fire."

"Her journals start a year after the murder," Liesl pointed out.

"She could have referenced something from the past. It's worth a shot."

Liesl eyed him with suspicion. "Why did you say you'll check the murder book? Are you taking it?"

Kurt nodded. "This is an amazing collection of information." He flipped through it. "Like this map." He pointed to a map of the levels of Winnie's house, marked with names, where everyone said they were when the murder was discovered. "It's genius. I need to review all of this and compare it to the actual investigation."

"She wanted me to have it."

"I agree, but we don't have any time to lose. Let me take it and make copies. I'll give you back the original. You don't have access to the cold case files, and I do. I need to compare the information. It's better if I take it now."

"But I have time to go through it."

Kurt held up his hand. "Please, Liesl. Let me win this argument. I'll get copies made and get it back to you."

She glared at him but gave up the argument.

He grabbed his phone. "I'm going to step out and see if I can reach Mr. Van de Berg to schedule an interview. He's our ticket to reactivating Winnie's murder case."

When he left the room, Nicole said, "We're almost to the point of having Winnie's murder and your aunt's death actively investigated. Much of it thanks to Kurt. You need to be nice to him."

With a sigh, Liesl said, "I owe him a lot." She gestured toward the statement list. "Ready to go through this baby and load the details into my spreadsheet?"

Nicole grinned. "It's what I live for." She started with the list, reading out the names of the witnesses who gave each statement, then giving the date it was taken. They also added what officer or officers were present. The number of statements taken over the years was huge.

When Nicole read out Joseph Bauer, Liesl paused. "Is that Joey Bauer, the man who rides his bicycle through town?"

She looked at the notes. "Yes, it must be. The address listed is where he still lives, at least for now. My coworker, Janet, has his home listed for sale."

"Why is he selling?"

"Janet said he's too old to live there by himself. He doesn't have any immediate family, so the house proceeds will pay for the nursing home."

"Does he need a nursing home?"

Nicole shrugged. "I think he's in good health, just not able to live alone."

"Aunt Suzanne said some of the mean kids called him 'bicycling Bauer' when he was young. She always thought he was a wonderful human being, regardless of his limitations."

Kurt came back, a big smile plastered across his face. "I've got an appointment tomorrow to take Mr. Van de Berg's statement. I'll need to figure out what to do with Ross. My mom will be out of town this weekend, but I'll find someone."

Liesl owed Kurt so much. It was her time to help. "I'll keep him."

Kurt and Nicole whipped their heads around and stared at her like she'd offered to fly to the moon. She straightened in her seat and gathered her shredded dignity. "I can keep him entertained and fed for a few hours. I don't have much practice with kids, but I like them, and they like me."

Nicole looked at Kurt. "As strange as it seems, Claudia thinks she's wonderful. I'd trust Liesl to watch her. I recommend you accept her offer for free babysitting services."

Liesl smiled. "It's settled then."

Chapter Forty-Three

Cain's descendant

Suzanne brought her death on herself.

I didn't want to kill her. She forced my hand. She *made* me.

Over the years, I told her to let it go. Winnie's murder wasn't something she needed to dwell on.

But did she listen? No. Not once. She wouldn't stop.

She got too smart. Made me nervous. I couldn't let her discover the truth. Not after all these years.

Then she found out about the money.

When she started asking around, I knew it was down to her ... or me. If she found out I'd embezzled money from The Butterfly House, it was only a matter of time. She'd realize I was capable of murder.

In the end, I chose myself.

It was easy to slip the medicine into her food. I needed it, but the need to stop her outweighed control of my gout.

I even played the part of caring friend as I watched her fade away. That old busybody almost ruined it, insisting on staying when she realized Suzanne was ill. Neither saw what was happening, right in front of their own eyes.

That biddy got in my way—stole my joy. I had to do more. I *needed* something to burn, so I let myself in when Liesl was out. Suzanne's coat was all too easy, hanging by the door.

I took it home. Imagine my disappointment when it didn't burn.

Now Liesl and her pesky friends are snooping into Suzanne's death. They need to leave well enough alone. I saw them gather in the dining room and plan something. They're trying to find me.

Next time, I'll have to do more than start a fire in the garage. No. They didn't appreciate my warning.

Once again, I will have to act. I will have to *kill*.

Chapter Forty-Four

Liesl

Liesl and Ross took advantage of sunny weather by playing catch in the front yard. Liesl waved when Doreen walked by with Barney. Doreen didn't seem to limp as much as she sometimes did, but Barney struggled to walk even more than before.

After pausing, Doreen called Liesl over.

Liesl turned to Ross. Although the sun shone, the wind was chilly, and her fingers resembled thin ice cubes. "Why don't you go on inside? I'll be right there to make us some hot chocolate."

He nodded his enthusiasm and ambled away.

She joined Doreen. "You're walking easier today."

Doreen nodded. "My medicine is giving me some relief." She pointed at Ross. "Found a lost boy?"

"The son of a friend. His father had an appointment this afternoon. Would you join us for hot chocolate?"

"No, thanks, dear. Barney needs to go home. He's struggling today."

Liesl held her tongue, resisting the temptation to tell her she was overfeeding him.

* * *

Inside the house, Liesl called, "Where'd you go?"

"In the kitchen."

When she caught up with Ross, she announced, "You get extra marshmallows for being so good today." They shared a high five, then Liesl started making hot chocolate.

Twenty minutes later, Liesl's phone rang, interrupting their competitive game of Go Fish. She glanced at the phone and said to Ross, "It's your dad."

"Hey, Kurt. How'd the interview go?"

"Great. Mr. Van de Berg makes an excellent witness."

Liesl smiled. "He's an attorney. I expected nothing less."

"He remembered so much detail from the night of Winnie's murder. I believe his statement will make an enormous difference to the case."

"Tell me all about it."

"I will. When I get there. The most interesting part was finding out where he was right before they discovered Winnie's body."

She gripped her phone tighter. "Where was he?"

"In the second-floor bathroom."

"What? I thought he was in the attic with Doreen."

"He needed a bathroom break when she was watching him. Doreen called Edgar over and Edgar took him to the bathroom."

"So when they left, Doreen stayed in the attic? Alone?"

"Winnie was with her. That's the last time Mr. Van de Berg saw either of them."

This assertion surprised Liesl. "That's not what Doreen told Aunt Suzanne all those years ago. My spreadsheet notes have Billy with her in the attic until the police took control of him and called his mother."

"I thought so. Very confusing."

"Could they have gone outside with the dog? Like Billy and Suzanne?"

"It's possible. Mr. Van de Berg said he went outside twice that night. The first time was to go out with Suzanne and the dog before Max arrived. The second was when his mother took him home."

"If Doreen and Winnie were outside and attacked, why didn't Doreen say that?"

He paused for a moment. "What if the attacker was Doreen?"

She gasped in astonishment.

Ross stood up and approached her chair. She realized he was listening to their conversation and seemed concerned about it. "I'll have to think about that. I've been playing cards with a fine young man who has enjoyed our day together."

"Glad he's happy. Do you mind if I swing by the station before coming there? I asked Roxy to make two copies of your aunt's murder book this morning. I'll pick those up and bring them with me. We can hash out where everyone said they were and go over that location map your aunt made."

"Good deal." She hung up and realized her phone battery was almost dead. She looked up at Ross, who was still standing next to her. "Will you be okay if I run upstairs and plug in my phone? My charger is in my bedroom."

"I'd rather go with you."

Liesl smiled. "Well, then. Let's go upstairs."

They scrambled up the stairs, making a game of Ross beating her to the top. Liesl then won the race to her bedroom. Once she took care of her phone, she led Ross to the guest bedroom that had been Myron's old room. Aunt Suzanne had a storage box in the closet filled with older boy toys such as plastic soldiers, metal cannons, Lincoln Logs, and plastic cowboys and Indians.

Ross squealed with delight.

"I'll carry this downstairs. You can play with these tonight. Your daddy and I have some work to do."

He chuckled, running his hands through the assortment of toys. He held up a plastic Indian with a big headdress. "These guys are amazing."

"Aren't they?" Liesl picked up the box and headed to the staircase, Ross skipping along behind her. Halfway down the stairs, she heard a sound that made her pause. Could someone have closed the back door? To Ross, she asked, "Did you hear that?"

He nodded.

She had a view of the front door from where she stood. She'd locked it when she came in. No one was there. "I know the back door was locked. Not to mention, I've locked all the windows. I don't understand."

Ross looked concerned. "You got an alarm. If someone came in, why wasn't there an alarm?"

"I didn't arm the system. Your dad was coming. But I know I locked the doors." She took a deep breath. "You stay here. I'll go check it out."

Ross shook his head, his eyes enormous. "I'm too scared. I want to stay with you."

She didn't want to leave him scared and alone. "Okay, but stay behind me." She carried the box down the rest of the stairs and set it on the hall table. She turned to Ross and gave his shoulder a quick squeeze. "It's probably Miss Nicole or your daddy."

He shook his head. "They would have yelled for us."

She couldn't argue with his logic. She called out, "Hello? Anyone there?"

No answer.

Ross stayed at her heels as they passed through the dining room and pantry. When they reached the kitchen threshold, her stomach lurched. Doreen Martin stood in the middle of the room, holding a large bag.

Doreen smiled. "Sorry to barge in, but the situation wouldn't wait. A neighbor stopped me on my way home. After that conversation, I needed to talk to you."

Liesl tried to keep her face neutral, without emotion. She couldn't let her discovery of Doreen's lies about her whereabouts at Winnie's party show on her face. That would be dangerous. The fact that Doreen let herself in the house increased Liesl's concerns. "We didn't hear you knock. We were upstairs."

"No one answered when I knocked, so I used my key." Doreen eyed her for a moment. "I was told you and Nicole scoured the neighborhood, asking who'd visited when Suzanne was sick. Is that true?"

How was that offensive to her? "Yes. So what?"

"What did you find out?"

"The only people noticed here were you, Patricia, and Dr. Johnson. Is that a problem?"

"It is, actually." Doreen glanced at Ross, then turned back to Liesl and frowned. "Do something with him."

Liesl reached for Ross's hand. "Let me get him settled somewhere."

"Don't go far." Doreen held up the bag she carried. "We don't want anyone to get hurt, now do we?"

Doreen's words and the tone she used caused Liesl to cringe. The tightening clasp of Ross's hand revealed that he sensed danger too.

"No, Doreen. Just give us a minute," Liesl said. She tried not to add to Ross's sense of fear as they turned and walked back through the dining room. She needed to get Ross out of the house. Her mind raced with options for his safety as they walked. Could she get him out the front door? It seemed a mile away. Could she hide him somewhere? She swiftly dismissed that idea. No hiding because of his claustrophobia.

Ross's whisper interrupted her thoughts. "I think that woman is scary." He looked at her with enormous eyes.

Liesl nodded. "Try not to be scared." She turned to see Doreen. From the dining room, Doreen stood watching them. If she had a pistol in that bag, it was too risky to run to the front door.

Inspiration hit Liesl when they reached the pantry. She spotted the laundry chute. "Do you like slides?"

He nodded.

"This house has a special slide." She pointed to the small door covering the laundry chute.

"Miss Nicole told you about the laundry chute. Remember?"

"Yes," he whispered.

"There is a slide behind this little door. It ends in the basement. You'll slide down and fall into a basket in the basement. You'll land, 'poof,' into all the laundry inside the basket." She'd put her own dirty clothes and towels down the chute this morning, and there should plenty to cushion him.

"It's scary and dark."

"You're right. It's scary. But it's scary up here too." She leaned down and whispered to him. "You're the bravest guy I know, besides your dad. And like your dad, you're going to help me, aren't you?"

He stared at her for a second and then nodded.

"When you land in the basket, I need you to get help. That woman is trying to hurt us. Climb out of the basket and run to a window with a red handle."

"Daddy wouldn't let me touch those."

"That's right. But we have an emergency now. Pull down the red handle. It will open the window and let you out. Don't be afraid of the bell that will start ringing. Climb out and run to any neighbor's house and tell them to call the police. Stay with them. Okay?"

He nodded.

She glanced back at Doreen, who reached into her bag and pulled out a white plastic container.

Liesl opened the little door and picked up Ross. "You are brave. Now, close your eyes. You're riding the coolest slide in town." *God, keep this boy safe.* She maneuvered his feet through the hole, and he disappeared into the stainless-steel-lined abyss.

Liesl held her breath. After a moment, she leaned into the opening and called, "Are you okay?"

"I think so," came the boy's tremulous voice from far below.

She sobbed as she closed the little door and turned to the threat who remained.

Doreen rushed up to her, her face red. "What have you done with him?" Gone was the sweet woman she'd known all her life. An ice cold, emotionless monster replaced her.

Doreen peered behind her, searching for Ross. "Where is he?"

"He's gone." Liesl smiled. "This house made him disappear."

"I'm going to make the *house* disappear!" Doreen held aloft the plastic container.

It took a moment for Liesl to realize the container was lighter fluid. She stiffened in surprise.

Doreen blocked her exit from the pantry, threatening her with the lighter fluid. Liesl glanced around for a potential weapon. She shifted slightly closer to a drawer that held serving utensils. Maybe she could get to a knife.

"I wondered how much you'd figure out about your aunt. Especially when your old flame started hanging around. Old flame." Doreen chuckled. "How appropriate. Too bad he's a cop. He's the reason you're wondering about Suzanne's death."

"Anyone would ask questions. She became deathly ill overnight."

How could Doreen have hurt her Aunt Suzanne? She was a lifelong friend. *Must call for help.* Her brain wasn't working right. Where was her phone?

Doreen waggled the charcoal lighter can. "Don't you think fire is the most beautiful thing?"

Liesl's stomach dropped to the floor. Her voice was a whisper. "No. I don't."

This woman has gone mad.

With more strength, Liesl said, "It was you. You burned Aunt Suzanne's coat and set fire to the garage."

Doreen frowned. "It wasn't fun to burn Suzanne's coat. Must have had some fire retardant on the material or something." Her face transformed with delight. "But the garage? Just a few squirts, and the place burst alive with flames."

The sound of an alarm began rhythmic screeches. *Ross! Good boy.*

He'd done it. He'd pulled the lever on one of the windows

the alarm company had wired separately for an emergency alarm. *Thank you, God!*

"What is that noise?" Doreen screeched.

"An emergency alarm. The police and fire department will be here soon."

Doreen's face clouded with malevolence. "They will be too late to save you. Fire takes away my anger. I was a teenager when I learned fire lifts my anger and leaves me in control of my emotions. When I discovered my Edgar was meeting Winnie in a shed, I burned it, so they'd never go back."

Doreen reached into her bag again, this time removing a long lighter, the type used to light a barbeque grill or a gas fireplace.

Liesl tried to reach into the drawer while keeping Doreen distracted. "Did you kill Aunt Suzanne? Your friend for decades?"

"That *friend* finally put all the pieces together. She figured out I killed Winnie. I saw it on her face."

"She loved you and trusted you. Why'd you do it?"

"Don't you understand? She forced me to kill her. I couldn't let her send me to prison. So, I took her phone and watched her until I could figure out how to kill her."

Liesl stared at her. "You wear a mask to hide the evil inside you. Why didn't anyone see it?"

"Because no one wanted to see it." She chuckled. "When Suzanne saw it, she had to die. Now I'm forced to kill you too."

The sound of another alarm coming from the kitchen area pealed. The heat sensors or smoke alarms had been triggered. Liesl didn't see smoke, but the scent of it reached her nostrils. At that, she grabbed the handle of a utensil and pulled it out of the drawer. She bashed Doreen with a soup ladle while she shoved her out of her way.

Liesl turned toward the kitchen. She ran but skidded to a

halt when she spotted a slight red glow toward the back of the room. Smoke curled near the ceiling, and the odor of smoke increased.

Fire! Doreen had started one in the kitchen while Liesl was figuring out where to hide Ross.

When she turned, Doreen was moving toward her, holding both the lighter fluid and the lighter. A chill ran through Liesl at the sight of the old woman's smiling face.

Dear God, she's going to burn down this house with me in it!

She would not allow Doreen to burn down her house and all her memories. She'd already lost her beloved aunt to this crazy woman. Liesl would fight for this home and the treasures inside it. They represented her history and Aunt Suzanne's gifts for her future.

She ran, dodging Doreen, to get back into the pantry. Hanging beside the window was a large fire extinguisher. She yanked it from its holster and struggled to pull the pin.

Doreen walked by, chuckling as she passed her.

Liesl raced back toward the kitchen. She braved the smoke, blasting the contents of the fire extinguisher on the flames licking the cabinets. The fire died down once she hit it a few times, sending foam to blanket the burning fixtures.

Now, where was Doreen? Liesl ran toward the front of the house.

She found the woman in the middle of the living room, squirting lighter fluid on the furniture. She aimed a spray of the liquid at the couch and rug of the living area. Some flowed onto the polished wood floor.

Doreen turned to her. "You think you're so clever? Just like Suzanne. I'll kill you too."

Liesl's nerve endings tingled at Doreen's tone. She remained silent and motionless, still holding the fire extinguisher and praying for help to arrive.

Her prayer was answered when the wail of approaching emergency sirens joined the cacophony of sounding alarms. *Thank God!*

Doreen reached toward the liquid with the lighter in her hand.

Liesl would not allow her to strike again. She ran at Doreen, swinging the fire extinguisher, which knocked Doreen to the floor with surprising force. In the skirmish, the lighter skittered away.

Doreen, on her hands and knees, scrambled to retrieve it.

Liesl lifted the fire extinguisher again and used the base to pound the hand reaching for the lighter.

Doreen howled and fell backward, clutching her hand to her chest. With a well-aimed kick by Liesl, the lighter disappeared under the couch.

Banging came on the front door, along with yelling from the emergency responders. Liesl ran to the door, trying to smother a cough, but didn't take her eyes off Doreen.

When she unlocked the door, two firefighters in full gear rushed in.

"Ma'am. Get out of here. Now!"

Liesl turned and pointed to Darlene. "She's a killer! She tried to kill us!" Then the room shifted, and Liesl fell to her knees.

Chapter Forty-Five

Liesl
November 27

The pleasant afternoon was sunny and unseasonably warm. Liesl was excited about a surprise to be revealed today. When Kurt's car pulled into the driveway, she strolled over.

Ross climbed out of the car first. He ran over and hugged her leg. "What's the surprise, Liesl?"

She chuckled. "I'll take both of you to see it in just a second."

Kurt approached with a smile. "So much happened this week. We've been able to gather financial information on The Butterfly House, and it's looking like Doreen was the thief."

"That's great."

"Mrs. Sizemore gave us a statement. She feels part of the reason for the theft was Doreen trying to make her look bad—her way to get Mrs. Sizemore arrested for theft. They've never been real friends. Also, Doreen didn't have much money, and

Mrs. Sizemore believes she took advantage of a chance to steal some."

"Has Doreen confessed to killing my aunt? Besides her confession to me?"

"She has a court-appointed attorney now. She's not saying anything. But don't worry. The fact that Doreen was prescribed gout medication is big evidence against her for your aunt's poisoning."

"What about Winnie's death?"

"The footsteps Joey Bauer heard running near his house were likely Doreen. Her father's apartment was near there, and she left the party without ever talking to investigators. She told your aunt she'd been questioned upstairs, in the attic, but the police investigation doesn't verify that."

He gestured toward the garage. "I heard they'd released it to you."

She nodded. "Fire department personnel have been frequent visitors since my encounter with Doreen."

"They put a rush on the samples they took from the kitchen and bedroom. Those samples match those taken from the garage and the coat. All positive for the light blend of kerosene commonly found in charcoal lighter fluid."

Liesl had spent hours cleaning the kitchen and living room, trying to eradicate every bit of the stuff.

She had a question for Kurt that nagged at her. "Why didn't I figure out the killer was Doreen?"

Kurt sighed. "We were getting there. Your aunt loved her, and so did you. It's nearly impossible to see the demon hiding behind a mask you've known and loved for decades. Don't beat yourself up."

Ross danced around the two of them. "Can we do the surprise now?"

"Just one second, Ross. I want you to see the progress they've made in the garage."

She took Ross's hand, and they walked to the structure, now shored up for safety purposes. "The garage itself will survive the fire, but the cars were toast. It was a sad day when the flatbed tow truck slid the lift under each of their twisted, melted carcasses and hauled them away."

Kurt looked at the new red Chevrolet Trailblazer. "I see someone bought a new car."

"Nicole and I went on an ultimate shopping trip to Pearl Motor Company. After much discussion and many test drives, this was the winner. It's a bit more practical than my old car but sporty enough to make me happy. Sadly, my best pair of sunglasses were lost to the fire. Melted right onto the dashboard."

He smiled. "I predict another shopping trip is in your future."

Ross yanked on her hand. "Will you take me on a ride one day?"

"I will. I promise." She smiled at Ross, then looked at Kurt, checking his reaction. He might never let her do anything alone with his son again. But Kurt wasn't looking at her.

He eyed the plans stapled to the wall. "What are you doing here? Looks like you're adding a room to the garage."

"More of a mini apartment. That's just a rough sketch. An architect is drawing actual plans for the place. I've talked with Joey Bauer. He's going to move in here. He needs an efficiency apartment on the ground floor. With none of his family left, he and I can be family."

"That's a really nice thing you're doing for him."

"It's a win-win. We're going to share a housekeeper. I believe it's something Aunt Suzanne would have done for an old friend like him."

Ross tugged again on her hand. "Are we ready for the surprise now?"

"We are!"

She led them to the backyard, where an overweight beagle named Barney lay on the grass inside a new fenced area.

Ross ran over to Barney while the dog rose from the grass and wagged his tail.

Kurt stared at her, stunned. "Doreen's dog?"

"It is."

"Why is it here?"

"His name is Barney. Animal Services picked him up after Doreen's arrest. When I realized he ended up at the Mexico Animal Shelter, I adopted him."

"Why? She tried to kill you and Ross."

"She did, but Barney didn't."

He stared at her. "I still don't understand."

"Aunt Suzanne gained a dog when Winnie was killed because Winnie's mother blamed the dog for her being outside that night. When I discovered Barney was homeless, it felt like my destiny to rescue him."

Laughter from Ross playing with Barney filled the air.

Kurt looked at her with soulful eyes. "I haven't thanked you properly for saving my son." He turned away.

Was he hiding tears? "You don't need to thank me. My greatest admirer is an almost seven-year-old boy with blond hair. Our adventure has bonded us. I saved him, so he could save me. I'm also glad you had Aunt Suzanne's murder book with you. It was one less thing to worry about during the fire."

"That book has led us to information the original investigators never knew. It's going to be instrumental in putting together Doreen's criminal trial, if it comes to that. We can't use it as direct evidence, but we can investigate the information ourselves."

"Will they offer her some kind of plea deal?"

Kurt shrugged. "Maybe, but they'll talk to you before they'd do that."

"Good to know."

They watched the boy and dog play for a moment.

"Your aunt had a succession of Jack Russell terriers. I remember two of them."

"When the last one passed, she said her heart couldn't stand the loss of any more pets. Since I'm going to stay, I thought it was time for a new legacy of man's best friends."

"I'm glad you're staying." With his eyes twinkling, he added, "Please continue rescuing dogs, but this tradition of getting a dog because of a murder must end here."

They shared a smile.

"Speaking of traditions, tomorrow I'll host my very first Thanksgiving in my new, old home. I pray this marks the beginning of a long line of Thanksgivings hosted by me. I'm quite proud."

"You should be. Who's invited besides me and Ross?"

"Since my family includes Nicole, Lee, and Claudia, and a million Schrader Aunts, uncles, and cousins, there will be a houseful of people I love. Also, Mrs. Sizemore will join us."

"Has she thawed a little?"

Liesl nodded. "We're going to be friends, real friends, one day. Joey Bauer will be with us too. He needs a family, and I have plenty to share."

"I'm sure he appreciates all you're doing for him."

"It's the giving that counts."

She didn't mention to Kurt that Justin was invited. He'd declined the invitation. His store is open on Thanksgiving, so he'd volunteered to work, giving some of his employees a day with their families.

They stood in the sun's warmth, listening to the sounds of

a laughing boy and a barking dog. Liesl felt joy in being comfortable with Kurt again. She was proud she'd moved past his former betrayal, and glad they were developing a fresh path together. Or perhaps reworking an old path to friendship. Either way, forgiveness was healing to the soul.

Author's Note

The Victorian home featured in this book is in Mexico, Missouri, currently used as a bed-and-breakfast. Built in 1893, it was owned for many years by Allen Percival Green, founder of A. P. Green Refractories. At one time, the owners divided the home into apartments. Two sets of my aunts and uncles lived there when they were newlyweds. The house fell into disrepair when it was over one hundred years old. Lura Williams and Tim Williams purchased the home and refurbished it when I lived across the street from them. Their hard work to restore this beautiful gem inspired me to make it the home of Suzanne and Liesl.

An unsolved murder in 1937 of Mrs. Margaret Mortimer was the inspiration for the murder of Winnie Whitcomb.

Acknowledgments

My sincere appreciation goes to friends and family who encouraged my writing. I'm grateful to speakers and educators who helped me improve my ability. A special thank you to my writer critique groups over the years because we've shared a foxhole in the war of words.

A Heavenly thank you to Dusty Richards for his encouragement and wise counsel. Every writer needs a mentor like Dusty. I've no doubt Dusty has continued to support my dreams from Heaven.

I am indebted to Linda Fulkerson, owner of Scrivenings Press, who made my publishing dreams come true. For writers who dream of writing a book, you can accomplish anything when you believe in yourself, and you're surrounded by people who believe in you. The proof of my dream is in your hands.

Special thanks to Dave (David) Snow, my Irish International Association of Special Investigation Units (IASIU) friend and fellow author. You proved investigators could also write books. Also, thanks to Gertrud Sandstrom, my Swedish IASIU fellow board member, and another champion of my desire to write. Thank you for all your encouragement over the years.

Thanks to John Burnell, who read the first manuscript I completed. It was a humble work and unpublishable, but your encouragement led me to believe this book was possible. I'm grateful to Peggy Blanton for sharing some of her life experiences to make this book more realistic. My deep gratitude to Laura and Steve Erdel for the use of their lake house in Mexico, MO, to complete research and writing in our hometown.

Thank you to my Mexico, Missouri resources: Mexico-Audrain County Library District Assistant Director Mare Prosso; Audrain County Historical Society Executive Director Lori Pratt, Assistant Director Janice Robison and all the wonderful ladies associated with the Historical Society (Pam Singleton, Jackie Kauble, Morgan, Nan Cox, Sue Fennewald, and Consuelo Baum).

About Ellen E. Withers

Ellen E. Withers is a retired insurance fraud investigator, a background that provides the realism and intrigue found in her new dual-time mystery series, *Show Me Mysteries*. Set in Ellen's picturesque hometown of Mexico, Missouri, each book features a historical structure, a dual-time plotline, and an intriguing mystery.

Ellen has earned over ninety awards for her short stories, including a prestigious Pushcart Prize nomination for published short fiction. She is a columnist for *Writers Monthly PDF*, a guide for professional writers about writing for contests. As a freelance writer, Ellen has written over seventy-five nonfiction articles published in local, regional, and international magazines.

Ellen serves as an officer of the Pioneer Branch of the

National League of American Pen Women and is a board member of the Arkansas Writers Conference. She is a member of White County Creative Writers, Sisters in Crime, and Tornado Alley, a local chapter of SIC.

More Mysteries from Scrivenings Press

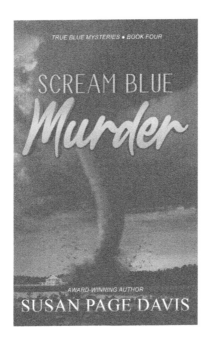

Scream Blue Murder

by Susan Page Davis

True Blue Mysteries—Book Four

An old photo, a twister, and a friend being stalked ...

A tornado rips through town, and Campbell McBride and her dad take shelter. Afterward, they try to help others who were hard hit, and a body is discovered in the debris of a cottage near their friends' home. Was the man dead before the twister struck? The owners of the ruined cottage hire True Blue Investigations to help identify the victim and find out how he got on their property. Meanwhile, among the volunteers, Campbell meets her mother's old school friend, Jackie. It seems Jackie married her mom's former boyfriend—and now she has eyes on Campbell's widowed father.

Get your copy here:

https://scrivenings.link/screambluemurder

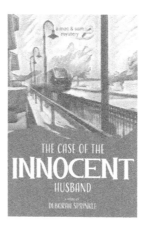

The Case of the Innocent Husband

by Deborah Sprinkle

A Mac & Sam Mystery - Book One

Private Investigator Mackenzie Love needs to do one thing. Find out who shot Eleanor Davis. Or else.

When Eleanor Davis is found shot in her garage, the only suspect, her estranged husband, is found not guilty in a court of law. However, most of the good citizens of Washington, Missouri, remain unconvinced. It doesn't matter that twelve men and women of the jury found him not guilty. What do they know?

And since Private Investigator Mackenzie Love accepted the job for the defense and helped acquit Connor Davis, her friends and neighbors have placed her squarely in the enemy camp. Therefore, her overwhelming goal becomes to find out who killed Eleanor Davis.

Or leave the town she grew up in.

As the investigation progresses, the threats escalate. Someone wants to stop Mackenzie and her partner, Samantha Majors, and is willing to do whatever it takes—including murder.

Can Mac and Sam find the killer before they each end up on the wrong side of a bullet?

Get your copy here:

https://scrivenings.link/innocenthusband

* * *

Stay up-to-date on your favorite books and authors with our free e-newsletters.

ScriveningsPress.com

Made in the USA
Monee, IL
23 June 2023

36951021R00181